I wish all old cars would write their memoirs. The 1934 Austin Tourer, Miss Daisy, has made a joyful job of it in her own somewhat curmudgeonly manner. Or is that something she's caught from her owner? Either way what we have from the "old girl", as the owner calls her, is a neatly interwoven pair of narratives, one relating the fascinating and sometimes moving life-story of a vintage Austin 7, the other recounting the car's entertaining adventures with her latest owner, a lady not much younger than Miss Daisy herself … all that with a few practical workshop tips thrown in. What a delightful read.

Chris Serle is a broadcaster and a director of the Atwell Wilson Motor Museum in Calne, Wiltshire.

Miss Daisy's Diaries is a splendid autobiographical account of the adventures and life of a 1934 Austin Seven car. Rather like a visit to an ancient aunt who regales you with the tales of her escapades, Miss Daisy reports on life with "Her Ladyship", these tales being interspersed with vivid flashbacks to previous owners and their exploits. We also see the changing face of motoring, the growth of vehicles on the road, the development of traffic lights, roundabouts and the MOT Test.

Abbreviated Review from The Austin Magazine.

Sue & 1334.
Thank you So much

Miss Daisy's
Diaries

Matador
9 Priory Business Park,
Wistow Road, Kibworth Beauchamp,
Leicestershire. LE8 0RX
Tel: (+44) 116 279 2299
Fax: (+44) 116 279 2277
Email: books@troubador.co.uk
Web: www.troubador.co.uk/matador

ISBN 978 1780882 079

British Library Cataloguing in Publication Data.
A catalogue record for this book is available from the British Library.

www.missdaisydiaries.co.uk
Twitter @missdaisydiary
Facebook http://www.facebook.com/missdaisydiary
You Tube http://youtu.be/p8xiaykG4pM

Typeset in 11pt Aldine401 BT Roman by Troubador Publishing Ltd, Leicester, UK

Matador is an imprint of Troubador Publishing Ltd

Printed and bound in the UK by TJ International, Padstow, Cornwall

To my sister Alannah who has this strange idea that I can write. Also to my grandson Toby who has promised to look after Miss Daisy after I have driven off on that great highway in the sky.

Acknowledgments

I am grateful to so many people. To my sister Alannah and my daughter Pippa who encouraged me start Miss Daisy's Diaries in the first place. To Yvette Brown who kept an eye on the book as it came together, usually suggesting far better ways of writing something than I could ever come up with. I must also thank Clare Hulton, a literary agent who while not representing me, encouraged me to keep going when I wanted to hit the delete button. I am especially grateful also to Ed Tanguay, the most talented of artists, who came up with the cover and the other illustrations that appear in this edition. I am also grateful to my dear friend, the late Chris Williams, who created a little film for Miss Daisy to go on You Tube to help with the book promotion. Twitter and Facebook are completely foreign to me, so I am grateful to Lorraine Allman who taught me how to use them. Then there are those many people who are as mad as me, for owning an Austin Seven; the members of The South Wales Austin Seven Club, Arthur White, John Williams and Harry Hales, without whom I couldn't have kept Miss Daisy running, and those of the Pembrokeshire Vintage Car Club who gave me reason to take Miss Daisy out regularly on our adventures.

Then of course there is Miss Daisy herself and her nemesis, Sir Herbert Orsten. Without them, there would have been no story and the diaries would never have happened.

Preface

I've always had a feeling that I first met Miss Daisy in another lifetime. So when she arrived at my home in 2004, I wasn't sure how our relationship would develop. But as I walked up the drive, the disapproving look that met my approach told me it was going to be a difficult one. She's twelve years older than me and I am no spring chicken. It didn't take me that long to realise she was quite a cantankerous old lady. For those of you old enough to remember them, she seems to be a mixture of Margaret Thatcher, Margaret Rutherford and Peggy Mount. A friend of mine likened her to one of those elderly people who delight in using their walking sticks to trip people over in busy supermarkets, then to wander away cackling.

Perhaps I shouldn't have given her a name, but it was a dear American friend, Marion Harshman, who on seeing her picture, said that she was undoubtedly a Miss Daisy and the name has stuck. So armed with that name, she seems to have developed her rather cantankerous and judgmental personality. If you think that naming a car is a daft thing to suggest, think back to your first car, usually an old banger that you personalised and invariably gave a name to. So although she isn't or indeed wasn't my first car, Miss Daisy could well have been. Austin 7s were first cars for many of my generation on a tight budget way back in the 1960s.

So here I am, retired to Pembrokeshire and sharing my life with Miss Daisy. We may have our differences but we do have a lot of fun together and we've had our scary moments. It was my sister's and my daughter's encouragement that made consider writing a book, but at first I couldn't think of a subject matter. I had been writing a series of short "Miss Daisy Diaries" in various vintage car club magazines over the years and those readers were telling me that Miss Daisy deserved a larger audience. Now, having written it, I feel that fuelled by the publicity, she will become insufferable.

Pam Hunt

Chapter One

I'm in agony, I'm pooped and I'm exhausted

Monday 15th March 2004

God! What a way to spend my birthday. I'm in agony. I'm pooped and exhausted. Indeed I am what those more uncouth among us might loosely describe as being knackered.

Mind you, I haven't been feeling very well for quite some time and he knew it, so why didn't he use a trailer? Indeed we could have used a trailer. No, correction, we should have used a trailer. But, oh no, no, no, no, let's save ourselves a few shillings. Let's haul the old thing over from Bristol under her own power. And that's exactly what happened. No consideration for my feelings nor was he concerned for the state of my health. But the biggest insult of all, and I suppose to make sure I got here, he asked a friend to follow along behind us with his 'modern' with a tow rope secreted away in its boot. Can you imagine the shame of it? A child of British engineering genius being escorted here by a pile of modern Japanese tin, all ready and primed to tow me if I broke down. This really is not the way I would choose to celebrate my birthday. Which one, I hear you ask. Well, a lady never likes to divulge her true age. Suffice to say that I am somewhere ever so slightly past my fiftieth birthday. But quite frankly, after a journey like that I feel nearer ninety.

When I arrived a boy thought I was Chitty Chitty Bang Bang, whoever that is, and asked my new owner if I could fly. 'No, it's a bit old for that sort of thing nowadays,' she replied.

3

It? IT? **IT?** Bloody cheek. I am not an 'it'. I'm a she. Miss Daisy is my name. Born in Birmingham on the fifteenth of March Nineteen Thirty Four. Three o'clock in the afternoon to be exact. How do you do? Oh pook! Now I've gone and given away my real age haven't I? You can see that I am emotionally drained at the moment. If he had bothered to sort out my engine before we set out from Bristol, I could show this youngster how I can fly. Now back in the thirties and forties, boy could I fly. I reached fifty, sometimes fifty five, miles an hour, downhill of course.

Well Boy, I made it all the way here on my own. I needed no help from that modern eyesore. The fact that I had to slip into first gear to climb the odd hill just showed my true Dunkirk spirit and in spite of my health and age I made it all the way here on my own and that's what really matters. Consequently, here I am sitting in my new home with springs so weak they are bending in the wrong direction and the bottom feels as though it's about to drop out of my engine.

So, what about my new home? More importantly I suppose, what about my new owner? Well my immediate reaction is... well she's a she for a start. All my other owners have been men. Mind you she is a bit of a wrinkly, quite tall, stout. We don't say fat in polite society. Oh yes – posh voice. My first impressions? To be honest, I'm not absolutely sure we'll get on. She has that look in her eye, which says, don't mess with me. She's rather haughty as well, so I think I will call her Her Ladyship. She also seems impulsive, you know, the sort of person who comes up with a wild idea, then draws others around her into her mad plan and after that you can be pretty damn sure that everything will end in disaster. But it shouldn't take me long to train her into my ways so that I can enjoy my advanced years in a degree of comfort. Now I've reached my three score years and ten, I intend to start writing my memoirs and for that I will need plenty of time and above all, peace and quiet.

Her Ladyship lives with her daughter and a five year old

4

grandson. I have to confess to liking them more than I like her. I especially like the boy. He reminds me of myself when I was younger. He comes over to me, climbs in and grabs my steering wheel. He slides forwards on my seat, stretching his feet towards my pedals until, that is, his bottom slips onto the floor. He hauls himself back onto my seat. 'Don't worry, Chitty Chitty Bang Bang, you'll fly for me won't you?' Of course I will Little One, as long as your Gran gives me some tender loving care first. I'm beginning to warm to this young chap. He has a mischievous smile. But then, like every child, he has to ruin it all by bouncing up and down on my seats hoiking at my gear and brake levers and why is it that children are always so fascinated with my horn and windscreen wiper? All right, all right, that's quite enough. They work. Now please stop it.

I cast a look around my new surroundings and out of the door at my new neighbourhood. Quite frankly it's ghastly, one of those horribly modern chintzy housing estates where lawns the size of postage stamps, are cut to perfection and there's not a blade of grass out of place. If that woman has chosen to live here, then it sums her up pretty well if you ask me. A bit of a Lady Muck. Why, there's not a weed to be seen anywhere, not even among her roses. On top of that the floor to my place is as neat as a new pin. In fact the whole place appears spotlessly clean. Still I can soon put that to rights. There, I've dribbled some oil onto her nice clean floor. I am sure it will upset her, but I'm more comfortable with a familiar smell around me. Anyway, aren't we oldies allowed to dribble occasionally?

It's time for bed I think. I've had an exhausting day and I dread to think what the future holds for me. But at least I am settled again and perhaps tomorrow I can make a start on my memoirs. I suppose I should really go all the way right back to the moment I first saw the light of day, that fifteenth of March Nineteen Thirty Four at three o'clock in the afternoon and actually my first sight wasn't the light of day but the back end of a relative. We were in this enormous building and looking around, I could see dozens of my relatives in different states of undress. They all looked very pristine. Surrounding us was a mass of humans doing all sorts of different jobs to us. When it was my turn to roll off the production line a man walked up to me and climbed in. 'Right me girl, welcome to Longbridge. Now let's see how well you drive.' At that, he started my engine and we drove out of some large doors into the daylight and I had my first glance of the world I was entering. The man took me on a ten mile round trip before bringing me back to Longbridge. As we drove in, there was a group of rather important looking men examining some of my relatives, who were now parked up by the big doors I had passed through half an hour before. The man parked me at the end of this row and a few of the important looking men walked over towards us.

'Hello Charlie. How does she drive then?' Charlie, I presumed was the name of the man, who had just taken me for a drive. He got out and touched the peak of his cap.

'Afternoon, Sir Herbert sir. She's fine, goes like a dream. This is a really nice little model sir. They all are.'

'Yes, but she's going to be the last of an era I am afraid. We have to move with the times. The public want something sleeker nowadays. So we'll be turning over to the new Ruby fronted versions with the Tourer as well as the saloons. Where's this one off to then?' Charlie checked a label attached to my windscreen wiper.

'Oxford, Sir Herbert. She'll be off there in a day or two.'

'Good, good. Well done. How's the wife by the way? Is she over that bronchial problem?'

'Oh she's fine now sir, thank you Sir Herbert.'

'Good, good, good. Keep up the good work Charlie.' Charlie touched the peak of his cap once more as the group walked away.

'Well car, I bet you don't know who that was.' Well of course I didn't, except for the fact that Charlie called him Sir Herbert. 'That was only the big boss around here, none other than Sir Herbert Austin. You are honoured to catch his attention. Now, let's get you polished up for your trip to Oxford.'

*****

I haven't slept well and I woke up with a start to find myself in a strange place. Then I remember. This is my new home. I am afraid that this place really doesn't look as though Her Ladyship is equipped to look after me properly, no workbench, no tools and no spares. What? There's no heater either? This place has no heating. The weather may be warming up now, but what is it going to be like next winter?

The door flies open and in strides Her Ladyship. She's clutching a notebook and she starts to look me over, too closely if you ask me. I can smell Marmite on her breath. Oh God, how I loathe the smell of Marmite!

She starts to mumble and take notes. I hate it when people mumble. Speak up! I want to shout out. Have you noticed that people just don't speak properly anymore and the younger they are, the worse they seem to be? For example, would someone please tell me what 'danowa-eyemin' means? I hear that used over and over again. And they use 'Nowah' which I thought was the name of a man in a biblical story, something about a flood, but apparently not. It is the modern way of saying no. If that's what they mean, then why don't they say it correctly? Now my first gentleman in Oxford, he was beautifully spoken. Well coming from there he would have been, wouldn't he?

It was a lovely sunny day as I was driven down from Birmingham to the dealer in Oxford, I don't want to sound too nostalgic, but driving on those tree lined roads was wonderful. No traffic lights, no roundabouts, no pedestrian crossings, no speed cameras, none of the awful trappings we find on the roads today. The driving was different as well. People weren't always in such a hurry; in fact the most important thing I noticed was that other cars would politely give way to let us out of the side roads. You could park wherever you wanted and I could fill my five gallon petrol tank for less than eight shillings. What's that in today's money? Just forty pence. Gosh, that's less than it costs to buy a litre of the stuff now.

Her Ladyship slaps her notebook shut. 'Well Old Thing,' she says. 'There's a fair bit that needs doing to bring you up to scratch. But we'll get there and I then have some big plans for us. But let's get you well first.' And she is gone, fortunately leaving the door open so that I can feel the warmth of the sun on my bonnet. Cheek. What does she mean 'up to scratch'? She looks in a far worse state than me. Snooty cow!

Then no sooner has she gone, than she's back, wrapped in a warm coat. 'Right Old Thing,' she says. 'I'm going to take you for a drive.' You'll be lucky. My battery is low; my engine is not what it should be. Quite frankly, I'm simply not up to it. And another thing, please do not call me Old Thing.

So without any consideration of my feelings, she gets in and rolls her fat bottom on my seat to get comfortable. 'So are you a one clothes peg starter or a two?' she mumbles. See? Mumbling again. I'm over seventy for heaven's sake. One day over to be exact, my hearing is not as good as it was.

Clothes pegs? Did I hear you ask? Why the clothes pegs? It's perfectly obvious: clothes pegs are currently the only way to hold my choke out when I am being started from cold. There was a time when my choke would stay out on its own. Choke? What is a choke? Oh good grief!

'I think we'll try two.' She says. I feel her tweak my spark control. Mm? Don't ask! And then... wurr – ur – ur – ur- ur –

ur. Wurr – rur – rur – rur – rurrr – rurrrrr – rurrrrrrr. My battery is completely dead now you wrinkled old fool. Now what are you going to do? Why don't you try waving a magic wand or sprinkling some fairy dust over me for all the good you are doing.

Then she's out of the seat and undoing the battery cover to check it. 'I think we'll put you on a charge for a few hours,' she says. Fat lot of good that will do, but suit yourself.

A few hours pass and she's back: this time with that look in her eye that says don't mess me around, you will start this time. So Lady Muck, it's going to be a battle of wills is it? I think I'll lead her along and then drop her in it. Wurr – ur – ur – ur – ur- ur – ur. Wurr – ur – ur – ur – ur- ur – ur. Cough, cough, brumm, brumm, harumm, cough. Wurr – rur – rur – rur – rurrr – rurrrrr – rurrrrrrr.

'I wonder what your spark's like? I've been told I should check that.' There was a tone in her voice suggesting that she hadn't a clue what she was talking about, probably read about it in a book somewhere. She gets out and starts to remove a spark plug, reconnects it and rests it over its respective hole on my cylinder head. In the old days we called this the eyebrow-singe test and it appears that she has decided to try it for herself, but not knowing exactly what she is supposed to be doing. This should be fun. She switches on my ignition and starts to turn my crank handle. Nothing happens. Well nothing noticeable. So now she leans over to look more closely. Then I did it. I allowed a large blue flame to shoot out the top of the cylinder, scorching her eyebrows. Gosh this is fun; I haven't done one of those for years.

Having recovered and brushed her scorched eyebrow hairs away, she cranks the handle again, this time keeping clear of the engine. I offer another small blue flame. 'Hmmm, must be something else then,' she mutters. Almost before I could blink, she's got my petrol feed off and is cranking the handle again. I allow some to flow through. Now what?

Then she's fiddling with my carburettor. It should be noted at this point Dear Diary, that I am discovering that Her Ladyship really doesn't understand us cars, let alone the vagaries of a carburettor or sparkplug. After messing around, she puts it back together and tries the eyebrow-singe test again. This time, I allow a few large blue flames to shoot out of the top of my engine. This time she stands well clear. Well at least she learns… I wonder if she will give up now, or will she have another go at getting my engine started? My money is on her giving up.

But no. I've underestimated her. She wraps a duster around my starting handle and starts to crank my engine. I decide to fire a few more times, just to ensure she keeps on trying. But there is no way I am going to let my engine run. I ponder a backfire in the hope that my handle will complete a full reverse spin and whack her on her knuckles. Oh hell, let's do it. It works and she whips her hand away rubbing it vigorously. 'Oh you are going to play that little game are you?' She snarls, I think I must have really hurt her. I feel a bit guilty now… actually no I don't. After all, she does need to continue her education, however brutal that might have to be.

I let her try to start me for another ten minutes and then I get bored. I start up and run with much coughing and backfiring and making lots of smoke. I'm really not well and she still doesn't realise it. Now please don't think I am a bit obsessed by my health, but this woman does need to appreciate just how unwell I am. I run myself to a standstill and think back to those happier times again.

Oh yes, my first gentleman. That's who I was talking about. I remember when he first walked into the showroom. I don't know who was the most eager, me to see him, or him to see me. He was a good looking young man, tall and slim and dressed very smartly.

'Mister Johnston, sir. We have your new car.' It was the salesman. 'She arrived from Birmingham yesterday afternoon. Well, what do you think of her then?'

'Oh, very nice. Very, very nice and you were right about that colour. I am delighted, thank you.' Oh how proud he was. He just walked round and round me, looking closely at every detail of his new purchase, while the salesman finished the paperwork. 'Right sir,' he said. 'The total comes to one hundred and twenty three pounds. That includes the seven pounds road tax, less of course your deposit. That makes ninety eight pounds due.'

The man pulled a rather crumpled cheque and handed it over to the salesman. 'My wife and I couldn't think of anything better to spend my uncle's legacy on than a little car like this.'

'Thank you sir. I will get one of the staff to take the car outside for you and then you can take it home. I presume that you are able to drive aren't you sir?'

'Oh yes,' he replies. 'I've had a few lessons with my brother in his car. I started them as soon as I ordered this one. I wanted to get myself motoring before they bring in that blooming driving test thing. I really don't want to be bothered with that. It's not long now is it?' The salesman nodded doubtfully.

'Voluntary tests start next month sir, and now there's talk it will become compulsory within the year. But you have to admit that driving is getting more dangerous, there were some seven thousand fatalities last year as well. The roads are getting terribly crowded nowadays. They reckon that there are a million and a half vehicles on them.'

'Well, one million five hundred thousand and one now,' observed the man wryly.

'Yes sir.' I think the salesman was getting rather annoyed at my new owner's attitude. 'So really, the driving test is going to be a good idea if it stops so many road accidents.' My new owner nodded his head. I think he was getting the message. I was.

'Hmm, perhaps you are right. Maybe I should have a go at the voluntary test when I think I'm more proficient.'

'Indeed sir, now let's get your car out of this show room.'

Once outside, the salesman handed over my keys and documents and my new owner climbed in. 'Wow car, you smell really nice. It must be the leather.' Then we were off. Well when I say off, we leapt up in the air a few times and I stalled. I could see the face of the salesman wincing at my every move.

'You won't forget to bring it back for its five hundred mile service will you sir? We'll need to tighten things down,' he shouted as my new owner finally got to grips with my foibles and we leapt away.

Heading to my new home was quite an experience. I think I was doing an impression of a kangaroo rather than driving smoothly like the car I should be, but my new owner was demonstrating that while he might have had some driving lessons with his brother, they had obviously achieved very little.

We eventually arrived at a place called Florence Park. My new owner swung me up a little drive beside a quaint semi detached house. He blew my horn a couple of times and a young woman came out of the front door. I don't think they had been married for very long. A year, two at the most.

'Oh David,' she said. 'She's beautiful, really beautiful.' She wandered over to me and peered in. 'Oh David, she's small inside isn't she? Is she all paid for now?' she asked as she wiped her hands on her apron.

'Don't worry Beatrice, it is all ours now.' He was flicking a duster over my bodywork. I mean, was I really going to pick up much muck and dust on a two mile drive, on a sunny March day in Oxford?

Oh yes, you might be wondering why he seemed to be called 'Oh David'. A strange name I know, but that was what she called him and he called her the even stranger name of 'Don't worry Beatrice'. In fact as the days passed, and we went out on little runs together, as soon as he started to speed up, it wouldn't be long before she would say 'Oh David, aren't we going too fast?' And he would always respond with 'Don't worry Beatrice. We are only doing thirty five.'

As she looked over me, Don't Worry Beatrice suddenly took a step back and looked at me rather quizzically. 'With those big spoke wheels,' she said, 'well it looks rather like two bicycles parked side by side from where I am standing.'

Oh David stepped back to see what she was talking about. I didn't think for one minute that I looked like two bicycles parked side by side. 'That's it!' Oh David became very excited. 'That's it. I've been wondering what name to give the car. We must give her a name mustn't we? We'll call her Daisy. That song, you know the one: 'Daisy, Daisy, give me your answer do. A bicycle made for two. Well this one is a car made for two. Car – I hereby christen you Daisy and God bless all who travel in you.'

'Oh David, you shouldn't take God's name in vain like that.' Don't Worry Beatrice feigned annoyance. 'Anyway she's just a motor car, built to carry us from one place to another. She doesn't need a name.' Doesn't need a name indeed. Personally I thought Daisy a rather nice name. After all, they could have called me Saffron or Xanthe!

'You see? You are already referring to her as "she". No we'll call her Daisy. Now what's for lunch? I'll take you out for a drive this afternoon if you like.' Then they were gone, into the house.

★★★★★

It seems as though I've been stuck in here for weeks, then all of a sudden I'm dazzled by the sunlight as the covers are whipped off. Yes, it's Her Ladyship. She's been coming and going for the last few weeks without so much as a by your leave. At least I've been tucked cosily under some nice clean sheets.

'Well Old Thing,' she says. 'I've got someone coming to see you.'

Uh-oh. Am I being sold again? But it seems not. It's one of Her Ladyship's friends. He's very tall. 'Go on,' she says. 'Try and squeeze your six foot six inches behind that wheel.' He clambers in.

'God in Heaven,' he exclaims. 'How the hell did people back then get into these things, let alone drive them?' THINGS? The cheek of it. 'Does the engine work?'

'With rather a lot of difficulty,' Her Ladyship replies. 'Let's have a go.'

NOT – I think to myself. 'Switch on the ignition will you? Two clothes pegs on the choke and retard the spark a bit.' Before I can blink, Her Ladyship grabs my starting handle and cranks it like a devil possessed. Of course I refuse to oblige. 'You have a go,' she says, once she has worked up a sweat. She would call it 'glowing', but we know the truth don't we? The man leans over and flicks the handle once and I spark into life. That'll show her. She looks very sheepish now.

'That engine doesn't sound very good,' he says.

'Doesn't it?' comes her reply, 'How can you tell?'

'Just listen to it. It's terrible. Can you hear that rumbling?' She nods. 'You are going to need to get that engine sorted and I would say, pretty soon.' Her Ladyship looks bemused. Well I have been trying to warn her. 'When's the MOT due?' he asks.

'I think it has to be done in the next few weeks,' Her Ladyship replies. 'Why?'

'She is going to fail on her steering,' he replies rocking one of my front wheels. 'That's a definite failure. But don't worry, I know just the person you need to sort things out, at least to get you through her MOT.'

With that, they were gone.

★★★★★

Oh David did take me out as promised that afternoon. He came out and started to dust my bodywork yet again and Don't Worry Beatrice appeared moments later, all dressed up to the nines.

'We are only going out for a little drive,' he said. 'Just in to the countryside. There was no need to dress yourself up.'

'Oh David, don't be silly. This is a very special occasion for me and this is my first drive in our car. I want to look right for your Daisy and you never know who we might see.'

How considerate of her, I thought. Dressing for the occasion. 'Please don't drive too fast. It might blow my hat away.'

'Don't worry Beatrice, I'll drive slowly.' Then we were off after the usual impression of a kangaroo, but this time we headed in to the country. The roads were quite narrow and not very well made. We turned up one and it didn't even have tarmac on it, just compacted stones.

'Oh David, do be careful.' Don't Worry Beatrice was gripping my door rather too hard; I could feel her nails digging in to my paintwork.

'Don't worry Beatrice, we are only doing ten miles an hour. Nothing can go wrong.'

At that point, I hit a very sharp stone. ! BANG !

I lurched to one side and Oh David pulled me up.

'Oh David, what's happened?'

'Don't worry Beatrice, you stay there and I'll have a look,' he said as he got out and walked round. 'Oh blast the thing, we've had a puncture. You'll have to get out I am afraid. We'll need to jack the car up.' Don't worry Beatrice got out and Oh David rummaged in my toolbox.

'I think we need this,' he said as he produced my jack. 'And this.' He produced a spanner. 'Now where do we put this jack? Where is the manual? Ah, I see. Right…'

Moments later my front left side was up in the air. Oh David removed my punctured wheel and swapped it for the spare wheel mounted on my rear end. I was back on the ground again, ready to go.

'Right,' he shouted to Don't Worry Beatrice who had been picking wild flowers from the roadside. 'Hop in, we'd better get home now. We don't want to have another puncture.' She got in and I sensed her nervousness. For her first ride in me, she had experienced a break down.

'We'll get back on to proper roads again soon.' Oh David was true to his word and just before we reached the outskirts of Oxford, he suddenly shouted, 'We'll drop the wheel in there. They should be able to fix it.'

He swung in to a place that had a large wooden building with lots of signs on it saying things like Champion Plugs, Wellsaline Motor Lubricants, Buy your Exide battery here and a big sign announced Weston's Garage and underneath, Vehicles serviced and repaired. In front of the building there were two vertical things mounted on a metal base, each with a large bottle near the top and a hose hanging beside it. On the top was a sign advertising that it was Dominion petrol. Surrounding the courtyard was a white painted picket fence with flowerbeds and in the corner of the yard was a small truck with a crane thing mounted on the back.

As we pulled up, a man in oily overalls walked out wiping his hands on an old cloth. 'Can I help you?'

'Yes, we've had a puncture,' said Oh David. 'I only picked up the car this morning and I was taking my wife out for her first drive when the front tyre burst. Can you fix it for us?'

'I'd be delighted sir. Let's have a look at it.' The man removed the punctured wheel from my rear end and examined it closely. 'Well it looks as though your tyre is all right, but I will need to take it off to examine it properly and see whether the tube can be repaired.'

'Will it take long?' I think Oh David was hoping it could be fixed there and then.

'I won't be able to do it today. I can attend to it first thing tomorrow morning and if the tyre doesn't need replacing, perhaps I can drop it back to you?'

'Oh that is very kind of you, Mister?'

'Weston Sir. This is my garage.'

'Well that is very kind of you Mister Weston. I will write down my address for you. What sort of time tomorrow, do you think?'

'Well if it is a simple tube repair, I can get it to you before midday. If I need to replace the tyre, it will take longer.'

'Oh that is wonderful. Thank you. I see you do car servicing. Do you do Austins?'

'Yes sir, most makes. But this is still under guarantee isn't it?' Oh David nodded. 'Then you should take it back to the dealer who sold it to you.'

'Well I think I shall be seeing you next year then. You are much closer to me than the dealer. Thank you very much Mister Weston. See you tomorrow.' Oh David hopped back in, obviously very pleased that he had found someone to look after me in the future.

'What a nice man,' said Don't Worry Beatrice.

'Yes he is and having Daisy serviced by him will be a lot more convenient than going across Oxford to the Austin people.' He started me up and to my total surprise we pulled away without our usual kangaroo impression.

★★★★★

'I've got a surprise for you Old Girl.' Her Ladyship cries as she whips the covers off a couple of days after the visit of her friend Rob. This time I see a man with a trailer outside. 'Don't worry, you are not being sold. Promise. This nice man is taking you away to do some work on you.'

At last, I think, she is going to have my engine done.

Then before I can blink, this man has jacked up my front end. Oh the ignominy of it all. What on earth is he doing?

'Rob was right,' he says wriggling my wheels to and fro. 'The king pins and bushes need replacing and unless I am very much mistaken, the front axle needs re-tempering as well.'

Her Ladyship puts on one of those faces that suggest she understands every word, but in truth she hasn't a clue what he's talking about. 'This car should never have passed its MOT.' With that, my front wheels are dumped unceremoniously back onto the ground. Ouch! Her Ladyship is looking deeply concerned. Not about me mind you. It's more that she is imagining that the cost for sorting me out is going to be more than she thought.

'Would you get into the car please,' the man asks and Her Ladyship clambers in. 'Now get out again.' After a bit of huffing and puffing, Her Ladyship obliges. 'Just as I thought. The springs have gone as well. Come and look at how the car is still leaning over. It's easier for me to replace them at the same time as I do the kingpins. Is there anything else you'd like me to do while I have her?'

'I think there is something not quite right with the engine,' comes her reply. Well done Madam, there is indeed something 'not quite right' with my engine. 'Would you just have a quick look for me? But I don't want to spend any more money than I have to at this point.'

The tight fisted old cow. Then I'm on to this man's trailer and gone.

★★★★★

I lived very happily with Oh David and Don't Worry Beatrice for the next five and a half years. Every weekend, almost without fail, we headed off into the Cotswolds for a picnic or perhaps lunch at an old thatched pub, passing through picture postcard villages. Then I would sit there enjoying the warm sunshine playing down on to my bonnet until it turned a gold and red and started to disappear behind the hills to the west. On the way home, we followed a sort of ritual. It was always exactly the same. First we'd stop at Weston's garage where Oh David would pull up by one of the pumps, beep his horn and The Nice Mister Weston would come out, rubbing his hands in that oily cloth. A cloth, incidentally, even grubbier than his hands already were. 'Just two gallons of Dominion this week please Mr Weston,' Oh David would say. It was always two gallons. The Nice Mister Weston would then proceed to pump the first gallon up into the measuring bottle by hand, before turning the valve and letting it pass down his hose and nozzle, which he had shoved in to my tank. Then he would repeat the whole action again for the second gallon.

'Shall I check your oil and water?' The Nice Mister Weston would then ask as he wiped my windscreen with his oily rag.

'Yes please,' Oh David would reply, getting out of me, grabbing a clean cloth and anxiously wiping the oil left by The Nice Mister Weston off my windscreen again.

The Nice Mister Weston did as requested. 'They seem okay, nothing extra needed today. Her service will be due soon, won't it? So that's three and tuppence please.' Then as we were on our way, he would shout after us, 'See you next week then?'

Oh David would wave an acknowledgment as we drove off and Don't Worry Beatrice would always remark, 'That Nice Mr Weston really does keep this place looking lovely, doesn't he? Those flowerbeds are beautiful at the moment. It's all so tidy and everything appears in its place, very spick and span, don't you think?' Oh David would always just grunt an agreement and we then headed for home in silence.

This same procedure every blooming week used to drive me

mad. I mean, why couldn't he buy three gallons just once in a while? But the ritual didn't end there. As we got home he would hop out and walk round to open the passenger door to let Don't Worry Beatrice out before he drove me into the garage. Then once parked up, he would produce a chamois leather and wipe me down.

'There we are Daisy,' he would say. 'Nice and clean now. All ready for next week.' In those days people would have called Oh David a creature of habit. Today they would probably say he had an obsessive compulsive disorder.

★★★★★

I'm back home now. I don't know how long I was away with the man who sorted my springs and steering, but I feel much, much better. The new springs make me feel higher and my front wheels don't wobble anymore. However, my engine still isn't right. As I am settled back in my home, the man gives Her Ladyship a piece of paper. 'Here's the MOT certificate. Now at least she's safe to take on the road. I've had a play with the engine. She's a bit better, but I think you are facing a big engine rebuild before too long. Oh yes and here's my bill.'

Her Ladyship blanches, totters slightly and through a cough says, 'Will you take a cheque?'

When he's gone, she looks at me. 'Well Old Thing, the sun is shining. I think a little drive is called for, don't you?' So in she gets, starts me up and off we go. The suburban roads of north Cardiff are quiet and we happily tootle off this way and that. It's still a struggle to get up hills, but my engine is feeling a bit better.

We swing around this bend. Uh-oh, there ahead is a string of road bumps. Do you know, I cannot understand for the life of me why the authorities think they are so necessary. Her Ladyship once remarked that they were supposed to be traffic calming. What a load of nonsense. I don't need calming for Heaven's sake. I am calm enough until you plonk those damned things in my path.

The apparent effect on me is nothing compared to the effect demonstrated by Her Ladyship. Now Dear Diary, this is in complete confidence. Please don't tell anyone else. Her Ladyship is a martyr to her bottom. Well, as a leading hypochondriac she's a martyr to just about every part of her anatomy. Particularly though, she suffers from haemorrhoids. Picture the scene. Road humps – my suspension – awkward seats – Her Ladyship's haemorrhoids. Yes, you've guessed. Bump – 'Ooh;' another bump – 'Aaaah;' yet another bump – 'Ouch, for God's sake car, can't you get over these more comfortably? Aaah!' On and on we go, turning the shocked heads of pedestrians as we bounce past.

No thought for me of course. I'm just the poor old dear who has to put up with Her Ladyship's fifteen stone plus bumping up and down on my seats and suspension. Is this what driving with her is going to be like? I'm not that sure I can cope.

I've remarked before that Her Ladyship has this terrible habit of throwing open my garage doors with some pronouncement or another and she always has that determined look on her face. It reminds me of the time when, gosh, I think I had been living with Oh David and Don't Worry Beatrice for a couple of years. Then it was the middle of the night when my garage doors flew open. Silhouetted in the light of the street lamps stood Oh David, dressed in his pyjamas and holding a suitcase.

'We've got to get to the hospital,' he cried. 'We are having a baby!' I peer anxiously past him and Don't Worry Beatrice appears, undoubtedly in some pain.

'WE? WE? **WE** ARE NOT having a baby.' She snarled at him. 'I AM having the bloody baby. Go and get dressed. You are not escorting me into hospital dressed like that.' So Oh David shot off to put some clothes on as she climbed gingerly onto my passenger seat. The normally timid wife of Oh David had become a snarling monster.

'Don't worry Beatrice,' he shouted as he returned. 'We'll be at the hospital in next to no time.' Then we were gone. In fact we were doing way over the speed limit and I am sure that I was taking some bends on two wheels. Every time Don't Worry Beatrice groaned, Oh David pushed his foot down on to my accelerator and we sped up even more. Of course, it had to happen didn't it? I heard the whistle, but I don't think Oh David did. He was still accelerating. I saw him first, up ahead of us.

The unmistakeable outline of a police constable stepped into the middle of the road, swinging his torch from left to right. It's on occasions like this that I wished Sir Herbert Austin had fitted us with hydraulic brakes. But he always argued that if you drove us properly, our cable brakes were quite satisfactory. Anyway, Oh David, realising that a policeman was ahead of us and rapidly coming closer, slammed his foot onto the brake pedal and I managed to start slowing down, but not enough. The constable was coming closer rather too quickly. Oh David now grabbed the handbrake as well and pulled that as hard as he could. My wheels locked and I slid rapidly towards this man who, while doggedly holding his ground, began to step nervously from one foot to another.

★★★★★

'Right Old Girl. It's a lovely morning and we're off for a day out,' Her Ladyship cries as she loads me up with picnic stuff. Goody, I think to myself, I was somewhat lost in the past in there. Then before I can say independent suspension, whatever that is, we are on our way. I have to say that I am feeling rather anxious as Her Ladyship steers me onto the motorway.

I hate motorways and while it might be early on a Sunday

morning, there is still a lot of traffic racing past. Would someone tell me please, why do lorries have to blast their horns at us while they drive past? They scare the living daylights out of me. Ah, Her Ladyship is signalling that we are turning off. Thank God for that, this is a very steep hill and I'm sure I am making rather a lot of smoke.

'Where's that damned turning then? The map says there should be a turning.' That's right, not only is Her Ladyship struggling with me, she has a map unfolded, flapping around in the wind. So now she is lost. Forty miles from home and this idiot of a woman is lost.

'Excuse me,' she enquires in her best crisp English of a rather hairy man standing with a shovel by the roadside. 'Am I on the right road for the Country Park?'

'No,' he replies and he walks away, leaving Her Ladyship mouthing the words 'But, but, but…'

I am beginning to enjoy myself. What's she going to do now? She pulls away and follows the road for another few miles. Then we see another man. She stops and asks again and we are told that we have to go back to where we met the hairy one and the Country Park is just round the corner from there.

So Her Ladyship, snarling now, turns me around and heads back to where this time she finds the entrance to the Country Park.

'Ah you made it,' says a man with a clipboard. 'So this is the infamous Miss Daisy.' Me infamous? Who on earth came up with an idiot idea like that? We are guided to a spot where we park between two of my relatives, a scruffy old dear and one who, while a couple of years older than me, looks fantastic. To be honest I don't care. I'm completely bushed and I just want to rest. Out Her Ladyship climbs and she wanders off.

'Some bits for you Old Girl,' she says as she returns. 'We'll get you back to full health pretty soon.' And she dumps a pile of unappealing and possibly surgical rubber bits and pieces onto my seat. Then she's gone again, this time to look at my other relatives.

'Would everyone taking the driving tests, please come to the ring.' The public address announcement sounds across the country park just as Her Ladyship settles in to her picnic lunch and she almost chokes on her smoked salmon sandwich.

'We'd better get going then. I hope you are up for this Old Girl.' She hops back into the driving seat and we are off to another part of the field, leaving the picnic hamper and rug where it was. We arrive at a big roped off area with poles planted in odd places in the ground. Lying on the ground is one weird contraption with a rope attached to it.

'Now we'll see how much you know your car', says a man who I think is the organiser and he proceeds to explain to Her Ladyship what she needs to do.

'Right, it's quite simple,' he says. Uh Oh, here we go. I hope Madam pays attention. 'Now, you see that horizontal bar across those posts? Well, from where you are now, you have to guess the height of your car and tell them whether you want the bar moved up or down, so that when you pull forwards your car just goes under it with the least possible clearance but without touching it either. Understand?'

'What bar? What posts?' Her Ladyship responds. I think she's doing this on purpose, but perhaps not. 'Oh those posts. Silly me. Oh, that's easy. Can I go over to them, my eyesight…' Becoming frustrated, the man interrupts.

'No you can't. So you stop your car so its highest point is just under the bar. The closer you are without actually touching it, the more points you get. Then,' he adds, before Her Ladyship can make another remark, 'then you need to drive into that gap by the cones and pretend it's a garage, but you must stop as close to the wall as you can without touching it. Okay? Then you do exactly the same but by reversing in. Finally you need to move to where that rope is attached to that other pole. You will be handed the end of the rope and you need to drive round in a big circle without letting it touch the ground. Then…'

But there's absolutely no point him continuing. Her Ladyship has completely glazed over. She's still thinking about the horizontal bar. He walks away shaking his head as Her Ladyship starts on her 'up a bit… there… a bit more up on the right… good… down on the left a bit…'

Quite frankly, it would have been easier if he had explained it all to me, then she won't make quite such a pig's ear out of it. While this was going on, I notice a man who seems to be watching us closely. I wonder what he wants.

He is waiting for us as we return from the driving test to our space. 'I was listening to that engine while you were driving around,' he says. 'It really doesn't sound at all well.' You can say that again. His conversation with Her Ladyship gradually reveals that I am about to go away yet again to have even more work done. This time to my engine. At last!

Their conversation is interrupted by an announcement over the public address: the awards are being given out and it seems that I have won second prize in my class. Personally, I think I should have been first, but I expect that Her Ladyship's lack of enthusiasm to give me a proper clean and polish this morning is the reason I came second.

Then shock, horror. What's that? Her Ladyship has won the cup for being the best lady driver in the driving tests. Of course she's the blooming winner. She was the only lady driver to take part.

Before I know it we are off again… I'd hoped for home but this time we are following the gentleman who had been chatting to Her Ladyship about my engine, a nice man called Mister John. It seems that I am going to be staying with him for a while.

*****

Now, back to that police constable. I bet you were thinking that I'd knocked him over, don't you? Well you are wrong, because I did manage to stop – just, with my radiator touching his tunic. What a brave man I thought to myself.

'Well, well, well, well. What have we here then?' The constable whipped out his notebook, obviously delighted that his night shift wasn't going to prove uneventful. He walked slowly round to Oh David's open side screen, confident that I was now unlikely to make a run for it.

Oh David collected himself and Don't Worry Beatrice groaned in agony as she looked pleadingly at the policeman.

'Officer, we… umm, my wife is having a baby and we have to get to hospital.'

'What?' The police constable quickly returned his notebook and pencil to his top pocket. 'Right I will come with you and clear the way.'

At this he jumped onto my running board, planted his whistle into his mouth, grabbed my windscreen frame and wing mirror. 'Off you go then and whatever you do, don't open the door,' he shouted through semi clenched teeth, trying not to lose his whistle. Oh David accelerated away again, with the constable clinging on to me for dear life and blowing his whistle for all he was worth to get any other cars that might be stupid enough to be out in Oxford in the middle of the night to move out of our way. Ten minutes later I pulled up outside the main door of the general hospital. The police constable ran in and returned with a wheelchair and a nurse. 'Oh David, I think its coming,' shouts Don't Worry Beatrice and all three and the nurse were gone into the hospital, leaving me standing there, all alone.

★★★★★

I've been with The Nice Mister John barely a month. But now I feel fantastic. I've been given a new engine. Well not a new one, but one that has been rebuilt and it's brilliant. Honestly, I feel as though I could climb Mount Everest at the moment. Her Ladyship arrives with her daughter and The Boy to pick me up and The Nice Mister John, who sorted my engine, hands over my key with a stern warning.

'Right,' he says. 'This new engine is a sports engine and it has a higher compression head.' Her Ladyship nods but has that look in her eyes again. You know Dear Diary, the lights are on, but there is no one at home. She hasn't a clue what The Nice Mister John is talking about.

'The old one was a standard engine,' he goes on. 'This one has fifty percent more power than that one.' Then, as he tells her that my old engine developed just twelve brake horsepower, while this new one develops eighteen, I can see that the whole thing is going over her head. She doesn't understand a word he is saying, but I do. I realise exactly what he is talking about. After seventy years of being a rather ordinary car, I have become a powerful sports car. Wow! Now I can really have some fun – forty, fifty, maybe even sixty miles an hour, here I come!

'Does that mean she will go faster?' Her Ladyship is still trying to grasp his message. 'I mean with cable brakes, these narrow tyres and so on, will fifty or possibly sixty miles an hour be a good idea?'

'Oh, she won't go any faster,' says The Nice Mister John. 'She'll just reach her top speed a lot more quickly. Instead of nought to thirty in thirty five seconds, she'll reach that in – gosh – probably twenty five seconds.'

'Is that good?'

'Yes it is good. But it means that you will have to be more careful as you get used to the increased acceleration.'

'Oh, right.' I really don't think that she has got the message even now.

Thirty minutes later, after a little run round the block with The Nice Mister John, I am on my way home again. Then something really strange happens and I feel as though I have wet myself. There is steam everywhere and Her Ladyship pulls over into a lay-by with her daughter in close pursuit.

'There was steam pouring out from underneath,' she shouts as she gets out of her car and comes towards us.

Her Ladyship lifts my bonnet to discover there is indeed steam emanating from a hole at the front of the engine. I feel completely flushed. 'I think she's blown out a core plug,' she says and pulls out her mobile phone. How does she know about core plugs I wonder?

The Nice Mister John arrives a few minutes later in his car. He takes a look at me and sucks in through his teeth. Have you noticed, Dear Diary, that men who fix us cars have this habit of sucking through their teeth? It's usually a precursor to bad news – You know the sort of thing – something that should cost ten pounds, will suddenly cost over a hundred.

'You are right, it's the core plug,' he says as he proceeds to remove most of my front end, my bonnet, my hoses and my radiator. He then opens a plastic box containing lots of different sized metal discs. 'That one should do,' he says as he starts to fit it in place. He then produces the most enormous hammer and whacks it in to place. Ouch!

'Try that,' he says as he puts some more water into my radiator.

Her Ladyship does and we are on our way once again. Five miles on, there's more steam, another lay-by and another hole, suggesting that another core plug has gone absent without leave. This time though it's at the top. Out comes the mobile phone again and The Nice Mister John is back, this time with a length of rope.

'You're beginning to make a habit of this,' he jokes to Her Ladyship and before she can come up with an answer, he goes on, 'I am going to have to check them all. Let's tow it back to my place.' I notice the colour draining from Her Ladyship's face. She hates being towed.

'Whatever you do,' says The Nice Mister John, as he ties the other end of the rope to his tow bar, 'don't let the rope go slack.' Then we're off, The Nice Mister John in front with his car, then attached to a length of rope is me and following along behind in her car is Her Ladyship's Daughter, keeping a discreet distance. We must look like a funeral cortège. I can feel Her Ladyship gripping my steering wheel uncomfortably tightly and her foot seems permanently on my brake. Oh yes, she is definitely not letting this rope go slack. After a couple of miles Her Ladyship notices much flashing of headlights from behind and having signalled The Nice Mister John, we all pull over.

'There's smoke pouring out from the rear wheels,' shouts Her Ladyship's daughter. 'Horrible smelly smoke.' All three gather around and stare at my rear wheels, which are still smoking happily away.

'When I said don't let the rope go slack,' says The Nice Mister John, 'I didn't mean that you should follow me with the brakes full on.' Poor old dear, she really is messing this one up isn't she? 'I think we should pause a little while. Let the brakes cool down a bit.' A few minutes later we are on our way back to The Nice Mister John's place.

'I'll need a week to sort this engine out. Come and get her next Sunday… and it might be a good idea to keep a few spare core plugs in the glove compartment in future.'

The Nice Mister John looks very concerned. My heart sinks; I want to be home now. I suppose there's one consolation; at last I can get back to my memoirs again.

★★★★★

Where was I? Oh yes. Outside Oxford General Hospital, waiting for Oh David and Don't Worry Beatrice to come back. But it was the police constable who returned first. He leant against me and lit a cigarette.

'Well car, I bet you haven't had to do a trip like that before. You didn't know you had that in you, did you?'

It's true, I didn't. It was rather exciting though. It wasn't long before Oh David returned as well. He had a wide grin stretching almost from ear to ear.

'It's a boy,' he exclaimed as he declined a cigarette that the police constable had offered him. Oh David never smoked. 'Thank you so much for your help officer. They are both doing really well. What's your name by the way?'

'Simpson sir. The same as that American woman who has run off with our King.'

'No, no, your Christian name. What's that?'

'It's Albert sir,' came the sheepish reply. I had the feeling that perhaps policemen were not supposed to give their Christian names to members of the public.

'Then that is what we'll call him. Albert Philip Johnston. Sounds really good doesn't it officer? Albert Philip Johnston. Philip was my father's name.'

'Was it sir? I am honoured, thank you.' The police constable was obviously delighted at that news. Then he remembered that he was still on duty. He dropped his cigarette and trod on it.

'Now sir, you were speeding back there and you nearly ran me down, didn't you?' He pulled out his notebook, paused, then smiled,

30

'But I think, I'll let you off on this occasion sir. I think there are some mitigating circumstances to take into account here don't you? The sergeant will probably yell at me when I get back to the station. But please, Mister… Johnston isn't it?'

'Yes officer, my name is Johnston – David Johnston.'

'Mister David Johnston… Sir; please don't do anything like that again. You go back to Mrs Johnston now sir, I am sure that she needs you.' He wandered away, obviously delighted that the new baby has been named after him. 'Well, well, well. Albert Philip Johnston eh? I wonder what the missus will say when I tell her.'

★★★★★

It's The Boy's birthday and it seems that I am to become part of the entertainment for his party. I hear the boy's voice outside my garage. 'Gran, can we go and play in Miss Daisy?' Uh-oh, alarm bells start ringing.

'No I don't think that's a good idea. Why don't you all go and play in the garden instead? It's a lovely day.' Well done Your Ladyship, that's what I like to hear, but you could be just a little bit more assertive.

'Pleeease?' The Boy knows that she'll weaken to his pleas. She always does. 'Oh Gran, pleeease can we just sit in Miss Daisy? We won't fiddle with anything. Promise.' Humph I've heard that before.

'Oh all right then. But only for a few minutes, because everyone's mummies and daddies will be along soon to take your friends home.'

My covers are whipped off and a bunch of excited children with sticky fingers and chocolate covered faces jump in and start bouncing on my seats, blowing my horn, yanking my gear stick back and forth, switching my wiper on and off and covering my steering wheel and other parts of my anatomy with chocolate and

31

jam. And she, Her Ladyship, just stands there smiling while I suffer this indignity. What have I done to deserve this? I think I'd prefer The Nice Mister Weston wiping me down with his oily rags to be honest.

Oh gosh, those oily rags. He never changed and quite frankly, it used to drive Oh David absolutely mad. I remember I had been there for my usual six monthly service; it must have been the winter after Albert Philip was born and it was a very cold January afternoon. Oh David arrived to pick me up. As he entered the workshop The Nice Mister Weston was wiping my bonnet down with that awful oily cloth. The thing is, oily cloths aside, The Nice Mister Weston looked after me really well and I think Oh David felt that he would upset things if he complained. So he preferred to say nothing and simply take me home and clean me up there.

'How is she Mr Weston.'

'Oh she's fine Mr Johnston, absolutely fine. You haven't done many miles since the last one, have you?'

'No – well, we only use her at weekends. I walk to work and Mrs Johnston doesn't drive. Why?'

'It's nothing, with this low mileage you won't need to worry about a decoke for a while, but when you get ten thousand miles on the clock, you'll need to think about it.' I think the Nice Mister Weston was keen to get his hands into my nether regions. 'Oh by the way, I've drained the water from the radiator Mr. Johnston. Don't put any more in until this cold weather has passed.'

'Is that wise?' Oh David asked.

'Well, we only need a really cold night and your engine would freeze up. The Austin Company advise that you empty the radiator completely in very cold and frosty weather. Apparently, there is a new additive called Glycol on the market. You add it to the water in the radiator. It's supposed to stop the water freezing, but it is quite expensive and I'm not convinced that it's any good. No, Austin recommend that we simply empty the radiator until the cold weather has passed.'

Oh David didn't seem that convinced, but he never questioned The Nice Mister Weston's actions. He paid his bill and took me home, where he once again washed me down and polished my bodywork.

★★★★★

Nowadays, I expect the winter months to be a time when I am wrapped up warm and resting in a cosy garage. But no, it seems Her Ladyship has other ideas. This morning, she throws open my doors, whips off my covers and announces that she has decided to take me into town for some reason best known to herself.

A cold blast of air from outside passes through my undercarriage. 'We haven't had a drive in such cold weather,' she says. 'Now what do you think? Is this a two or a three clothes peg start up?'

I know I've mentioned this before, but she really does need to find a better way to hold my choke out while she starts me up. I mean, would a new choke cable be too much to ask? You see, not for me the ease of blipping the remote locking device on the key fob and the computer-controlled starting up procedure. No, starting me requires a degree of dedication and a considerable sense of ceremony and even then I only start up if I feel like it. I don't bother with remote locking. In fact I don't even bother with locking. In my day people just didn't steal cars. So in today's criminally inclined world, Her Ladyship has taken a tip from a Second World War regulation – she disables my engine by removing the rotor arm from my distributor whenever I am parked up, even in my garage. This means any potential young thief will be unable to take me off on a joy ride. I've always wondered why they call it a 'Joy Ride' by the way.

So the first thing she does is to restore the rotor arm into its rightful place. She pulls out my choke and out come three clothes pegs. It is so very cold that two would simply not have been enough. Then, without switching on my ignition, she cranks my starting handle for the recommended twenty turns. Well, that was her intention, but as usual she only reaches about twelve. Totally unfit you see. With that little job done, she gets in and adjusts my advance and retard spark control… not now, Dear Diary… not now. Another day… I'll explain another time. Finally she switches on my ignition and grabs the choke control with her left hand, pulling it out even further than the three clothes pegs will allow, and pulls the starter button with her right. Only now, should I actually feel so inclined, might I allow my engine to start. This is the time for me to have a bit of fun, so I run sweetly for a few moments and as she gets ready to pull away, I simply let the engine stop.

The sight of her frantically adjusting everything without the slightest knowledge of what she is doing, and continually failing to start me up again, is just lovely. Then just as she thinks she has exhausted everything that she wants to try and is seriously thinking of giving up, I simply start up again. Oh such fun.

We head off into town while Her Ladyship's fingers turn blue. What on earth am I doing driving into town a week before Christmas? Still it all looks very glittery, the shop lights sparkle in a myriad of colours and the place is heaving with well-wrapped human bodies scurrying to and fro. We pull up by the pavement and I can't help thinking how pretty the road looks with two lovely yellow lines stretching away into the distance. 'How Christmassy', I think to myself. Then along comes a little man with a hat band that matches the colour of the lines. I wonder if he is one of Santa's little helpers.

'You can't park here, Madam.' Is he talking to Her Ladyship or to me?

'Why not?' comes Her Ladyship's sharp reply. I sense some tension, but I agree with her. Yes you little man with the yellow band on your hat. Why not?

'No parking at any time. Can't you see the sign? Can't you see the yellow lines?'

'Now look Constable,' she says. Gosh haven't the police changed? They always used to wear blue serge. I don't think the yellow sends out the right message for a policeman. 'There's no need to get shirty with me,' she says. 'I just want to pick some maps up from that shop – look, that one over there – and then I'll be gone. I will just be two minutes at the most.'

'First of all Madam, I am not a Constable.' Oh not a policeman, that's all right then. 'And secondly I am not getting shirty. Move that car… please madam… now!' This bit is said through clenched teeth and I wonder whether there is a degree of exasperation in his voice, or is it irritability?

By now, a small crowd is gathering to see what is going on and, sensing defeat, Her Ladyship climbs in and takes me to some sort of car parking place. Personally, I can't understand what all the fuss is about. I've always parked at the roadside. All I can surmise is that this little man must be responsible for keeping the yellow decorations clear ready for Father Christmas to land his sledge. Obviously the fact that I have parked on it has upset him. What a silly little man.

He reminds me of someone. Oh yes… Those wonderful few years, those early years of my life. It seemed as though we didn't have a care in the world, save for that nasty little man with the toothbrush moustache in Germany. I kept overhearing people talking about him with really grim looks of their faces. Then that awful day. I'll never forget that day. Oh David came into my garage. He was wearing a sort of khaki brown suit.

'Hello Daisy girl,' he said. 'Umm, I am afraid that I have to go away for a bit and I think that you are going to be stuck in here for a while. I don't know when we'll all be able to head out into the countryside for lunch again. But all being well it won't be for very long. Anyway, in the meantime I have to make you safe and secure until I get home again.' He then proceeded to hoist me up into the air and rest my axles on some blocks of wood. He then removed the rotor arm from my distributor. 'I have to do this Daisy girl. It's the law now. All unattended vehicles must be disabled.'

He then disconnected my battery, drained my radiator and stepped back; I am not sure whether it was to admire his handiwork or to think he had missed something. He stroked his chin. 'I know, that's what I'll do…'

Suddenly he was gone, back into the house, and returned a while later with a small brown envelope. I managed to see that it had 'To whom it may concern' written on it. He pulled my passenger seat forwards and proceeded to empty my toolbox. He secreted the envelope under the matting at the bottom of the toolbox, returned the tools, shut the door and finally he covered me over with some sheets.

'There, you'll be nice and comfy now. I'll try to get back to you all soon. I promise.' He then left, making sure he shut the garage doors properly.

I never saw 'Oh David' again.

Chapter Two

I enjoy the odd little tootle around the countryside,
but all that way into foreign lands?

Tuesday 15th March 2005

So here I am. I've survived a year with Her Ladyship and I've made it to seventy one without major mishap. There are a few minor embarrassments mind you, but nothing too disturbing. I suppose if the truth be known, I am beginning to get used to Madam's somewhat extreme foibles. Hasn't it been a long winter? Well I think so and apart from a few little outings with you know who, I've been quietly sitting here thinking about what I should be putting in those memoirs of mine. I had got as far as… yes, that's it, life in Oxford with Oh David and Don't Worry Beatrice.

'Good morning Old Girl… Happy seventy first,' Her Ladyship cries as she throws open my garage doors. 'What a lovely day for your birthday. I've got a couple of surprises for you.' At this point, The Boy appears and together they start to sing Happy Birthday to me. Oh for Heaven's sake, do I really want them telling the whole world that it's my birthday? This is so, so embarrassing. The situation might be improved if they actually sang in tune. Oh God, please hide me someone. Now there's a group of children walking past and they are laughing their heads off. I am not sure whether their ribaldry is aimed at Her Ladyship or me. Anyway, shouldn't The Boy be on his way to school?

'There you are Old Girl, that was our first surprise,' announces Her Ladyship after that terrible rendition. What? Is there more?

Surely not? I can't take so much excitement all in one day. I am seventy one you know.

'But here is the big one and you are just going to love this. I have decided to retire next year and since I will be just sixty, twelve years younger than you by the way.' All right, there is no need to rub that in. 'And the fact is, well I don't want to vegetate, pruning roses and knitting bootees for newborn family babes and all that. So I've decided that you and I are going to drive round the world!'

WHAT? Is that what you call a nice big surprise for my birthday? And what's all this about me 'going to love it'? The world? Us? Drive round the world? She's lost it. Her little oddities I can take, as I said, but now she's completely lost it. Does anyone out there know the name of a good home for the insane? I'd noticed that she'd been buying maps, maps of Algeria, Libya and Egypt. Indeed I thought they were for educational purposes. Then the other day, I overheard her on the phone talking to someone about shipping services between Singapore and Australia. I thought that she was thinking of importing some illegal substances. I never had an inkling that she was planning something like this.

Well if she thinks I am going with her, then she had better think again. I am no spring chicken; I enjoy the odd little tootle around the countryside, all within fifty miles or so from home. But that far into foreign lands? I mean, they don't have roads much further than Europe do they? I've seen the documentaries: people carrying goods on their donkeys on rough, stony roads. So all I can say is that she has a rather long walk ahead of her. If she tries to take me along, she had better remember whom it is that has the fuse to blow, the carburettor to get a mysterious blockage, a tyre to puncture, or a spark plug to oil up.

'We won't be going immediately,' she says. 'We have to get this right and it will take a few years to get everything organised. For a start, we need to do a lot more to you to make you capable of such a journey. So I think we should head off on some shorter trial runs to start with. You know, five hundred miles here or a thousand miles there and with that in mind, I've booked you onto your first trip to north Wales in a couple of weeks time. There's a few mountains to climb up there and it will be a good start for us both to get to know each other on a longer journey, but I would like to think that within the next few years we would be able to head off down through France, Spain and possibly into North Africa. Oh yes, that's another thing. I thought it would be a good idea to take in every continent. As far as I know no one has done that in an Austin Seven before. We've started to get you up to scratch and now you have your new luggage rack. We are going to need that.'

Ah yes, my luggage rack. Now that was a nice present. Talk about fashion accessories. You should see it. It really finishes off my rear end. Smart or what? Of course Her Ladyship would have made a complete mess of it if she had tried to fit it herself. For once she'd had the good sense to take me down to see The Nice Mister Arthur. He's good at things like that, a dab hand with his welding torch. I'll tell you what though; a very smart little Austin Seven van lives with The Nice Mister Arthur. He looks very smart and stylish in green. A good manly colour! He can try his starting handle in my engine any day!

The smell in The Nice Mister Arthur's garage reminded me of that time, gosh all those years ago, of those never-ending days and nights covered in sheets and blankets in Oh David's garage. It was all so quiet after Oh David went off to war. I did hear the occasional very distant explosion and I presumed that they were bombs, but they were a long way away. I think that the Nasty Nazi, as Don't Worry Beatrice used to call him, had decided not to drop his bombs on Oxford. Nevertheless Don't Worry Beatrice would appear without fail every few weeks to take my covers off, check I was all right and then crank my starting handle, turning my engine over a few times. Once that little ceremony was over, she would cover me up again and leave. She never said a word, but I sensed that she desperately missed Oh David. It was if she was in some sort of a dream. By coming in to check me over, she felt a sort of link to him.

Then suddenly one morning my covers were whipped off and the sunlight came pouring in. I saw the silhouette of Don't Worry Beatrice and with her was a man. But he wasn't Oh David. It took some time for me to get accustomed to the light and slowly I was able to make him out. He was quite tall and very thin; he wore a badly fitting suit and he could only walk with the aid of a stick.

'Well this is it,' said Don't Worry Beatrice. 'This was my husband's car. He called it Daisy, you know. He christened her that on the day he collected her from the showroom. It was after I had remarked that with those big wheels she looked like two bicycles bolted together. It seems rather silly to give a car a name, don't you think?' Well I didn't think so, I thought we all had names. The man limped over to me.

'So Daisy, let's have a look at you.' He turned to Don't Worry Beatrice. 'He looked after it well and it seems to have survived the war pretty well too. But the proof will be in the pudding.' He opened my door and got in. 'It's pretty comfortable isn't it? Only seven thousand miles? Is that all? In all those years? That doesn't seem very much.'

'Well we only went out at weekends. My husband cycled to work and I used the bus for shopping and things. We had planned that I would start driving her myself, but then they brought in the driving test just after we bought it and I really didn't want to go through all that. Then of course he put it up on blocks before he left to join the army.' She paused and stroked my radiator cowling; then, 'Did you know my husband quite well then? When he was serving in…'

'Yes, we were in North Africa together. We were good mates, in the same platoon. I was with him when he stepped on that... that...' He paused, and then bit his lip as if thinking that he shouldn't be talking about this. 'I'm sorry, I shouldn't have...'

'No it's alright,' she said, then suddenly changed the subject. 'So would you like it?' Oh why did she have to keep calling me It? I was not an It. At least I now knew what had happened to Oh David and to be honest I was warming to this new man. He had a tenderness about him.

'Yes, I think I would. I imagine that things have been pretty tough for you since, umm... How much are you asking?'

'I am afraid that I don't know what it's worth. We paid over a hundred pounds when it was new.'

'Well it is over ten years old now and we don't know if she'll even start.' He was stroking his hands over my steering wheel. You cannot imagine how good that felt to have a man touching me again.

'Tell you what,' he interjected suddenly. 'Since your husband and I were good mates, I will offer you twenty five pounds. I have seen cars like this go for less, fifteen pounds sometimes. But she is economical to drive and with the petrol rationing... well for old times' sake... and she does seem to be in pretty good nick. Twenty five pounds, how about that? But can I keep her here for a while and pop down next weekend to try to get her going again? Then, hopefully, when she is ready, I will be able to drive her home.' He'd got out by now and had come round to the front and tried my handle. It turned over. 'I see that you have been looking after her then. That's a relief.' The man limped back towards the door, but she stayed behind with me as if she was trying to cling on to the memories of the outings with Oh David just that little bit longer.

'Yes my husband asked me to check it every couple of months. He said I was to be sure to turn the starting handle over a few times. So I did.' She was murmuring vaguely and then she seemed to give him her full attention. 'Oh sorry, the twenty five pounds and coming back next Saturday. Yes that's fine. You can leave it here until you are ready. Leave it as long as you need. What's your name again?'

'Oh, Chalk, Eric Chalk. I'll see you next Saturday then. I'd better bring a new battery. That one has probably had it. Bye...' He'd gone before Don't Worry Beatrice could respond. She muttered a 'bye bye', but had returned to her deep thoughts again.

'Do you know Daisy, or whatever your name is. Apart from Albert, you are my last link with, with...' She started to sob.

'What's wrong Mummy?' A little boy was standing in the doorway now. 'Who was that? Wow is that Daddy's car?'

So that was Albert. I hadn't seen him since he was a baby.

'Nothing Darling, I'm fine. That man was a friend of Daddy's, before, before...' She straightened herself up, brushed some dust off her apron and turned towards the garage door. 'He is buying the car. We have no need of it now. Come along, it's time for lunch.'

'Can I play in it? Just while you are getting lunch ready?'

'No you may not. You'll get yourself dirty. Come along in now.' At that she turned on her heel and was gone. The boy Albert paused and peered inside me.

'Albert, come along now. Lunch!' The boy scurried away.

True to his word, Eric Chalk returned early the following Saturday armed with a new battery, a can of petrol and a tool kit.

'Well Daisy, we'd better get you going.' It took him most of that morning. But how wonderful it felt to have my engine running again. 'Now we've got some forty odd miles to do to get you home. Do you think you will be able to make it?'

What a thing to ask, of course I knew I could and my new driver, having given Don't Worry Beatrice five crisp white five pound notes, jumped in and pulled me out into the daylight. For the first time in years we hit the open road and headed north to my new home. As we drove through and then out of Oxford, we went past the garage owned by the nice Mr Weston. It was deserted now. The once lovely flowerbeds were full of weeds, the windows were broken and there was a For Sale sign hanging precariously on the door. I couldn't help wondering what had happened to him, had he been killed like Oh David? So much change and I, with a new driver and now going somewhere else to live, couldn't help thinking that I was entering another very different world.

Now what was I talking about? Oh yes, Her Ladyship's latest and by far her craziest scheme. Hopefully, her daughter will step in and make her see sense. Mind you, I am not the only one who thinks she's falling off her trolley. I overheard The Boy talking to a couple of his friends who had come to play the other day. 'Don't worry about my Gran,' he said. 'She's just bonkers.' Out of the mouths of babes and sucklings. Oh how true.

★★★★★

I headed north out of Oxford with Mister Eric Chalk. I had been wondering where we were going and eventually we passed a sign saying we were entering the village of Hardingstone.

'We'll be home soon Daisy,' he shouted above my engine noise. 'Not far now. Do you see that monument over there? That's Queen Eleanor's Cross. It's one of only three left now. She was the wife of the first King Edward. Apparently when she died, her funeral went through this way and the king built a number of these to mark the route.'

I've always wondered why he felt it necessary to tell me all that. I wasn't the slightest bit interested. We turned up a side road and pulled up outside a small house. He got out, grabbed his walking stick and limped up some steps to a front door. Rat-a-tat-tat. 'Missus Chalk,' he shouted. 'Come and see our new car.'

A plump woman, whom I presumed was his wife opened the door and came out to see what her husband was on about. Mister Chalk made a grand gesture with his walking stick and pointed it towards me.

'Oh Mister Chalk, is that what you've spent your demob money on? You said you were buying a car for us, not an old wreck like that.'

'It's only just over ten years old, dear, and most of that time it was in storage. She's called Daisy and she's only done ten thousand miles. She belonged to my mate. You know, the one who was killed in Libya. It was his car before the war. She's not that bad and a bargain at twenty five quid.'

'Hmmph, well she looks very old and she's very small isn't she? Are you going to be alright driving her, with your leg?'

'Well,' he said. 'I had no trouble driving up from Oxford. I am hoping that I can get her in to the big shed at the back of the garden. This'll be perfect when I start that job with the county council. Apparently she'll do forty miles to the gallon.'

'Well Mister Chalk, I still think you could have bought something better for the money, but since you are the one driving it, I suppose it's up to you what you drive.' She turned and went back in to the house. Mister Chalk started me up, took me up a little lane behind the house and plonked me in what was no more that an old shed. It wasn't as nice as Oh David's garage, but at least it was dry.

★★★★★

'Good night Old Girl. You completed that little trip with flying colours. Well done.' Her Ladyship switched off the light and was gone.

Well, I'm home from North Wales and it was not without incident. Last Friday, very early in the morning, Her Ladyship loaded me up with various spare parts, a can of oil, another of water and she plonked a suitcase on my back seat. She was then joined by her two

46

girlfriends, the Nice Miss Clem and the Nice Miss Claire. They also piled loads of luggage on to my rear seat. For a moment, I did briefly wonder judging by the luggage whether this might be the trip round the world she'd been planning. But no, this was as promised, one of her 'trial runs', the one she had been talking about a few weeks ago; the one north with the South Wales Austin Seven Club.

Fortunately for us all, she had absolutely nothing to do with the planning. The Nice Mister John, who had sorted out my engine last summer, was in charge of us all and it seemed that I was joining eleven of my relations on this adventure to Llandudno and back. I supposed that I better try to enjoy it. But first we had to get to Carmarthen, ninety miles to the west to meet the others, before even thinking about heading north.

Much to my surprise, it was a nice journey, no motorways and no speeding traffic. The roads seemed remarkably quiet. 'Isn't this wonderful?' Her Ladyship cried to her friends. 'The open road in front of us...'

The Nice Miss Clem cut her short. 'That's because we have about twenty vehicles stuck behind us.'

'What?' Her Ladyship retorted, 'Oh... I suppose I'd better pull over and let them through, don't you agree?' Murmurs of agreement emanated from her friends.

We'd completed most of the one hundred and eighty miles north without major incident, and I was beginning to think that I could manage this trip of Her Ladyship's around the world. No, no, whatever was I thinking? A comfortable two hundred trouble free miles is hardly the same as the thirty odd thousand troubled miles in inhospitable countries that a certain Madam had in mind.

As we headed north, Her Ladyship's confidence had been growing, that was until the Nice Miss Clem's scream alerted her to a very large and very fat bumble bee, which had flown in through my side screens. All three of these supposedly sensible, career women started to flap at it. On top of that Madam succeeded in swerving alarmingly on the road until the by now terrified bee buzzed off out of my other side screen. I didn't blame it. Who on earth would want to be travelling in the same car as these three alarming women?

Eleven hours after leaving Cardiff we arrived in Llandudno,

'God, I need a gin and tonic after that,' Her Ladyship announced as she levered her frame out of my seat. 'But I'll tell you something. I thought Miss Daisy would have given us a load of trouble, but it was everyone else who seemed to be breaking down. How could I ever have doubted her?'

Just give me time dear lady, I thought to myself. I will find the right moment.

They were all up bright and early on the Saturday morning. Her Ladyship, having devoured Manx kippers for breakfast, dutifully attended to my needs. Well she thought that was what she was supposed to do as all the others were examining their cars.

'It seems that we have a bit of a climb today Miss Daisy. We are going to drive through the Sychnant Pass. You'll enjoy that,' she announced as she polished my windscreen. 'But first we need some petrol.'

We all paraded into the petrol station on our way out of Llandudno. I thought of those days gone by when Oh David would beep my horn as we pulled into The Nice Mister Weston's garage to summon him to come out to shove his nozzle into my tank and then ask if I needed my engine compartment examining. Well, a little man did come out at this one, but only to show Her Ladyship how to put her credit card into a slot so that she could fill me up. He might have known about credit card slots but I certainly wasn't going to let him examine my engine compartment, not at my age.

Now to get to the Pass, we had first to head through the Conwy Tunnel. This was a motorway sort of road with the all the other traffic going incredibly fast. I think I've already mentioned that I don't like roads like this. Well, I like dark tunnels even less. This one was about a mile long and half way through I felt unwell. The air was awful and I started to cough and splutter. I thought of conking out there and then, but even I wouldn't do that to Her Ladyship and her friends in such a dangerous place. A badly lit tunnel with nowhere safe to stop was alarming to say the least and Her Ladyship and the Nice Misses Clem and Claire all willed me to pull us out of there. Almost as quickly as I started to feel unwell, I felt better again and we emerged, much relieved, from the other end of the tunnel. But our relief wasn't to last.

After about a mile we turned up a narrow road towards the Pass. The hill got steeper and steeper, I was finding the climb a real struggle and I could barely make five miles an hour. There were four relatives behind us and behind them I spotted a lengthening queue of modern cars. Then it happened. Cough, cough, splutter, splutter; right on the steepest part of the hill, which also happened to be a very sharp hairpin bend with a vertical cliff in front of us and a sheer drop behind us.

A couple more coughs and my engine died. Madam slammed on all the brakes and the Nice Miss Clem bailed out. Was she concerned for her safety? Did she think I was going to roll back down the hill and over the edge? But no, it seems she was intending to start pushing me out of the way. The queue of cars behind got longer as the other relations' drivers behind also gallantly jumped out and helped to push us to safety at the side of the road. Who said that old-fashioned road courtesy was dead?

Okay, so here we were halfway up a mountain and now stuck. Her Ladyship hadn't a clue what to do. Mind you, neither did her friends. But we needn't have worried. The other relatives' drivers descended upon my engine compartment like bees round a honey pot. It was a bit like a scene out of a hospital drama, with The Nice Mister John as consultant surgeon…

'Points need adjusting. That should work. Try it now.'

Yer-yer-yer-yer-yer went my starting motor. 'Nothing! Change the distributor. Anyone got a spare distributor?' One was produced, installed and…

Yer-yer-yer-yer-yer. Nothing again.

'Put the old one back in. Leads. Recheck all the leads. Blast and Bollocks, we should have set the timing…' The drama continued and I just sat there looking complacent and remained very, very quiet. Well, it was a nice sunny day and I was enjoying the scenery.

Then ninety minutes after stopping so suddenly, and you might be imagining that I am an attention seeker, I felt that the time had come for me to cough back into life.

'You've got dirty connections,' someone said to Her Ladyship. How did they find out about her Uncle Charlie? I wondered. Then someone suggested that we went to the pub. 'Good idea,' says Her Ladyship. 'I'll need a gin after that.' Now Dear Diary, I really don't you want to start thinking that Her Ladyship is an alcoholic, but I am discovering that she does enjoy her occasional little tipple.

After lunch, Her Ladyship decided that attempting the Pass was perhaps just a little too much after that and we headed into Conwy for a tour of the castle. Far more sensible if you ask me. What a load of stuff and nonsense trying to get me to climb steep hills at my age. Put that in Your Ladyship's 'let's go round the world' pipe and smoke it.

Fortunately The Nice Mister John had planned a shorter and easier trip for the next day. No steep hills this time, just a nice gentle meander through some of north Wales's beautiful scenery. There was only one snag, it was raining and well… I don't like rain. I simply don't like getting wet. Well, who does?

We sailed down to Betws-y-Coed but then as we climbed out the other side of the town, the rain got heavier. I was determined to prove to Her Ladyship that her new found doubts at my aging and therefore failing abilities were unfounded and I ploughed on with that sort of gritty British determination we used to see in the old war movies. Not even a Volvo who tried to drive us off the road could stop me.

'That driver's premenstrual,' chorused The Nice Misses Clem and Claire in unison. Her Ladyship just resorted to that oft-used two fingered hand signal that suggested she found serious fault with the other car's driving.

But just then we drove into a load of low cloud and I couldn't see a thing. Please stop. I wanted us to stop. I was not happy, but Her Ladyship seemed determined to keep going and they were all chatting away ten to the dozen, completely ignorant of my feelings. Then I had an idea.

I flicked my windscreen wiper blade off and into a ditch, leaving the arm swinging from left to right on my windscreen, giving out a sound not unlike that of a fingernail being dragged across a blackboard. That finally achieved a result. Brakes on, everyone out and look for the wiper blade. The chaps, who had been following us, were out and grovelling about in the ditch as well. The Nice Miss Clem found it first and before the men could take over to attend to this little difficulty, she had triumphantly refitted it to my wiper spindle.

But I wasn't to be beaten. I simply decided to make sure my wiper motor didn't work from now on. So what did Madam do? She completely ignored the fact that the wiper wasn't working and to annoy me, drove me back to the hotel without using it.

'Who needs windscreen wipers in cars like these?' She announced this to the others while leaning forwards to peer through my rain droplet covered windscreen. I felt really sorry for the relative in front, especially as it was being driven by The Nice Mister John. What if Madam didn't see him stop until it was too late?

Monday was our last day in North Wales and it was time for us all to go home. Her Ladyship was out of the hotel straight after breakfast. Thank God this time it wasn't the kippers. They have such a derogatory effect on her digestion. This time it was just a good old fashioned Welsh fry up. She checked my oil and my water and then wandered around my tyres, pretending she knew what to look for. What a shame she didn't check the wheels a bit more thoroughly. I was sure that one of them had started to feel a bit loose towards my rear end. I did wonder whether that, or something else, might be the cause of my throwing a wobbly on the drive south. But this wasn't to be the leisurely drive of the past few days; I had to get these three ladies back home to Cardiff, and preferably that same day, so I thought I'd better behave.

It was a sunny day and The Nice Mr Williams decided that we would take another route south, one where we could pick up the faster roads. Why on earth should one want to use a faster road for a car with a top speed between forty-five and fifty? It all seemed rather daft to me. But Dear Diary, you know what humans are like. Some of the relatives threw the odd wobbly. Me? I just wanted to get home. I was getting quite worried about this looseness towards my rear – we were getting nasty clunks every time we went round a right hand bend; nevertheless Her Ladyship blithely drove on without a care in the world.

We arrived home well after dark and, thank God, I didn't have to rely on my headlights. The streetlights are much, much brighter and Madam was able to find her way around quite happily without any assistance from my lights. Anyway, she has never set them up properly and they were pointing in every direction but forwards.

'Do you know girls? We've done five hundred and ten miles in the past four days,' Her Ladyship announced after consulting my odometer. 'Not bad huh? Who's for a coffee?' Making their excuses, the Nice Misses Clem and Claire climbed into their moderns and were gone.

'We didn't do too badly did we Old Girl? Now don't you agree that between us we could conquer the world?'

For goodness sake, we had a crisis on Saturday and could she fix it? No! Then we had another admittedly smaller problem on Sunday. Could she fix that? No! Now I feel a real looseness in one of my rear wheels and she hasn't even noticed that something is wrong. Then she has the gall to suggest that we are ready to go round the world together. Well, in her dreams. At the moment, I don't think we could even make it safely over the Severn Bridge. And I wish she wouldn't call me Old Girl. A bit of respect wouldn't go amiss. I was always referred to with respect in the old days. Now Mr Eric Chalk always treated me with respect. He took great care of me and every Saturday without fail, he rolled me out of the shed for a clean and a polish. Then he would check me over to see if I needed more oil, a touch of grease, even a minor repair. He never took me to see anyone like The Nice Mr Weston; he always did everything himself. I rather liked that.

I used to take Mr Chalk to work every day. He worked for the local council, something to do with the sewers. He was very fond of his drains and sewers. In fact he almost had an unhealthy interest in them. Certainly, he loved to talk about them but others, especially Missus Chalk, seemed completely uninterested. Sometimes on his days off, he would come in to my garage looking rather down.

'Sorry Daisy, we can't go out today – petrol rationing and all that. We've got less than a gallon in your tank. It's more important that you get me to work than take a pleasure drive. Anyway, my new ration cards will be here soon. Then we'll be okay and we can go out for a nice long drive. Perhaps we could persuade Missus Chalk to come along as well.' He said that last bit with a total lack of enthusiasm. Sometimes though, I rather wish we had petrol rationing today. It would temper Her Ladyship's enthusiasm for this crazy world trip she has in mind.

I couldn't help noticing that getting petrol had changed from when Oh David took me to The Nice Mr Weston. Eric Chalk took me to a place that had posh electric pumps with illuminated signs on top. I remember them well; the sign proudly announced it had National Benzole Mixture. No longer did the man who sold the petrol have to use a hand pump. This time he just plonked in his nozzle, pressed a lever and the petrol pumped in.

But the roads were also changing. Those strange erections at the side of the road that flashed red, orange and green lights and could force us to stop. There were one or two around before the war but now they were breeding. We also had to stop for humans to cross the road. I did remember some of those when I was younger, but there were many more around in Eric Chalk's day. My relations were beginning to change as well. They had sleeker bodies and could apparently go much faster than me. Whenever we were stopped at one of these erections with the coloured lights, one of these sleek things would pull alongside and growl at me, 'You should be on the scrap heap. You pre war lot are always getting in our way. This is the bright new world and it hasn't got room for the likes of you.' As nice as Eric Chalk was, I was beginning to think that I wanted to go back to Oh David and Don't Worry Beatrice.

★★★★★

'Right Old Girl,' Her Ladyship cries. 'It's MOT health check time.' Does she really think I am ready for it? Since getting back from the north, the looseness in my rear wheel has reached a point that I make rude noises when going round both right and left hand bends. It sounds a bit like I'm breaking wind, or more likely it sounds like Her Ladyship breaking wind. Have I mentioned before that she is a martyr to her bottom? Her flatulence can be legendary. But these noises were sharper than her usual blurps. Yet she still doesn't notice. Either that, or she is ignoring the problem and hoping it will go away. That's more like it.

Then in she hops and starts me up. 'Come on Old Girl, we mustn't be late for your health check. I'm sure you'll be fine. Nothing wrong with you.' There is a roundabout within a few hundred yards of home and as we went round, 'G-G-G-G-G-G-R-R-R-Rind. Nothing, no reaction from Madam. Good grief, she still hasn't noticed.

We've barely done a mile when an old van behind us starts flashing his lights. Her Ladyship pulls me over and the van stops behind us. The driver gets out. 'I do hope you don't mind me stopping you like this,' he calls out as he walks towards us.

'Well it is a bit inconvenient,' comes Madam's curt reply. 'We have an MOT appointment to keep.'

'Well Missus if I was you, I'd sort out that wheel wobble before you go much further. Otherwise I reckons it'll fall off.'

Her Ladyship bristles as she sits bolt upright. 'Wheel wobble my man? What on earth are you talking about?'

'That nearside rear wheel. I just followed you around that roundabout back there and I thought your wheel was going to fall off, it was wobbling so much.' The man is obviously very concerned. Her Ladyship throws my door open and leaps out.

'I'll have you know that this car has no such problem.' She walks round to my rear nearside wheel. 'That looks absolutely fine to me. Look nothing wrong with that.' She pushes my wheel with her foot. CLUNK.

'Ah. Oh. Oh dear. It seems to have come loose.' Bingo. The penny has finally dropped. How many weeks is that? She has finally realised that I have a problem. Not a little problem either, but a very big one. Why does she always seem to go into denial every time I have a problem? She lets them build up and up until they get really serious. If she had done something about this in north Wales, just checked my wheel nuts, this wouldn't have happened now.

'I think I need to tighten these wheel nuts,' she says to the man.

'And you didn't notice anything?' he shouts as he walks back to his van. 'Lady, you don't deserve that lovely old car.' He jumps in and drives off, leaving us by the side of the road. There you are Your Ladyship. You don't deserve me.

'Let's get those nuts tightened. Then we can go and get your MOT,' Her Ladyship mutters while rifling through the tool kit. 'Aha, that's what we need.' And she proceeds to tighten my wheel. But two of the wheel nuts will no longer tighten. They just spin around.

'Somehow Old Girl, I don't think you are going for your MOT after all. Hopefully, your wheel is safe enough to get us home.' Her Ladyship is now subdued as we head back home. Hopefully she will learn that I mustn't be taken for granted. Somehow though I think it's more likely she won't. And she's still calling me Old Girl. Damned cheek!

'Right, let's have a look at this wheel and its nuts,' she announces after making herself a mug of coffee. 'I think we need to get you up into the air first.' My normal subdued demeanour is ripped away as my rear end is hoiked unceremoniously upwards. 'I'm going to have to make a phone call. These nuts are just spinning around and won't undo.'

'You'll either have to try to saw through the studs or drill them off.' It was the voice of that Nice Mister John on the speaker phone. 'You know what's happened don't you?'

'No,' says Her Ladyship quite dryly. 'I haven't a clue. What has happened?'

'It was probably the trip to north Wales. Vibration and the direction of rotation of the nearside wheels on an Austin Seven means that the wheel nuts can work loose and it sounds to me that is exactly what has happened. You are supposed to check them every day. These cars don't have as many wheel nuts as a modern. I expect that you'll need a replacement hub. I'll talk you through taking that one off.'

Picture the scene Dear Diary, an anxious Ladyship being instructed over the speaker phone on how to remove my damaged hub. Then, 'I've got it off. What do I do now?'

The Nice Mister John's voice comes back. 'I've got another one here. Just bring the old one to me and I will swap them over.'

Two hours later I am lowered gently to the floor, all finished and as fit as a flea once again. Her Ladyship, while elated at her achievement in changing my hub, is covered in grime and oil.

'Do you know Miss Daisy; that's the first major repair job I've ever done on a car. I'm quite pleased with that. Let's go for a test drive, just to make sure you are okay.' So in she gets and off we go… My goodness that feels much better, no more noise and definitely no pain in my rear end.

I do remember something similar but more dramatic happen to me when I was out and about with Eric Chalk in Northamptonshire. He had been sent out to look at some problem with one of his sewers. Apparently a road gave way and subsided when a heavy lorry drove over it. Eric Chalk's boss told him that he reckoned the part of the road where it happened had been badly repaired after a stray bomb had hit it in the war and left rather a large crater.

For some reason, Eric Chalk decided this was an emergency and we roared off to where the incident had taken place. He was going far too fast when we swung round this bend and before we knew it, we too had lurched in to the crater just behind the lorry. More haste, less speed was the phrase that came to my mind at the time, but not before we heard a nasty metallic crack and one of my front wheels fell outwards. This whole experience was not helped by the fact that we were sitting in a foot of sewage and there was an awful pong.

'Morning Mister Chalk. That wasn't supposed to happen was it?' Talk about understatement, but I had already discovered that the men who worked for Eric Chalk had a particularly dry sense of humour, which was ironic as they spent most of their time wading through water. Eric Chalk pulled out a handkerchief to try to suppress the stench.

'This is all I need, Fred. Let's hope the insurance will cover it.' He squatted down to examine my damage. 'Crikey, it's the axle. It's snapped off by the hub.' He looked over to see that a tow lorry was already towing the lorry out. 'There's a garage up the road. I'll ask the tow truck people to lift Daisy out of this mess and take her there to be fixed.'

Fred nodded. 'Your Missus ain't going to be pleased though is she? Weren't you supposed to be taking her to see her mother this weekend?'

'Thank God for small mercies,' sighed Erick Chalk, realising that my damage had saved him from a weekend with the mother in law. Then he paused. 'Missus Chalk is going to be livid isn't she?' Fred nodded again. He'd met Missus Chalk once before. As it turned out the garage had a new axle in stock and were able to fix me in a couple of days, enabling Eric Chalk to make the trip to his mother in law after all.

★★★★★

It's quite late in the afternoon when Her Ladyship throws open the garage door.

'Hey Miss Daisy. We are off into town,' she shouts and hops in the driver's side, while The Boy gets into the other. I am not that fond of modern city centres at any time, there are just too many vehicles, but for some strange reason the streets today are absolutely heaving with people.

We arrive at a public house where Her Ladyship's daughter and her friends were waiting for us. There are humans everywhere and there's just nowhere for me to park. Then the pub owner comes out.

'Can you get through that gap between those two cars there?' he shouts. 'We'll move the tables and umbrellas, then you can park on the pavement.'

So gingerly, Her Ladyship manoeuvres me through the gap between the two parked cars and onto the pavement.

'Glass of wine Pam?' Well, I've never known Her Ladyship refuse an offer like that and she didn't disappoint on this occasion.

'Just one. I'm driving.'

It is a rather strange experience sitting among pub customers on a pavement. It's certainly not a lonely one. As I sit here among the tables and the umbrellas, to my delight I am getting admiring looks and comments from every quarter. Occasionally someone gets in to me while someone else takes a photograph. Then they swap over. Her Ladyship seems to be ignoring all these goings on.

'Another wine Pam?' someone shouts.

'I'd better not, as much as I would love one,' comes her reply. Then she gets up, along with her daughter, her three friends and The Boy.

'Right Miss Daisy, we're moving on.' I wasn't that sure she would achieve it, but she manages to get me out through that gap without a scratch. At least she's sober. But the friends are certainly full of bonhomie. Then we are off to our next port of call.

Another hour or so passes before Her Ladyship, her daughter and The Boy reappear. At the same time a taxi pulls up and they start to get in.

'Just a minute,' says Her Ladyship, 'I just want to check Miss

Daisy is okay.' It slowly dawns. She's just going to leave me here. Alone. In this street with all these strangers.

'Look Old Girl, I've had a couple of glasses of wine now. In any other circumstance I would drive you home, I'd probably be absolutely fine. But there are rather a lot of police around and I don't want to be stopped and breathalysed. As she speaks, a large crowd of rather drunken humans comes round the corner singing Sospan Fach, very badly by the way. Madam hesitates. Then…

'Look, you two take the taxi home,' she shouts above the noise. 'I am not leaving Miss Daisy here with all this going on. I just can't risk it.'

'Well on your own head be it!' says the daughter. 'Don't blame me if you are stopped by the police.'

'I'll see you at home,' cries Her Ladyship after the departing taxi. She plants her large frame onto my front seat and off we go.

Isn't it funny? As soon as we pull off, the place suddenly seems to be crawling with policemen. They are everywhere. I've never seen Madam drive so carefully. The police ignore us completely, I think they have far more important things to worry about and we make it home without incident.

It's funny how attitudes have changed towards drivers having a drink and then driving their car since I was young. It reminds me of a story a relative told me many years ago, just after the war in fact. She had been left outside a pub and her driver, the local vicar, had left her lights on while he popped in for 'a little quickie'. Something about thirst after righteousness, he told her. That quickie had turned into a three hour drinking session and by the time he came out, her battery was virtually flat. He was completely sozzled and there he was in the middle of the night, unable to use his starter and cranking her for all he was worth. He was, however, achieving absolutely nothing.

Then up rolled a shiny black car, just like many others of that time. But this one had a shiny bell at the front, an illuminated Wolsely badge on the grill and on its roof a glowing police sign. Out got two policemen, one a sergeant and they slowly put on their hats and walked up to this character, still cranking away like someone possessed.

'Are we having a problem sir? Oh it's the Reverend Smithson isn't it? Good evening sir. Can we help?' The sergeant towered above this hapless figure, still madly cranking away, beads of sweat now dripping from his forehead. In those days Dear Diary, local policemen did seem to know everyone on 'their patch', as they called it. His colleague watched from a little distance with a knowing grin on his face.

'Can't get the damned thing shtarted Shargent Thomas… can't undershtand it, it worked fine on the way here,' came the good reverend's reply.

'It's Thompson Sir, I'm Sergeant Thompson. You christened my boy last month. Let me see now Sir; first of all, have you considered trying to start it from the other end?'

'Other end?'

'Well Sir, you are cranking the exhaust pipe at the moment and correct me if I am wrong, but I don't think that's what it was intended for.' The sergeant was enjoying this as much as his colleague…

'Oh? Am I? Silly of me,' came the reply.

'Here sir, let us help,' and the sergeant gently withdrew the starting handle from the exhaust pipe and handed it to his colleague.

'Constable would you mind?'

The constable obliged and my friend's engine burst into life. 'I shay offisher, that's awfully good of you.'

'No problem reverend, no problem at all. All in the line of duty. Now you mind how you go then.' He saluted as my relative drove erratically off and that, Dear Diary, was how the police seemed to deal with drivers who had imbibed one or two too many when I was young. Later on, they would get drivers to walk along the white line in the middle of the road, then to touch their nose with their middle finger. And finally to say 'The Leith Police dismisseth us.' Fail one or more of those tests and the driver was up before the beak the next morning and down for a ten shilling fine and possibly an endorsement on his licence.

★★★★★

'Wake up Old Girl!' It's Her Ladyship. 'Come on snap out of it. I have a new friend for you. She pushes the garage door wide open and there staring at me was a complete stranger.

'Yes, that's right Miss D, I've finally got rid of that awful pile of Japanese rubbish. This is my new car, it's a Skoda.' They have a good reputation and I expect this one to see me into my grave.'

Now why would I want to know what sort of car it is? I really don't care. The name seems familiar, though, but I can't at the moment think why.

'The Skoda is built in Czechoslovakia.' She adds that, almost as an aside. Her mind seems elsewhere. She wants to say something else to me. Please God don't let it be something about going round the world. She grabs a duster and aimlessly starts to clean my windscreen which, incidentally, is already very clean.

'Miss Daisy, there is something I need to tell you.' She's going to sell me. That's it. She's had a good offer for me. Come on woman out with it. What is it you have to tell me?

'Miss Daisy, you know that I've decided to retire. Well I've now also decided to sell up here and move back home to Somerset. It's where I grew up and I have this sort of feeling that I need to go home.'

What is so sensational about that? I'd love to move to Somerset. No more queues of cars, no more traffic lights. Well, fewer traffic lights than here I am sure. But best of all, no more speed bumps. I can't wait to go.

'I just want a change Miss Daisy. I just want to move out of this city.'

Listen you old fool. Watch my lips. I'm ready to go. When can we leave?

'I don't suppose it will be until next summer and I have to sort this all out with my offspring. I don't suppose they would want to come to Somerset with me. Not with all their friends here.' As far as I am concerned, there's no need to discuss this any more. Just deliver me safely to my new home.

★★★★★

It was a few weeks after being repaired that I overheard a row coming from the Chalk household. Missus Chalk was telling him I had to go.

'I might have let you take me to mother's the other day, but you are not getting me into that car again. It's probably dripping with awful germs from that sewer.' I thought she was being quite unreasonable.

'Oh come on dear, she isn't that bad. They gave her a really good clean at the garage and I did another one when we got home. She'll be fine, honest. Anyway, I can't afford to replace her yet. I'm fond of the old car.'

'You can take it out on your own if you want to, but make sure you leave your shoes in the porch when you come back. I don't want you bringing pestilence and disease into our home. Mother is coming for Christmas and you know how she is about germs. And don't think you are going to pick her up from the station in that thing. She can take a taxi instead and you will pay for it.'

'Yes dear.' I am afraid that Eric Chalk was rather under the thumb of his good wife and I got the impression that he wasn't that keen to have his mother in law staying over Christmas as

63

well. He'd be under the thumb of two harridan women then. I'm afraid that it wasn't a very Happy Christmas for my Mister Eric Chalk.

Christmas is coming here now and the Goose is getting fat… So is Her Ladyship. I saw her coming back from shopping with a box of mince pies and several boxes of chocolates last week.

'They are not for me Old Girl, they are Christmas presents.' Oh Yes? Pull the other one.

Talking about Christmas, I have noticed that our owners are less inclined to take us out for a drive when the cold weather arrives. It strikes me that the generation of today's car owners are complete wimps. Now in the good old days, I was out and about all the year round.

I remember that cold winter of forty-seven. It snowed for weeks and weeks and then it was here for several months. I was stuck in my shed in Hardingstone for a while but it didn't seem that long before Eric Chalk opened my creaky shed doors, shovel in one hand and a brush in the other. 'Well Daisy,' he cried, 'we are not going to let a little bit of snow stop us getting out are we?'

I looked behind him, at first fearing that Missus Chalk was hovering not far behind. But there was a pile of snow on the road outside and it seemed almost as high as me. 'We'll soon get rid of that little lot won't we?' I had my doubts; there was a thick sheet of white covering everything. It took him several hours, but he did it and cleared a way for me through to the main road.

'There,' he shouted triumphantly. 'Now we can get out and I can get to work in you again.' He started me up and I tentatively rolled out onto a very cold and icy surface. Eric Chalk seemed to be aware of my nervousness and he drove me very slowly. Out on the road others were sliding about, pedestrians and cars alike. In those days, they didn't put all that salt and grit down on icy roads. After a while, Eric Chalk decided to turn me back for home.

'I think we need to get you some chains,' he said. 'You'll take to the road as if there was no ice there at all then. Yes, I will get you a set of chains.'

The next morning, even though there had been another dusting of snow, I proudly wore my new chains on my wheels and I drove him to work as if the roads were completely clear. Mind you he still had to wrap himself up nice and warm and by now I was using that antifreeze stuff in my radiator. We had gone about a mile when we came up on one of those sleek new cars. It had buried its nose into a snowdrift. Its driver was out of the car and walking up and down, occasionally slipping on the ice, and when he saw us he started to wave us down.

'Problem?' Asked Eric Chalk as we pulled up.

'Yes, yes… My wife has broken her arm. She was walking on the pavement outside our house and slipped on the ice. They can't get an ambulance out and I have to get her to hospital.' Golly gosh, I thought. Is this a case of deja vu? Now all we need is Constable Simpson.

'I can take you,' shouts Eric Chalk. 'I fitted chains this morning. Goes like a bomb on this ice.' The man having helped his wife from his sleek modern thing into me, climbed in himself and Eric Chalk pulled away. I glanced at the sleek thing that was looking rather sheepishly at me. Bright new world indeed. No room for the likes of me on these modern roads indeed! I was beginning to think that in another life I should have been an ambulance.

So it seems to me that since the present modern monstrosities provide a heater, even air conditioning and loads of other gizmos, it's understandable I suppose that our drivers prefer not to take us out when those piles of tin and plastic provide such creature comforts. But are they really more reliable than we are? There is certainly more on them to go wrong.

★★★★★

Since I am to spend most of the winter months shut away in the garage it would be nice if I could have some peace and quiet to work on my memoirs. But she won't even allow me that. This morning for instance, Madam appears with a machine that she plugs into the wall and attaches to the garden hose.

'It's a pressure washer Old Girl,' she announces. Ah I think, she is going to give me a really good wash. But don't you think I should be outside the garage rather than in it?

'Don't worry I'll shut the garage door so you won't get splashed with mud while I use it.' People never cease to amaze me sometimes. How can she wash me with that machine inside the garage with the doors shut?

'This won't take long. The drive is really filthy.' At that she slams shut the garage door.

The penny drops. She's going to wash the drive. But can't she see the gap at the bottom of this garage door where any muck that bounces up from the ground will fly straight through and smother 'guess who'? An already filthy 'guess who' in fact, about to be covered in yet another layer of muck and mud as a result of Her Ladyship's wild rampage with her confounded machine.

The door flies open. 'Okay Old Girl. Your turn now.' At this, Her Ladyship pushes me out onto her now clean, yet very wet drive.

'It'll be a very quick job with this machine,' she remarks as she manoeuvres it into a suitable position. 'You'll be bright and clean in no time at all.'

And she's off, squirting the water onto my bodywork, my windscreen, into my running boards – ooh that tickles. Then she pokes the hose under my wings and onto my suspension – now that hurts. Can't you turn the pressure down a bit? Ouch. But I am to be ignored and before I know it a soggy chamois leather is slapped on my bonnet and she is removing the last of the water and polishing me up.

The job completed, she rolls me back into the garage, turns to leave and spots that the recently clean drive is once again covered in mud; this time it's my mud.

'Oh Pook! I suppose I should have done you first,' she says looking back at me.

No, I want to reply. Because as soon as you would have pressure hosed the drive, the muck would still have flown under the garage door.

'Anyway you look very smart now, smart enough for our trip over to Bristol.'

Bristol? Why are we going to Bristol?

'Oh I haven't told you have I? We have to pop over to Bristol to see some people about our trip round the world. They think they can raise some sponsorship money for us.'

So, Madam has plans for a doubtful trip to Bristol with wild hopes that she will come back with a promise of money. I think I'd rather stay at home. It's too cold and wet out there.

'We'll call in the petrol station and fill you up before we head off,' she says. 'Petrol prices are rocketing at the moment. I'd better fill you up before it gets any more expensive. It's worse than petrol rationing.'

Oh no it isn't. She's never had to experience that. There were so many occasions back in Eric Chalk's day when he simply couldn't take me out because of the rationing. 'Sorry Daisy,' he would say. 'No trip out today. Not enough petrol.' Apart from the occasional trips to her mother for an eventually relenting Missus Chalk, I only ever had enough petrol to take him to work and back. But there again I also remember the day when it all came to an end. It was a bright day in the late spring of nineteen-fifty and he burst into my shed.

'Guess what Daisy,' he cried. 'They've ended petrol rationing! At last after years of restricted supplies of petrol, we can drive when and where we like without having to worry about how much fuel we have left. He was jumping up and down like a little child and tearing up his ration book. I thought he was going to wet himself in his excitement. 'Come on then. Let's go and fill you up!'

'Three shillings a gallon? Three shillings? That's fifteen shillings to fill the car up! Why the price hike?' Eric Chalk's excitement had completely abated. It seemed that they might have stopped rationing, but to make up for it the price of petrol had gone from two shillings to three shillings overnight.

'Don't blame me Guv. Blame the Labour Government. They dropped the rationing and doubled the tax.'

I remember the first time that Oh David bought petrol for me; it was just one and five pence a gallon then. Now it had more than doubled to three shillings and in those days you could buy a whole load of groceries for three shillings. So it is little wonder Her Ladyship is grumbling as she pumps my petrol into my tank at nearly four pounds a gallon.

We are soon on our way again and sail down onto the motorway that will take us to Bristol. Oh gosh how I hate these roads. The traffic roars past me at seventy miles an hour and I cling to the hard shoulder for all I am worth. But when a big lorry roars past, I still feel as though it is going to suck me under its wheels. And why do they have to blow their horns at me? It's really frightening. The trouble is that if Her Ladyship navigated me over the normal roads, it would take us ages to get to Bristol. They've closed down the Aust Ferry you know.

We arrive in Bristol and Madam negotiates me through the streets of Clifton to a very smart building. As we pull up a rather large, rather pompous man in an expensive suit marches out, followed by three minions who almost disappear behind his mountainous frame. He wears a forced smile and proffers a sweaty right hand as he marches up to us. Madam is hardly out of the car.

'My dear lady, welcome, welcome. I'm Rick Smales. Welcome to Smales Public Relations. This is Steve Adams and this, Richard Annis and here, my PA Joanna Davies.' After much handshaking Madam introduces me.

'So this is Miss Daisy is it? You really think that this old thing can drive round the world?' He looks at his assistants with a smirk and one eyebrow rising above the other. They all dutifully murmur agreement. Madam bristles and although I really don't want to drive round the world, I bristle with her and straighten myself up to my full five foot and give him a look of total contempt. He didn't notice. Mind you my real objection to this obnoxious man was more because he called me an old thing. I've sort of got used to Her Ladyship calling me that, but not this awful man.

'Of course she can,' Her Ladyship snorts. 'Of course she can. Other Sevens have done it before, but we shall be the first to take in all five of the continents.'

'Yes, yes, yes, you can give us a ride in her later. Joanna, be a sweetie. Run along in and make us all some coffees would you?' Joanna heads off and after a further look around me with the odd knowing sneer towards his other colleagues, Smales walks back into the building with Her Ladyship in tow. Now I really have taken a dislike to this man. He reminds me of the spivvy car dealers of yesteryear.

About an hour later, Her Ladyship returns with Rick Smales, his two male assistants following dutifully behind. 'In you get then,' she says. Now I know she has a large frame, but golly gosh Fatty Smales almost needed a shoehorn to get into my seat.

'Right Old Girl, let's show them what we can do.' And we are off, driving through the streets of Clifton. With a malicious grin Her Ladyship steers me over a pothole, I bounce into the air and the four bottoms on my seats momentarily ascend before landing heavily again.

'Jesus, doesn't this thing have any suspension?' Fatty Smales obviously wasn't expecting that.

'Of course she does,' retorts Her Ladyship. 'It's just that you are not used to hard suspensions. I imagine you probably drive something more comfortable.'

'A Beamer. Four by four actually. I find…' He was interrupted by Her Ladyship slamming her foot on my brake, grabbing the hand brake and pulling it for all she was worth. My wheels lock hard and we skid to a standstill just in front of a dog that has strolled into the road. The man called Steve is ejected from his seat and his head lands heavily on Fatty Smales's shoulder. 'The jacket Adams, the jacket,' he shouts, brushing the face away.

'The brakes are pretty effective too,' Madam retorts, but for a few moments Fatty Smales becomes very silent, obviously trying to regain his dignity, not that he had any in the first place. Then, sensing what he was going to say next, she adds, 'Would you like me to take you back to your office?'

'Yes, yes, if you wouldn't mind.' They all remain very quiet as Her Ladyship heads back to the Smales empire.

'Well,' Fatty Smales says. 'All I can say is that you are very brave even to contemplate a drive round the world. I wouldn't even drive that thing a mile. Nevertheless I think I might be able to find you some sponsorship. I'll be in touch.'

'Well Miss Daisy, that went well didn't it? You were brilliant by the way. I think you really impressed him.' Oh for heaven's sake. He was terrified, but judging by the way he treats his people, he deserved every minute of it.

Chapter Three

*All I have to do is push the brick through the hole in the floor and if
the rope goes tight in less than five seconds,
then I'm doing more than thirty."*

Wednesday 15th February 2006

Good gracious, doesn't time fly? It's already a month into another year and while every one else was enjoying their Christmas break, I spent mine in a darkened garage. That was because Her Ladyship had decided to desert me and hightail herself off to West Wales for those few days, partying the night away with her friends no doubt. She has often told me that she plans to grow old disgracefully, but I really wish someone would tell that woman to consider slightly less 'dis', and just a little more 'grace', thereby not embarrassing the rest of us.

Madam has also admitted to friends that she is not an enormous fan of winter. She claims to be a sun lover. And that is why she had barely got home from the trip to west Wales when she was off on another; this time to her favourite little haunt in the Caribbean. I suppose she would describe it as her annual dose of Sun, Sea, Sex and Slippy Nipple. Actually she is rather past it for that third 'S'... Well look at her... Slippy Nipple, by the way, is a cocktail she indulges in when she's on holiday. She claims that she is a completely different person over there, far more carefree, if that is at all possible judging by her behaviour back here. She says that she enjoys the raw and wild excitement she finds on the island.

Well, she got back last week and I could see that she had enjoyed herself. 'Well, Old Girl, that was a trip and a half,' she announces as she plonks several bottles of over strength rum on the shelves.

'This stuff would make your engine run, I can tell you. Where was I? Oh yes… two days after I arrived, my friend Marion, you know, the American Marion who I always stay with? Well two days after I arrived, she had a massive heart attack and popped off to the next world. I didn't know what to do. Should I find somewhere else to stay? But her friends on the island were able to contact her family in New York and they said it was all right for me to stay on at the villa for the rest of my holiday. But staying there on my own was rather creepy to say the least. It's not only rather remote; it is very close to the jungle and therefore snakes and tarantulas occasionally wander or is it slither in. Put simply, it wasn't much fun. So I got out of the villa as much as I could and then I met this fabulous American guy, his name was Bill and he looked after me for the rest of my stay. He's really nice.'

What a tart! Your friend Marion is barely cold in her grave and you are out partying the nights away and flirting with any man you lay your eyes on and a man from the colonies at that, God help us!

'Well,' she went on. 'We'd gone out to dinner at this nice restaurant. He insisted on my paying for my share. I thought that rather tight of him, but he assured me that was the American Way. Anyway, we ended up in Sam's bar. I was drinking Slippy Nipples…' Now there's a surprise. 'I must have been on my third, or was it my fourth? Well it doesn't matter, what did matter is that a gunfight started right outside in the street. I suppose that our American cousins must be used to this sort of thing, you know when bullets start to fly around, because they all dived onto the floor, taking their beers with them. I was still wondering what was happening when Bill grabbed my hand and pulled me down on top of him. "Get down onto the f*****g floor, you stupid idiot. Do you want to get yourself killed?" He seemed quite angry with me and there was I thinking that he wanted to have a kiss and a cuddle. I didn't know it was a gunfight, I thought it was fireworks.'

God give me strength, picture the scene, the cream of the colonies across the Atlantic take cover from flying bullets while a flower of the British Empire remains seated at the bar, resolutely refusing to let a little spat of gunfire ruin her evening. Well that is how Her Ladyship will tell the story when she has had a chance to think it through. The truth is that she hadn't a blooming clue what was going on. And this is the woman who thinks that she is going to drive me around the world? My God there will be death and destruction in our wake.

Then yesterday she comes into the garage, takes off my covers and says to me, 'Come on Miss Daisy, let's burn rubber.' Excuse me, what's all this burn rubber? For a moment I consider that she has finally lost it and is now a candidate for the nearest insane asylum and then The Boy appears behind her with one of his young friends and I realise that she is showing off, pretending to know modern street language. Judging by the way that The Boy's eyes go skywards, I realise that she has got that well wrong. I believe that is the parlance he would use.

They all get in and the boys settle on my rear seat.

'Right Old Girl, we are going posh today. We've been invited to tea with friends at the St. David's Hotel in the Bay. It's five star you know, so best behaviour if you please. And that goes for you boys as well.'

That's fine coming from her. We are off, through the streets of the city and Cardiff Bay. She turns off into a side street.

'There's something we need to pick up first,' she says as she gets out and goes into a shop.

'This is for your petrol can,' she announces to me as she returns waving a new leather strap and she proceeds to remove the old piece of rope that is holding the can onto the luggage rack and replaces it with the strap. So with petrol can and picnic basket now firmly in place, and looking very smart mind you, we sail up to the front door of this very flashy five star hotel. As Madam applies my brakes, a flunky in a great coat and a top hat far too big for his teenage head runs out and offers to park me, a job apparently he is supposed to do with all cars that arrive at the hotel. As the boys clamber out, Madam pauses, looks from me to the by now eager flunky and then back to me. She walks round to my front to make sure there is nothing he can drive in to, once he discovers that my clutch is not what he might expect. She then checks for similar obstructions to my rear before handing over my keys with a glint in her eye.

'But Gran, Miss Daisy's not very easy to drive,' says The Boy.

'Oh he'll be fine,' she replies, the glint in her eye now brightening.

The Top Hat is of course overjoyed... I am probably the first vintage car he has ever driven. But this joy comes rapidly to an end as soon as he gets in and starts my engine. First of all he grates my gears, then once he has worked out how not to do that, he stalls me a few times. Then he grips my wheel, pauses and mutters something to himself. I catch some comment about not being like an Escort. Now I didn't think they would allow people like that at this hotel. He then has another go. I start up and he proceeds to engage first gear and lets out the clutch – rather too suddenly I am afraid. I take off, thinking he expected me to make a world record attempt to jump over Cardiff Bay, but instead I land heavily a few feet away. Finally, Her Ladyship takes pity and suggests that perhaps it would be easier if she parks me instead. His top hat now decidedly lopsided, the crestfallen young man hands back my keys. But I have the last laugh; I make her grate my gears before moving off and the Top Hat walks off with a grin from ear to ear.

This reminds me of the time when Eric and Missus Chalk took me to a very posh country house hotel for a dinner dance – I can't remember the occasion. He appeared at the entrance to my shed in a penguin suit that had seen better days and stank of camphor. He drove me round to the front of the house where Missus Chalk was waiting in a gaudy brown and yellow ball gown, a moth-eaten fox stole tossed around her shoulders. I thought that she must have hired both from a theatrical costumiers, but it seems not.

'If I damage mother's dress from having to squeeze into this thing, you'll be for the high jump Eric Chalk.'

'Yes dear. It will be fine I am sure. Just make sure you have brought all your skirts in to the car before closing the door.'

'Hmmph… And another thing, you should have aired that suit for a few days to get rid of the smell of the mothballs. You stink.'

'Yes dear. But I fear that father's suit would have needed more than a few days to get rid of the smell after twenty five years of mothballs. But it looks all right doesn't it?'

'If you want to look like some faded nineteen twenties, second rate gigolo, then yes it's all right. But since this is nineteen fifty one Eric Chalk, then no it doesn't look all right, but it will have to do. Come on. We don't want to be late.'

We arrived at the country house hotel to be greeted by two liveried door attendants. I couldn't help thinking that the Chalks were about to appear very much the odd couple at this particular event.

One of the door attendants opened my door for Eric Chalk. 'May I park your car for you sir?' Then he took a step backwards as the smell of camphor hit his nostrils. The other attendant stepped forwards to open the passenger door for Missus Chalk.

'That is very kind, thank you. Be careful though, she has a harsh clutch.' Eric Chalk replied

'It's all right sir,' liveried attendant number one said, trying to maintain a discreet distance. 'I've got one of these myself. I know their quirks.'

Missus Chalk was still struggling to get out of my passenger seat while liveried attendant number two proffered his hand. She grabbed it ungraciously and hauled herself out.

'Why you couldn't have hired a taxi rather than make me suffer the indignity of this old car, I don't know.' Even at an event like this, poor old Eric Chalk was still in for a tough evening. Missus Chalk took Eric Chalk's arm and they proceeded up the steps.

'Poor bugger,' said liveried attendant one. 'Fancy being married to that!' At that point Missus Chalk tripped over the hem of her skirts and fell heavily. Eric Chalk helped her back to her feet and Missus Chalk immediately started to berate her husband.

'He's in for a fun evening then,' smirked liveried attendant number two.

★★★★★

'Good Morning Miss Daisy,' Her Ladyship announces with a particular verve as she throws open my garage doors. Go away, I think in reply, I'm busy. However, I've got to know that look on her face, the look that suggests she is about to have the opportunity to show off. But hang on a minute, who are those people? I peer past her at three rather charming young men. One is holding a clipboard; another holds a big camera and the third a pole with a strange furry thing at the end of it.

'We are going filming,' she announces. Filming? Me?? Me going filming??? So that's why she's been spending hours cleaning and polishing me for the past few days. She could at least have said something. I mean – you cannot expect me to go into such a demanding role without preparation. I need to prepare myself emotionally. A proper actor does not suffer the indignity of being woken up in the morning, handed a script and told to be on set within the hour to perform his lines. Dame Judy and Dame Helen would not be prepared to perform like this. So why ask Dame Daisy? She really should have warned me. Still, like any good professional, I decide to give it my very best. If only I knew what they wanted me to do.

'Yes, you remember the visit to Bristol last year? When we met

Rick Smales?' How could I forget that awful man? But what has he to do with this? 'Well, he wants us to make a promotional film to show to all the potential sponsors he hopes will put money into our round the world trip and that is what we are going to do today. You just wait there for a moment while we go in to the house for a coffee and a chat.'

And they were gone. It reminds me of when I was first filmed. Oh yes, Dear Diary, I have been filmed before, several times in fact, but the first time was really special and on a very special day.

It was the morning of the second of June 1953. Eric Chalk and Missus Chalk appeared in the shed door. This was a very significant day and for some reason Missus Chalk had stopped objecting to travelling around in me. I think it was something to do with her mother being mowed down on a pedestrian crossing by a brand spanking new car that the driver couldn't control. Apparently, mother didn't survive. But it left Missus Chalk with a very different attitude to me.

'Well Missus Chalk, we are going to go and see the Coronation today,' cried Eric Chalk. 'But first let's make Daisy look a bit more appropriate.' He produced a box from off a shelf and between them; they started to decorate me with flags and bunting, all red, white and blue. I have to say that I felt rather like a painted Jezebel, but the Chalks seemed happy with their efforts. As we drove along, the streets were also bedecked in red, white and blue flags and bunting. Everyone seemed really happy. I remembered the time when King George was crowned before the war. I was only three then and we heard it all on the wireless. Don't Worry Beatrice had decorated our house and garage with red white and blue as well. They even joined in a big party in the street.

But I was also confused. You see I had thought they had these Coronation things in London, not in Northampton. Nevertheless we pulled up at a pavement outside a row of shops and there was a small crowd gathering in front of one of them. Inside the shop window were a number of small glass screens, like fat framed pictures. But each one had the same picture flickering on it.

'There you are Missus Chalk, that's the Coronation,' said Eric Chalk as they both got out. 'It's on the television.' At that point a voice in the crowd shouted that he had a portable wireless in his car and that they could hear the sound on that. Everyone seemed really excited at that prospect. Personally, I couldn't see what the fuss was all about, but the crowd got bigger and eventually I couldn't see anything anymore.

It seemed that I waited there for hours, interrupted only by the odd gasp, 'Aah', and occasional applause. Eventually Eric Chalk and Missus Chalk returned to me. Both seemed very happy, especially Missus Chalk.

'Well Daisy girl, did you enjoy that?' Thank you for asking, but no. I couldn't see a blooming thing.

'Right. Now we're going to take part in the Coronation Carnival, but first I want to do a bit more to your decorations.'

The day, which had started rather dull and wet, was beginning to brighten up and Eric Chalk folded down my hood. Now it seemed it was my turn to be part of the celebrations. He produced two large stuffed dolls from my back seat; one was a lion and the other a bulldog that Missus Chalk had made. He secured the lion between my left-hand headlight and bonnet while Missus Chalk did the same with the bulldog on my other side. Then, suitably decorated, we went off to join a group of similarly decorated vehicles forming up in the road. Everyone was brightly dressed with men, women and children everywhere all waving flags. It was getting warm and the men had taken off their jackets, something I thought was rather unusual. It was not the done thing for a man to remove his jacket in public, but times, I suppose, were changing. The mood was incredible, everyone seemed happy and the children especially were terribly excited. All that is, except one little girl sitting on the back of the lorry in front. She was staring intently at me. The parade started and we made our way slowly through Northampton with cheering crowds on both sides of the road, but this little girl just couldn't take her eyes off me. I was feeling rather uneasy at her staring, but Eric Chalk and for once a very happy Missus Chalk were thoroughly enjoying themselves.

'Look Missus Chalk,' shouted her husband. 'It's Movietone News. Look there's a camera over there. I'll slow down so they can clearly see us.'

I spotted the camera as the man in charge pointed us out, said something to the cameraman and he swung the camera towards us. The man was gesturing to Missus Chalk to get her to stand up inside me and to wave her flag. She nervously got to her feet and obliged, but sat down again very quickly.

We eventually reached a big field, which was already full of people and a fairground was in full swing. We were guided to a parking spot beside all the other carnival vehicles. As Eric and Missus Chalk got out of me and wandered off, I became aware again of the little girl who had been staring at me. She had got off the back of the lorry and seemed to have been separated from her family, but she didn't seem too upset. I then realised that her eyes weren't exactly fixed on me, but on the stuffed bulldog wedged beside my headlight. At this point the Movietone people approached and seeing the little girl, asked her if she was lost.

'No,' she replied, 'that's my daddy's lorry there. I think I am supposed to wait here till he comes back.'

The cameraman was setting up the camera in front of me as his colleague was talking to the little girl.

'What's your name then?'

'Emily,' came the reply and she pointed at the stuffed bulldog.

'Do you want that toy doggy then Emily?' She nodded. 'Tell you what, I am sure the owner won't mind. Why don't you lift it off the car and give it a cuddle while we film you.' She obliged and once having removed it, she did not to want to let the toy out of her hands. The Movietone people walked off delighted with their shot.

'That'll make a great closing shot for the sequence,' said the man who had been talking to Emily. 'Little British girl, little British car – shame it was so old – and lots of red white and blue.'

So old? I wondered what he meant by 'so old'.

'But we are filming in black and white,' mutters the man with the camera and they were gone. Emily, still clinging to the stuffed bulldog, seeing some cushions on my rear seat, climbed in, settled down and went to sleep.

So there I was sitting at the edge of the field, it seemed for hours while Emily was curled up fast asleep on my back seat and clutching her new toy bulldog as tight as she could. I became aware of a beam of torchlight making itself slowly towards us, accompanied by a squelching sound of feet slowly progressing on soggy grass. Whoever it was, the torchlight seemed to swing in time to the squelching feet. Who on earth, I wondered, might be making their way along the edge of the field, here in the dark when all the celebrations were happening over on the other side of the field? I became concerned for the little girl, curled up inside me and on her own.

★★★★★

My reverie is disturbed by the return of Her Ladyship and her camera crew. For some reason Madam has decided to smarten herself up by putting on a rather low cut top. What a tart, and in the middle of February as well. She'll freeze.

'Pam, can you come out of the house, open the garage door and get into Miss Daisy please,' shouts the director while the other two set up their camera equipment in the road. Where is his megaphone, I wonder? All proper directors have megaphones don't they? 'That will be the establishing shot and then we'll show you starting the engine in close up.'

'But I wouldn't do it like that. I always stop and have a chat to her and then crank her handle a few times to suck the petrol through. I'd need a motivation to just get in and start her. What's my motivation?'

'Just do what you are told. We are not doing a remake of Genevieve. Just come out of the bloody house, open the bloody garage door and get in to the bloody car,' came the exasperated reply. Oooh dear, he's getting ratty with her already and we haven't taken a single shot yet. Anyway, what's all this about bloody car, might I ask? I'm not sure I want to take part now.

But what a fuss they make with this filming. I've lost count of the number of times Her Ladyship keeps walking out of the front door and opening my garage door. I'm getting rather fed up myself and I can see that she is getting cold. Then, 'Hang on, I've a great idea. Let's take the hood down,' shouts the director. Phil's his name by the way. Hood down? My God now she'll really freeze! One look at Her Ladyship and I can see that she is not happy with this decision, not one little bit. She marches over to him.

'Look,' she cries, 'this is not the weather nor the time of year to take the hood down! I'll freeze.' Phil strides over to his car and returns with a shiny white megaphone. Now that's more like it. He marches up to Her Ladyship and places it within a couple of inches of her ear.

'JUST DO IT!' She marches back over to me and as she takes my hood down she's muttering. 'Who the hell does he think he is? Take the hood down indeed. It's bloody February for heaven's sake. We never take the bloody hood down during bloody February.'

'CUT! Pam, if you have anything to say, at least say it in a way that we can all hear you, not just to the car.'

Then we are off, apparently to see The Nice Mister John. This turns out to be a very unusual drive. I sail out of Cardiff and up the Tumble past Wenvoe with little difficulty. What style, I think to myself, but only because I know that the film crew are just around the next bend and I want to impress them with my abilities to pull madam's nearly fifteen stone up a steep hill. Then we stop and we wait while they pack up and move on to the next point, where they set up the camera and start to film us all over again. Finally, Phil decides that the cameraman should get into me to get close up shots of Her Ladyship and get what he calls 'POVs' from the car. This goes on until we reach the house of The Nice Mister John.

'Right what I want you both to do now is to walk slowly around the car and discuss what sort of things will need to be done to Miss Daisy prior to going on an arduous trip like this. You know, "do I need a bigger petrol tank?" Or "should I be fitting wider tyres?" That sort of thing. Play it by ear, but make them intelligent questions.'

Intelligent questions? She tries, bless her, but hardly intelligent.

'Right now we'll do it again from another angle,' shouts Phil. 'But Pam you need to remember what you said last time so we can cut these shots together.'

'But I cannot remember. I didn't realise.' Her Ladyship's subdued. Not only is she cold, I think she's getting tired.'

'Don't worry, I can remind you.' Gosh, Phil has started being nice to her. He must be tired too and just wants to get home. Anyway I sit here with my best disapproving look while they do all this work. I also cannot help noticing that it is getting dark. That is not good.

'That's a wrap folks,' shouts Phil. 'Thank you everyone. He turns to Her Ladyship. Don't forget that we still need to do some filming in the centre of Cardiff and we need to do the master interview. I'll call you.' Well at least I can be prepared now I know what is going on.

As the film crew pack their things away, Madam is looking decidedly worried. At least she is finally able to put my hood up again.

'I'm worried about your lights Old Thing. We have to drive home in the dark.' Now I haven't used my headlights for a while and they are so dim that any time we have to drive through an area without streetlights, you can barely see the little yellow circles in the road ahead of me. But it turns out not to be a problem as there are streetlights all the way home. Gosh, it wasn't like that on Coronation day, there were very few streetlights then.

★★★★★

That field was dark, but the sight of the fairground with its coloured lights across the field did at least bring a warm glow across to us. But then there was this torch and the squelching sounds coming towards us. Who was the person with the torch? It seemed to be flashing over every vehicle in the row. I couldn't help wondering if this was a thief looking for what he could steal. Eventually, the beam of light reached me and it flashed all over my bodywork and into my seats. If I could have, I would have shaken like a leaf.

'Well, well, well, what have we got here then?' said a man's voice. He walked round to my rear and shone his torch on the still sleeping child. 'Oh dear, oh dear, oh dear, a child left on her own.'

He then walked round my rear end and came back to the front. He then fumbled for something in a pocket and in the torchlight, I saw a policeman's helmet. Oh thank God for that. There was I thinking by now that this was some sort of child molester. Anyway he started to examine me, noting my number, checking my tyres and my doors.

'Hey, what are you doing with my car?' It was Eric Chalk, and the now somewhat tipsy, but still happy, Missus Chalk.

'Is this your car sir?' The policeman once again opened his notebook.

'Yes it is. What's the matter Constable?'

'In which case sir, why have you left a child unattended in the car?'

'What? No. No constable, this is not my child. We have no children. I couldn't. An injury during the war... killed my best mate... and it er,' he glanced at Missus Chalk. 'I couldn't... after the war.'

'Oh I understand sir. I'm sorry. Then whose child is she?' At this point, the little girl woke up and rubbed her eyes.'

'Who are you?' she asked.

'More importantly,' said the policeman, 'who are you little girl?'

'Oh, I am Emily. That's my daddy's lorry there.' She points at the lorry next to us. 'I was very tired and I saw this dolly.'

'Well, you've been sleeping in this gentleman's car. I am sure he doesn't mind, do you sir?'

'No of course not. I just hope you were comfy.' Emily nodded her head and continued to clutch tightly at the toy bulldog. Eric Chalk noticed this. 'Would you like to keep the dolly? My wife made it and I'm sure she wouldn't mind.' He looked towards Missus Chalk who smiled and nodded acquiescence. I simply couldn't believe the change in this woman.

'I think you'd better come along with me and we'll find your mummy and daddy.' The constable opened my door and took her hand to help her get out. 'Oh sir, just one more thing. I've been taking a look at your car. How old is it?'

'It's nineteen thirty four, nearly twenty years old. Why?'

'Well sir, it has seen better times. I think you need some new tyres. Those are very worn, and those brakes... cable brakes; I mean sir, don't you think it is time you replaced it? This one is a bit past it now.'

Better times indeed... Change? Me? That was the second time in one day that I had been called old.

As Eric and Missus Chalk clambered back into me and got ready to take me home, I watched the silhouette of the policeman holding the hand of Emily, who in turn was holding the paw of the stuffed dog as they walked away towards the fairground.

★★★★★

'Gooood morning Old Girl. Fabulous news. I've been chatting

with Rick Smales. You know, the PR man in Bristol?' How could I forget him? 'Well he thinks he has some potential sponsors interested in funding our trip. Anyway, it seems that they are saying that we will have to take out something called completion insurance before they will back us. That is a special insurance that will pay out if we don't make it all the way round. The one small problem is that I have to undergo a medical examination!'

Well that has put the kybosh on it then. Madam passing a medical? For Heaven's sake, she has to stop for a rest halfway up the stairs. She has about as much chance of passing that medical as I have of winning Le Mans. What she really needs to do is shed a few pounds by spending the next few months working out. And let's face it. That is just not going to happen, is it?

'Come on Old Girl, let's go for a drive. It's a lovely sunny day and I'm bored with being stuck here.' Now, as a result of her regular trips out with me, Madam knows where they have positioned the city's speed humps and to save my embarrassment at her undoubted award winning haemorrhoids, she endeavours to navigate roads where they haven't yet been installed. Sadly, we still occasionally hit upon a road where they have been newly plonked down but short of us turning round to go another way, we have to grit our teeth and think of the Empire.

To be honest, I don't quite know why she continues to insist on taking drives around the city, apart from speed humps; it is a traffic environment that I really hate. First of all, there are just too many vehicles around and you cannot stop at the side of the road anywhere, because a little man in a yellow hat will leap out at you with his little book. You cannot move more than a few yards without being stopped by a set of traffic lights and then other lights make you stop to let humans walk across the road. What's the point of that? I mean, why keep making us stop? We were made to go, to carry people from one place to the next. We were certainly not made to be stopping the whole time. And we all know that I usually overheat if I have to stop too often.

We are brought to a sudden stop by yet another set of traffic lights. Madam hadn't been concentrating and we have rolled a bit over the line. Well nothing wrong with that. But then two young rather ragged urchins arrive either side of me. One holds a tattered sponge and the other has something that looks like a windscreen wiper blade attached to a stick. Urchin One proceeds to wipe filthy water all over my screen while the other starts to pull his wiper blade over the same area.

'Push off', screams Her Ladyship. 'Go away and leave us alone.' The urchins continue their task with an increased urgency. This time Madam stands up inside the car. 'I said bugger off. Don't you understand simple English?' We are now a source of entertainment for the others watching Her Ladyship's performance. The urchins continue their task until it is finished. My screen is now dirtier than it was before they started.

'You give us two pounds pliz.' The older of the two is now holding out his grubby hand having just wiped his nose with it.

'WHAT?' screams Her Ladyship. 'Two Pounds? Two Pounds for what? What have you done apart from making this car significantly dirtier than it was a few minutes ago? I am not giving you a penny. Now get out of my way.'

The traffic lights go green and the smaller of the urchins plants himself in front of my radiator and shows no intention of moving. Then the car horns behind us start to blare, as those either side of us drive off. Madam sits down again and starts to rev my engine. She even puts me into gear and starts to move forwards. The little urchin just stands there looking defiant.

'Blast and damn the little creatures,' she cries out as she reaches for her handbag and pulls out her purse. 'Here I've only a ten pound note. Can you give me change?'

'Thank you lady,' says the larger urchin, grabbing the ten pound note and running off with his little friend.

'WHAT? They've robbed me! They've stolen my money! Did you see that?' Where are the police when you want them?'

By now the traffic lights have gone red again. Madam doesn't notice and starts to move us forwards over the junction.

It's a large lorry that brings her to her senses as it blows its horn and stops inches from my side. 'Oh pook!' is all she can say. Then almost miraculously, a policeman appears, notebook emerging from his pocket.

'I think you jumped the lights there madam.'

'Where were you?'

'What do you mean madam?'

'Where were you when those two little creeps stole ten pounds from me?'

'I don't know what you mean Madam. I only saw you jump red lights and nearly cause an accident.'

'But, but, but, there were two kids who threw filthy water all over my windscreen, look there is still some of it on my bonnet. Then they took ten pounds off me for wiping it off again.'

'Oh those two. They'll be a couple of squeegee kids, Romanians probably. I've seen them here before.'

'But why haven't you arrested them? They stole ten pounds from me.' She softens her irritation. 'I was so upset at being robbed, I didn't notice the lights had changed.'

'Well Madam, no damage has been done, I suggest that you drive on – when the lights go green – and take that lovely old car home before it gets damaged.'

We drive off. Madam's nose has been put firmly out of joint and we head home with rather a lot of 'harrumphs' and 'damned kids' and 'Police force has gone to the dogs' and for heaven's sake, he is younger than my own son.'

'I think we'll give city centres a miss from now on. Don't you agree Miss Daisy?' To be honest, I couldn't agree more. I will be thankful when I have been able to take Her Ladyship away to a quieter and more civilised place when she retires. I don't think she can cope with modern cities anymore. Well at least we won't have to indulge this nonsense when we move to rural Somerset.

★★★★★

I think those comments made by the policeman at the Coronation, about me being old, had sown a seed of thought in Eric Chalk's mind, although he did continue to use me for another few years. Then one frosty morning he came into my garage.

'Well Daisy, I am afraid the time has come for you and me to part company. We've been together for nearly ten years and I am changing my job so I really need to get something faster and more reliable.'

I thought I had served him well. We'd had our odd little breakdown and there had been that incident a week or so before when he was late for an important appointment after I had conked out. But I thought all was fine afterwards.

Later that day, Eric Chalk pulled me up on a car dealer's forecourt.

'Good Morning Sir, can I help you?' We were greeted by a rather fat moustachioed man wearing a loud check suit, a wide multicoloured tie and brown suede shoes. His moustache was heavily stained with tobacco.

'Yes, I hope so. I need to change my car. I've had this one ten years and before that it was in storage during the war. Even so, it is twenty years old now and I need something newer and more reliable.'

'Six years stored in a damp garage? Did you have it professionally serviced?' Eric Chalk shook his head. 'Well, what do you expect?'

The man had this horrible habit of curling his stained

Moustache upwards every now and again, as if brushing the tip of his nose.

'The engine'll be shot by now. Suspension's probably had it. And the brakes – crikey cable brakes. The body could do with a lick of paint as well.' He kept kicking my bodywork, knowing it would cause a shower of rust to fall out. I think that's where I developed my distaste for large men in loud suits.

'You've been asking for trouble for ages. Fancy buying a pile of rubbish like this.' He started now to suck through his browned teeth and then he kicked me again. This time it was the tyres. 'Tyres perished – See? It's gonn'a cost a lot to put right. Gosh – twenty, maybe thirty quid to sort it out and then you don't know how much other damage there is. Tell you what, I'll give you a fiver for this one against that nice little Morris Minor over there. One lady owner, goes like a bird, only three years old.'

Eric Chalk went over to look at it.

'Would you like to take it round the block sir?'

Twenty minutes later, Eric Chalk came over to collect his few things from me. 'Well Daisy, we've had a lot of fun and strange as it may seem, I am going to miss you. Good luck old girl.' Then he was gone in his Morris Minor, leaving me there with this horrible moustachioed man.

'So you're called Daisy are you? Well Daisy, you are pretty well past it, but I'm sure that I can make a few bob out of you. Fred, have a look at this one will you? Sounds like the engine needs some attention. And give it a lick of paint. It should make twenty, maybe even thirty if we are lucky.'

I hadn't been there for very long when one afternoon a young man came onto the forecourt.

'I need a car to get me to and from college. I don't want to spend a lot of money, no more than twenty pounds.'

'I have just the car for you young man. Came in only last week.

Laid up during the war and since then only used for local driving. She's a nice little car, an Austin Seven. Called Daisy by the way.'

An hour later I was parked up at this young man's home. It turned out that my new owner, Richard Benson was his name by the way, he was a mechanical engineering student and enjoyed tinkering with cars. I had a horrible feeling the first time he approached me gripping a spanner that I was about to become spare parts for another relative. But it wasn't to be; I was the only car he had. Instead, he started to get me sorted out and smarten me up. It felt good.

★★★★★

'Right Old Girl.' Her Ladyship flings open my garage doors yet again, disturbing me from my innermost thoughts. 'I have some news for you. We are not retiring to Somerset as I'd originally planned. I've decided that we will be moving to Pembrokeshire instead. We will be sixty miles from the end of the motorway, there will be plenty of leafy country lanes for us to enjoy and the best news of all is that there are hardly any traffic lights there.'

I don't know Pembrokeshire. But it sounds a bit like the end of the world.

'You'll like the quiet roads down there,' she adds. Oh yes? How the hell does she know whether I will like the roads or not? Who's the poor seventy two year old creature who has to drag herself along them? Not Her Ladyship, I can tell you that. She just plants herself on my seat while I do all the work.

'But before we go down there, I have another trial run planned for us. This time we are going to the city of your birth for a big rally. They say there could be as many as two thousand of your relatives there.'

Twenty four hours later, we are on our way to Birmingham with Her Ladyship's friend, the Nice Miss Clem. It is a lovely sunny

July day and as we tootle up the motorway I can't help noticing with delight several modern contraptions broken down, their bonnets pointing skywards at the side of the road. Then as we turn down the Old Bristol Road on the outskirts of Birmingham, I begin to feel excited as we get closer to where I was born. I spot familiar sights from all those years ago. This was the road upon which I took my first test drive. Then there it is, the place of my birth. But there's no hustle and bustle of workers and new cars now. The building stands empty and grey with nearly every window broken. It's really sad. I had been so excited about coming here, but this is awful. The place is so decayed and silent. Her Ladyship seems subdued as well, but not for long.

'Now where the hell is this Cofton Park place? That's where we are supposed to go isn't it?' I think Her Ladyship expects the Nice Miss Clem to be navigating.

'Haven't a clue,' shouts the Nice Miss Clem in response. 'Just follow that old car over there. They must know where we are supposed to go.' Old car indeed! A few minutes later we arrive on this field where there are already lots of my relatives all lined up. We stop by an official.

'Austin Seven? What year?'

'Nineteen thirty four,' replies Her Ladyship.

'Oh there's lots of you here. The Sevens are lined up year by year, just up there.' He points to where there are rows upon rows of my relatives. 'Park at the end of the row. The one marked nineteen thirty four. Got that?'

'How many of us are there?' Her Ladyship enquired. 'Oh there's over two thousand five hundred Austins due to come here. They're coming from all over the world, Switzerland, Germany, France;' someone is even bringing a Seven Racer from New Zealand. It's the same age as yours.' He walks over to the relative that has stopped behind me, and we move on. Her Ladyship doesn't head straight for our parking place; I think she is going to have a look around. We drive over a big hump in the field and there, stretched out before us almost as far as I can see, are all the relatives he mentioned. Thousands of us. Her Ladyship stops to take in the scene.

'My goodness, so many,' she says. 'Oh look over there.' Her Ladyship spots something else. 'Look, there's some strange looking Sevens by those tents and they are flying a German flag. Let's go and talk to them.'

'Whatever you do,' says the Nice Miss Clem, 'Don't mention the war.'

'Of course not,' says Her Ladyship. 'I wouldn't be so insensitive.' So over we go and it transpires that the 'strange looking Sevens' are actually German relatives and there are differences between us. They look rather Teutonic, but have nice lines. One of them seems to be eying me up. 'Guten Habent Fraulein,' he says.

'I am sorry, I don't speak German.' I reply. 'How far have you come?'

'Ve haff comen all ze vay from Hamburg. Since feer tags. Four days it took us,' he replies with a warm smile.

'Gosh that's a long way. Look, are you a relative? From a distance you look like me, but when I get closer you are very different.'

'Zat iss because ve are Dixies. Ve are born at ze Barvarian Motor Verks, ve are ze same, but ve are also different.' Now I was really confused and then Her Ladyship, deep in conversation with their drivers interrupts us.

'What happened to all those lovely big luxurious Mercedes built in the twenties and thirties? You don't see many around nowadays,' she enquires of one of the German gentlemen.

'That is because at the end of the war, the Russians and the Allies helped themselves to them. All that was left after that were cars like these.'

'Don't go down this path,' hisses the Nice Miss Clem quietly into Her Ladyship's ear, hoping the Germans couldn't hear.

'Well,' she replies, 'they look fabulous, probably considerably better engineered than this old thing, knowing the quality of German engineering.'

This old thing? THIS OLD THING? Excuse me. Have I not just dutifully carried you all the way from Cardiff to Birmingham without a hitch? And if you remember, Madam, two of the cars we saw broken down on the motorway were built at ze Barvarian Motor Verks. This old thing indeed!

Then with a wave and a cheerio, we are off again. 'You were flirting with that man. You tart,' the Nice Miss Clem comments as we head back to our nineteen thirty four row.

'I was not flirting. I was simply indulging in polite conversation. Anyway did you notice that it was he who mentioned the war, not me. Come on, rather than park up, let's go and find our hotel.'

I wake up to another lovely sunny day when Her Ladyship comes out with a bucket and sponge to give me a good clean.

'Well Miss Daisy, let's get some of this motorway dust off you. So how do you feel about coming home after seventy two years? I expect there are many familiar sights for you to see.' She's obviously in a good mood. Maybe I can forgive her for calling me 'an old thing' yesterday. There again, perhaps not. But I have to chuckle at her friend calling her a tart. It's nice to know that I am not the only one who thinks that.

With me all spick and span, Her Ladyship loads me up and with the Nice Miss Clem, we prepare to head back to the Cofton Park field again.

'Before we go back to Longbridge, let's just pop in towards Birmingham's city centre. We need petrol anyway.'

Her Ladyship swings me towards the town. It's not long before we find ourselves racing down the Bristol Road into the city centre, Her Ladyship is so deep in her own thoughts that she isn't thinking where, exactly, she is going. We shoot into a tunnel.

'Oh my God, Pam. That sign said M6 North back there. Where are we going?' The Nice Miss Clem grips my door so tightly that I wonder if she is going to rip it off.

'What? What? What are you on about? Ah. Yesss… we shouldn't still be on this road,' shouts Her Ladyship as we speed out the other end of the tunnel with very large lorries growling and hooting at us. 'Oh dear, I think we are about to hit Spaghetti Junction. Where do you want to go? North to Manchester or south to London?'

'We need to be in Longbridge,' hisses the Nice Miss Clem. 'Not on the bloody M6.'

'Ah right. We need to find somewhere to turn off and to go back.' Stating the obvious aren't we? I think to myself.

We are nearly an hour late when we eventually arrive at the field. Just about everyone else has already arrived and Her Ladyship duly plonks us in our line. She unpacks the picnic hamper and puts it in the shade. 'Right. Lets have a wander. Miss Daisy will be fine here.' And they are gone.

As the day passes, people come up to me, peer inside and make nice remarks. Others point at something and declare that it is wrong, not original. I don't care though. Then some officials turn up and move the relative next to me and replace it with a monstrosity that looks like something from outer space. Suddenly all the people lose interest in me and go to look at this new arrival.

When Her Ladyship returns, she looks at the new neighbour with a degree of disgust. What's this I wonder? Is the Wrinkled One showing some taste at last? She speaks to one of my neighbour's admirers.

'What on earth is that?' She is told that it is a Special, used for racing.

'Well I think it's awful. Nothing like a proper Austin Seven at all.' But her comments fall on deaf ears.

'G'day?' ventures the monstrosity. 'How are you then?'

'Are you speaking to me?' I enquire. I have to confess to being rather flustered. 'Have we been introduced?' Well, I cannot think what else to say to him.

'Name's Bruce. I'm from Wellington in New Zealand.' And I always thought that Wellington was a boot.

'I'm Miss Daisy and I'm from Cardiff in Wales. How do you do.' Well what else would I say to a strange gentleman?

'How do you do, Miss Daisy from Cardiff in Wales,' he replies.

'Well I was fine until you arrived on the scene. I was enjoying some admirers. Now all they do is hang their tongues out at you.'

'Ah but we are all the same under the skin,' he replies. Well I suppose he is right, but I still think he's ugly and for once I am in full agreement with Her Ladyship.

The afternoon seems to pass all too quickly and Madam starts to pack me up to go home. It's still a lovely summer's day and she decides to join a group of relatives going home on a cross country route through Worcester and Hereford.

We make our way home towards a setting sun. Then I recall how Her Ladyship had described me to those Germans. 'This Old Thing,' I think she said. Now picture the scene. We are the last car in the convoy and are about to go round a very sharp bend. If something happens now, it would be some time before the others realise we are no longer with them.

So I decide to blow out a rear tyre. This time Her Ladyship does notice, but as she always does when I have a problem, she pretends not to. But you cannot drive on a flat tyre for very long and inevitably she has to stop. I couldn't have planned it better. She pulls me up at the side of the road, gets out and looks around for a possible knight of the road. None forthcoming, she has to remove her luggage, all so carefully strapped onto my luggage rack, and then remove the spare wheel. I wonder how she will handle a wheel change out on the road.

As I expected, it is some time before the others realise that we are no longer with them and turn back to see how we are. As they arrive, Her Ladyship has completed the wheel change and is lowering the jack with the spare wheel in place. I have to say, I am impressed. They have changed a wheel between them without any help from the male of their species.

Her Ladyship puts the wheel with the burst tyre on the back and replaces her luggage onto the rack. 'Now, Clem and I need to clean up. Where are we going to eat?' All of a sudden, I am quite impressed with this woman. But it won't last long, it never does.

★★★★★

Now where was I? Oh yes, my third owner. Well I liked this young man. He not only knew how to look after ladies like us, but he seemed to have a really good sense of humour. I remember us being stopped by the Northamptonshire Constabulary one day. They wanted to check me over. How long I wondered, would it be before they discover my speedometer or rather the lack of my speedometer? Unfortunately, there was just a big hole in my dashboard. Well, it didn't take long and one of the policeman told Richard Benson that he had to bring me to the police station within seven days and prove that he had the means of telling I was travelling at 30mph or less. 'That's the law sir.'

Accordingly a week later we turned up at the police station still without a speedometer. 'What's all this then?' said the policeman, peering into my passenger compartment.

'It's a coil of rope officer, with a brick tied to one end. The other end is tied to the handbrake,' came Richard Benson's reply.

'And?' said the policeman, stretching to his full six foot with his boots on.

'Well, you see that hole in the floor? All I have to do is push the brick through the hole in the floor and if the rope goes tight in less than five seconds, then I'm driving too fast.'

Oh no, I thought. We are heading for the cells, and pretty damn fast at that. I looked at the policeman. He straightened up a bit more, six foot one this time and looked at my owner. Was that a hint of a smile I wondered?

'Well sir, very amusing. We must have our little joke mustn't we? Now go and get a proper speedometer and if you aren't back with it working properly before I go off shift at two o' clock, you will be well on the way to a fine. That car will be confiscated and looking at the state of it, you will be required to scrap it.'

Scrap it? SCRAP IT? Me, smashed into little pieces and melted down? I couldn't bear the thought. Don't worry officer he will go and get my speedometer working. Promise.

★★★★★

'Well, what do you think of your new home then?' Her Ladyship flings open my garage door. We've only been here in Pembrokeshire for a week and she says that to me every day. Does she really care what I think? 'There you are Miss Daisy,' she adds. 'Now you can see Dumpledale.' Then she goes back into the house. Why I ask myself, does she think I want to keep on seeing Dumpledale? I mean, once one has seen Dumpledale in the sunshine, then in the rain, at dawn and at dusk, then what on earth is the point of looking at it anymore?

'No time to just sit there and stare out at Dumpledale you know,' she says when she returns moments later. 'Come on, time to get moving.' Then with keys in hand, she starts me up. I wonder if we are we are going for a little drive? Well it seems it's to be a very little drive, fifteen yards in fact to a far corner of the yard where she parks me again. 'Sorry Old Girl,' she says. 'We've got to keep you out of the way of the builders. We don't want dust and cement falling all over you do we?' Then she is gone, back into the house with no explanation whatsoever. So here I sit and now it's starting to rain.

I sit here for a couple of hours before Madam appears yet again.

'The builder's just called,' she says sheepishly, 'to say that because of the rain he is going to start tomorrow.' She starts me up and puts me back in the garage. 'There you are,' she says as she climbs out. 'You should be able to see Dumpledale when the rain stops.'

Then she stomps off muttering something about the Pembrokeshire Promise. Did I catch a comment about bloody builders? Oooh dear, she's beginning to get herself stressed again and I thought that the whole idea of retiring and moving down here was to avoid stress. Somehow, I don't think I shall be going on any drives in the near future. Perhaps I can get on with my memoirs. So, back to Richard Benson.

Well after that little contretemps with the police, he did sort me out to their satisfaction and I sighed with relief. At least I wasn't to be scrapped, at least not for the time being. Then one autumn morning, I think it was in nineteen fifty six, Richard Benson told me that we won't be going anywhere for a while. Apparently it looked as though the country was about to go to war again. This time it wasn't a little man with a moustache causing it, but a big man with a moustache that was stopping us getting at our petrol supplies. So as well as preparing to invade the big man's country, the Government had decided to reintroduce petrol rationing. Once again, I was to be parked up, but not this time under warm blankets in a cosy garage; no, this time I was just parked up outside and left to my own devices. I sat there all through the winter months and into the spring. Richard Benson completely ignored me, until one morning he appeared with a petrol can.

'Good news Daisy Girl. Petrol rationing is finished and we can start to go out together again.' He poured two gallons of the lifeblood into my tank. 'Now are you going to start for me?' He opened my bonnet. 'Let's just check everything is in order.' I hoped that he would check my battery, but no. He closes my bonnet and cranks my handle a few times and gets in. 'Right Daisy let's have a go.' He pulls my starter knob and nothing, I was completely lacking in any energy.

'Hmmm. Then it's the starting handle isn't it? Well I hope this is going to work Daisy Girl.' It took a fair few attempts, but I was soon ticking over again. 'Now let's go for a good drive, fill you up properly and charge that battery. I can use you for college again now.'

So each college day for the next couple of years, I would carry Richard Benson around. Eventually he started work at a big garage for one day a week and the other men there would always joke about me.

'Don't jam on your brakes too hard Richard. Your foot may go through the floor.' One would shout.

From another of them, 'At least you can shower on the way home. There's more hole in that hood than cloth now.'

'Still doing hand signals, Richard? Battery not strong enough for you to have indicators?' Richard Benson took all these insults with good humour, but they upset me.

Still, nothing changes in fifty odd years, because here I am and I still don't have any indicators. But you will laugh at this, Dear Diary. Her Ladyship has obviously decided that it's time to fit some on to me and she's been searching around for some nice original semaphore trafficators to fit to my bodywork. Personally I think she is just too lazy to do hand signals. All my drivers for the last seventy odd years were happy with that. Anyway, she succeeds in tracking down a brand new set, still in their original box. So what does she do? Having paid rather a lot of money for them, she tells me that it would be a shame to fit them now, especially as the set is so original and perfect. Now she is looking for a second hand set. For God's sake, what is the matter with her? A trafficator is a trafficator isn't it? What made me digress about that? Now I was thinking about Richard Benson wasn't I? Oh yes, we were about to part company.

It was like this. It was one sunny autumn day, you know, one of those days when there is a crispness in the air, every shadow is long and the world seems covered in golds, oranges and reds. Well, Richard Benson was getting ready to take me home and the garage boss came up to him.

'Richard, when you finish college, I would like you to come and work for me full time. Charlie is retiring and I will have a vacancy for you to fill if you want it.' I could see that this news delighted him. I was pleased for him too. 'But, you are going to have to get rid of that old car. It's a bad advert for the garage. How old is it?'

'Twenty five years boss. But I do enjoy driving and looking after her. I could smarten her up. Then she could be a good advert, attracting people's attention and all that.'

To me, Richard Benson was clinging onto a straw here. I think his boss thought so too. I knew these modern garage owners; I had experienced something similar when Eric Chalk parted with me.

'Sorry Richard, no one is interested in old cars and anyway, it would cost you a fortune and the car would still only be worth ten pounds. Tell you what, when you start here, I will provide you with a nice second hand car. You can take your pick and you can gradually pay for it out of your wages. But you'll have to get rid of that thing.'

The very next morning, parked in the college car park, I had a 'For Sale' sign on my windscreen and it wasn't long before Richard Benson appears with a young friend.

'Daisy, I would like you to meet Dave Saunders. Dave, this is Daisy.'

I looked this newcomer up and down. He seemed pleasant enough, but he was dressed really strangely, rather scruffy I suppose.

His hair was unkempt and he wore an apparently oversized roll neck jumper and a crumpled duffle coat was hanging round his shoulders.

'Do you really give cars names, man?' the friend enquired as he looked over me. 'That's daft.' Well not to me young sir. I couldn't think of anything more normal.

Richard Benson ignored that comment. 'Well do you fancy her? My new boss has offered to let me have a newer car and there is a rather nice little MG that I fancy. Would you like to test drive her? She goes well and I have looked after her.'

Dave nodded in agreement, 'Well man, I am going to need some sort of transport when I go to university and this old car would be really cool. That seat in the back will be big enough for my tea chest when I do the skiffle gigs. And I could carry another band member as well. Okay, let's go.' Both young men climbed onto my front seats.

As we pulled away, rather too quickly and erratically if you ask me, Richard Benson had an afterthought. 'You have passed your driving test, haven't you?'

'Yes, yes, yes. Tell you what; can we try out the new motorway? It is open now isn't it?'

Motorway, what was a motorway? I had never heard of a motorway before. We headed south out of Northampton and there up ahead was an enormous grey road, curling gradually and stretching all the way over the horizon. Vehicles were zooming along in both directions. We passed a blue sign that said M1 in large white letters and below that there was a list of vehicles not allowed to use the road. Unfortunately, I couldn't see twenty five year old Austin Sevens on that list. Dave Saunders swung me onto a sort of wide feeder road that connected the main road to the motorway, which itself was an even wider road, one with three lanes in fact. Everything was so large, straight and fast. So far so good, but I was surprised at just how fast everyone was going. One good bit was that there seemed to be a big grass verge separating us from the cars coming in the other direction. To my left there was another stretch of tarmac, a fourth inside lane, which I later understood was where we were supposed to break down. That's a good idea, I thought at the time.

Dave Saunders had his foot pressed down on my accelerator and we were travelling at over fifty miles an hour. Even so, all the other vehicles still seemed to be roaring past us. I was giving his test run all I could, but I had never gone so fast and for so long. Quite frankly I was terrified. Richard Benson seemed terrified too judging by the way he gripped on to my door. The big lorries added to the terror by blowing their horns as they raced past us. I was so pleased to get off at the next junction and when we parked back at the college car park, I was a nervous wreck.

'Hey man, that was so cool. I'll take her. How much do you want?' Dave Saunders sat there absolutely elated. He was still gripping my steering wheel rather too tightly. And Richard Benson sitting in the passenger seat? Well, the pupils of his eyes were dilated and he was still gripping my door so tightly that his fingernails were cutting into my paintwork.

'Umm, what did you say?' He was eventually able to speak. 'Oh yes, umm how about ten pounds?'

'Too much man. I will give you seven pounds, that's all I can afford.'

'How about seven pounds, ten shillings?'

'Seven pounds?' He reached into his pocket, pulled out a few coins and thumbed through them. 'Seven Pounds, six shillings and, and four pence ha'penny. That's all I've got.'

Richard Benson, now slightly recovered, gets out.

'Okay then, that's a deal; seven pounds, six shillings and four pence ha'penny. I'll bring in the logbook tomorrow. Can you get the money together by then?'

Dave Saunders nodded his head and they shook hands. Then my about-to-be-new-owner sauntered away, humming tunelessly to himself and clicking his fingers. I decided I would call him Hey Man Dave from then on. Me? I was still shaken from that driving experience and thus started my enduring hate of motorways.

★★★★★

Her Ladyship came out this morning and finally allowed me back into my garage after an ignominious two months dumped outside in the yard. 'The builders have replaced the roof.' she said. 'You can go back into your home.' Needless to say it wasn't long before I had my revenge for being deserted for so long.

It was like this. She must have been feeling guilty when she put me back inside the garage, because she gave me a nice wax and polish. Then after brushing a load of autumn leaves out of the garage, she left the door open.

'There you are Old Girl, Dumpledale is looking particularly lovely today. I think I am going to leave your engine running for a while to charge your battery.' Now anyone normal would have just plugged me in to a battery charger, but this woman? No she had to start my engine and leave it running. Rather than use my starter, she decided to use my starting handle. That's odd, I thought; there's no one about to watch her showing off. What's her point? Now there will be those among you who might just think that by way of revenge, I would refuse to start. But nothing could be further from the truth; I sailed into life almost immediately. I had a far better idea. Since my brake lights come on when the handbrake is on, Madam put some blocks in front of my wheels and let the handbrake off. That way the brake lights went out and my battery could get the best possible charge. So here I sit ticking over happily.

After about half an hour she comes out again and switches off my engine, pulls on the handbrake and takes the blocks away. She mutters something about the view and heads back into the house, leaving the garage door wide open. Now picture the scene, Dear Diary. Here I am sitting in the garage. A few feet away is Her Ladyship's new Skoda. It is too good an opportunity to miss. But I don't do it straight away. She comes outside a couple of times to empty wastepaper baskets and shake rugs. She glances over and satisfies herself that all is okay. Meanwhile here I sit in the garage doorway as if butter wouldn't melt in my radiator and apparently enjoying the sunshine. Then once Her Ladyship is convinced that all is well and goes back into her house, I flip off my handbrake and gracefully roll into the back of the Skoda. From the house it looks as though I have rammed my starting handle straight into the back of that modern car's rear valance.

Out she runs fearing the worst and a big repair bill, only to discover to her relief that it is my front tyre that has rammed itself into the Skoda and not the starting handle. She wedges herself between me and the Skoda and struggles to push me back into the garage, where she secures the handbrake again. She seems annoyed; obviously she cannot take a joke.

'You bad, bad car,' she shouts wagging her finger a couple of inches from my radiator. 'What did you think you were doing? You naughty car. You naughty, naughty car. You might have damaged the Skoda.'

It was just at this point that a young family walks past the end of our drive on their way home from chapel. They stare up at us for a moment, mouths hanging open. Then the astonished parents hurry the children away, obviously now under the impression that there is a mad woman who has moved into the village and who talks to cars.

Laugh? I nearly shook my headlights off!

Chapter Four

But it was all in vain as I rolled across the lawn
and straight into a rose bed.

Sunday 9th January 2007

Well, I am glad that's over. The festive season that is. I've been here barely six months, but I already have two problems with Pembrokeshire. One, there seems to be a lot more wind and rain here in this county; and two, my garage doors are not so protective against the weather as they were in Cardiff. So, if it isn't wind and rain howling under my garage door, then it's either just the rain or just the wind. I'm fed up with it. Today for instance, we head out for a nice belated New Year's lunch with friends in Little Haven. When it's over, Her Ladyship totters back out into the car park. She seems rather too cheerful if you ask me and experience has taught me that I usually have cause to worry when she is rather too cheerful. It frequently means that there is some wild idea brewing.

'Come on Old Girl; let's go home before it gets dark. Shouldn't take long. Looks like rain actually.'

We climb this long winding hill out of the village, seemingly on the way home; well it was the way we came here I suppose. Then as we reach the top it starts to rain. Actually that's putting it mildly. It starts to tip down. We reach a turning and Madam puts my brakes on. I can barely see the other side of the road for the rain.

'I don't recognise this junction Old Girl, do you? Is this the way we came? Do you know where we are?'

Why does she ask me? How on earth would I know?

'Tell you what, let's go left and see where that road takes us. My senses tell me that is northwards and from where we are at the moment, that is roughly in the direction of home.' With that she hoiks my steering wheel and we are off into the great unknown.

After a couple of miles, she slows down to a crawl. 'I don't recognise any of these place names Old Girl, do you? I should have looked at a map before we came out.' Far be it for me to suggest Your Ladyship, but it does make sense to discover how you are going to get home from, as well as how you are getting to your destination when in a part of the world you don't really know. She suddenly takes a right turn.

It takes us nearly an hour and a half to get home. I am soaked and it's dark when we finally make it. It took us just thirty minutes to get there this morning. 'Perhaps I should treat you to a satellite navigation thingy before we embark on a strange journey like that again,' she ponders more to herself than me. What would I want with a navigation thingy, whatever that is? Good Lord, I don't even have indicators yet.

'The thing is Old Girl, with us going to France in May, our biggest test drive yet...'

Excuse me? France? Who said anything about France? That's foreign isn't it? Have I no say in this? I mean, a trip from Pembrokeshire to Cardiff or Swansea is one thing, even a trip to North Wales or Birmingham and back. But FRANCE? Good God woman, that's abroad and I don't do abroad.

'Oh I forgot to tell you didn't I? Yes we are going to cross the channel to France. You'll enjoy that won't you?'

Will I hell. What's wrong with a gentle drive to the Lake District or the New Forest? That's about the same distance as France. Anyway, what do we find when – I mean IF – we ever get to France? I'll tell you what we'll find, a load of garlic eating, Gauloise smoking and beret wearing Frenchmen who shrug their shoulders a lot and purse their lips when trying to express themselves. The worst thing of all is that they drive on the wrong side of the road because Napoleon said they should. Anyway they've never forgiven us for Agincourt!

But she completely ignores my concerns. 'You see Old Girl, a Sat-Nav would be very useful over there, but they are rather expensive. But hey, it's only Normandy. We'll probably manage with a map. Anyway I'd better start practising my French,' she pauses a moment and then muses, 'I wonder how one says to a garage attendant, "You are welcome to put your nozzle into my tank?" I know, "Vous êtes bienvenu – to put – pour mettre – your nozzle – votre bec – into my tank – dans mon réservoir." There you are Old Girl, you see; I've still got a grasp of my O level French.' Well of course, the smart tart had to know that didn't she?

'We won't be going alone Old Girl. There will be about eight of us. We'll be fine.' Famous last words, which will come back to haunt us all I am sure. 'Now here's a phrase for you to learn when you meet those French relatives… "Bonjour je m'appelle Madamoiselle Daisy et j'habite dans le Pays de Galles. Qu'est que vous appellez vous?" There you are Old Girl. A good chat up line for any French car you meet.' Personally I fail to understand why on earth I would want to speak to a French car in the first place. If I have to communicate, I will do it very slowly and very succinctly in English. Anyway how would I know what a French car looks like? Does it smoke Gauloise and wear a beret?

Hang on, what am I saying? This is no good. It's all part of her crazy 'let's go round the world' plan again isn't it? I've never been abroad before. When I was younger, taking a drive to the Continent was a pastime only for the very rich in their Rolls Royces or Bentleys and who probably had chauffeurs to attend to their every need. But for the likes of most of us, 'abroad to foreign parts' just wasn't the done thing. Actually, come to think of it there was that time when

Hey Man Dave contemplated finding himself in India, but I'd rather gloss over that to be honest. He was enough of a problem back home in Warwick. Now where had I got to with him?

Oh yes. He was my newest owner wasn't he? My fourth in fact and I was hoping I could forget about him. But no, he turned out to be a rather important part of my past. He'd bought me for just seven pounds, six shillings and fourpence ha'penny. He had left me in this car park, well it seemed for ages. Then one morning he turned up, still wearing that old jumper and duffle coat and once again he was humming and clicking his fingers, but now his walk had changed. At every step he seemed to bend his knees, so now he bobbed up and down as he walked along humming and clicking fingers. I have to say that I never did recognise the tune he was humming. But it was always the same one.

'Hey Daisy Girl.' He slurred his speech as well, but I'm sure he wasn't drunk, unless it was something else. He did rather enjoy those funny smelling cigarettes. There again, perhaps it was just his manner. 'Hey! We are off to uni in Warwick and you are going to carry my luggage and the tea chest. I'm hoping that I can join a new skiffle group down there; or maybe I'll start one of my own.' So he was going to take me somewhere new. What the hell, I was getting bored with Northampton anyway. But where was Warwick? Well I discovered the answer to that question quite quickly as the next day he turned up with a load of luggage. Among all the bags and cases was this strange big square wooden box with a broom handle attached to the side of it. There was also a piece of string stretching tightly between the top of the broom handle and the box itself. I couldn't help wondering what on earth he would want to do with that.

'Now Daisy Girl, how am I going to get this tea chest onto your back seat? 'Fraid it's going to be a bit big. I suppose I could take down the hood, but then it might rain. Hold on, I have an idea.' At that point Hey Man Dave pulled out a penknife and cut a slit in my hood.

'There that should work.' He then proceeded to poke the end of the broom handle through my hood so it stuck out of the top rather like a radio aerial, the sort of thing I had seen on newer relatives.

He then pushed his cases and bags in beside the tea chest. 'There we are, ready for the off.' Hey Man Dave climbed in and attempted to start my engine, but my battery was completely flat.

'Hey Man. What's wrong with you Daisy Girl? I wonder what happens now.' He got out and walked around me. 'Hmmm, what's this thing? I know, it's another way of starting you isn't it.' He was talking to my starting handle. He fingered it and attempted a half hearted turn, but it just span around. I was beginning to think that Hey Man Dave didn't have a clue how I worked. In due course it became very apparent that he did not.

'Okay, Daisy Girl, I think I need some help here. Don't go away now, I'll be back.' He wandered away, clicking fingers, bending knees and humming tunelessly to himself once more. I couldn't help wondering if a complete idiot had bought me. I was also becoming aware of a feeling of impending doom.

★★★★★

There is of course a similar feeling of impending doom living with me in my retirement. She's been away for weeks on one of her jaunts to the Caribbean and I've been deserted yet again. So while she's away and cannot know what I am writing, I can reveal some serious concerns I have for her and how she's dealing with her own retirement. It goes without saying that it all causes me some considerable embarrassment.

It was like this, and we'd only been here a few weeks when she confided in me that she was struggling to come to terms with slowing down. Slowing down? She doesn't seem to know whether she is going forwards or backwards at any speed. She certainly seems to have lost track with what day of the week it is. I've also noticed that when she is in full verbal flow with a friend, she will suddenly stop abruptly mid sentence. That's not because she has spotted a large hairy spider on her friend's shoulder, it's because she cannot think of the word she wanted to use. Then to top it all, while she is struggling to find that word, she completely forgets what she was talking about in the first place. For Heaven's sake. She's not even sixty one.

Talking of hairy spiders, Her Ladyship really doesn't like them, not one little bit. She's convinced now that Pembrokeshire is full of tarantulas, as she calls them. We had an incident while out on a run when one decided to take an afternoon stroll across the windscreen. In response Madam whipped out a can of WD40 from the glove pocket and drenched it with the spray. The result is that the windscreen got covered in oily goo and Madam couldn't see out. Anyway she was then far more concerned with the comatose spider, which had fallen into her lap. We shot off the road and ended up hovering over a deep ditch. I tell you, I am worried for that woman's good sense. It was only a little spider, minding its own business, probably looking for a fat fly for lunch. Mind you, I still remember with shame that incident with the bumblebee two years ago.

But her dislike of spiders is as nothing compared to her DIY abilities. Since moving in she has been having work done to the house and inspired by all the professional work going on around her, she attempted to hang some wallpaper. She'd seen it done on TV and thought it looked so easy. In fact she ended up covered in wallpaper paste and the final result appeared to be like something from one of those old Laurel and Hardy films. 'One would think,' she confided in me, 'that in the age of non-drip, one coat, gloss paints that it wouldn't be beyond the wit of wall paper manufacturers to come up with something easier to hang.'

She then turned her attention to decorating the new utility room at the back of my garage. I listened with interest as she shut the door behind her so that she could paint it. That, it seems, was where her problems began. When she had finished painting the door, she couldn't open it anymore. Not because it was stuck with the paint but it seemed that the handle would turn and the catch just would no longer open the door. It was six o'clock in the evening and there she was stuck inside and no one around except me to hear her cries. The window was too small for her not insufficient frame to get through and all she had to aid her escape was a tin of paint, a paintbrush, a small radio and a screwdriver. She wondered if Blue Peter had ever explained how to escape from a room with those implements. She couldn't recall, so she panicked. It seemed, she explained later, the best idea.

After about ten minutes she realised that panicking would achieve nothing, so she decided to think instead. Apply herself. Be practical. Personally I couldn't see her achieving anything by thinking and I was right. She proceeded with the screwdriver to remove the door handle. Why she thought that would help, I haven't a clue, but she said later that it made her feel better. Then she put it back on again and wiggled the door handle, ferociously this time, while pulling at the door with all her might. Nothing. So she chose to panic once more. She called out to me at one point. I mean, what on earth did she think I could do?

You know how it is when one is at the pit of despair; a germ of an idea appears over a sunny horizon. Well in our case the sun had already set and Madam realised it was best to stop applying her brain, she jammed the screwdriver into the gap by the door catch, wiggled it around while also pulling at the door for all she was worth. This time it worked and she was free, no longer incarcerated near to death in a cold, half decorated utility room. The next day she was telling a friend of her predicament. He offered no sympathy.

'Silly arse,' he said. 'Why didn't you have a phone in there with you?' I didn't catch her full answer, but as she stomped away I heard her muttering something about 'bloody men stating the bloody obvious!'

That I suppose is why she's now hightailed off to the Caribbean. I wonder if she realises that she'll meet some real big hairy tarantulas over there.

But I digress; I was talking about Hey Man Dave. Well he didn't leave me there in that car park, filled up with his tea chest and suitcases for long. He soon came back with my old owner, the now fully qualified motor mechanic, Richard Benson.

'I'm not surprised you couldn't start her. How long has she been parked here?'

'Hey man, how would I know? Coupl'a months, I suppose.'

'She's been here two months and you haven't run her?' Richard Benson looked at Hey Man Dave as he sullenly shook his head. 'The battery will be flat. I am surprised you left her here and didn't take her home.'

'Couldn't do that Man. The old man doesn't know I've bought a car.'

'Well I think you would be well advised to get a new battery fitted before you go off to university.'

Hey Man Dave didn't seem to be listening. 'What's that handle thing at the front?' He was staring at the lower areas of my radiator shell.

Richard Benson let out a shout of surprise. 'That is her starting handle. Didn't you know that?'

'I thought it was, but it didn't seem to work? It just span round and nothing happened.'

'You are supposed to push it inwards so that it engages with the crank. Then it turns the engine over.'

'Listen man, I'm a musician, not a mechanic. I don't understand engines and things.' Hey Man Dave was irritated.

Richard Benson switched on my ignition. 'Well there is enough life in the battery to crank her. Then I suggest that you get in and pump the accelerator and let's see if we can get this engine started.

Unless of course you fancy walking to Warwick?' Hey Man Dave climbed in. 'I presume she is not in gear.' Richard Benson added almost as an afterthought as he bent down to grip my handle.

'Hang on man, it is. Well I think it is. There, should be okay now…' At that point, Hey Man Dave started to pump my accelerator while Richard Benson started cranking me. I fired once.

'Give her a bit more choke. I think she'll start then.' Hey Man Dave duly obeyed and I quickly roared into life.

'There you are,' Richard Benson said as he climbed into my passenger seat. You can take me back to work now and I'll try to get you a discount on a new battery'

'No point, man. I'm broke, I'll get one soon.' He slammed me in to first gear and we were away.

★★★★★

What? What? What on earth is that? I am jolted out of my reverie yet again by a vision that is turning my sump. Peering out of my garage I can see Her Ladyship lurching across the yard clutching firmly onto a bottle of rum and singing the Banana Boat Song. I ask you. A woman of nearly sixty-one! Whatever next? To top it all, she is wearing a hat made from banana leaves and a pair of shorts revealing her not insubstantial cottage cheese thighs. Can you imagine it? I rather wish that this vision was actually a nightmare and I am still asleep. Unfortunately I am not.

'Good Morning Old Girl. Did you miss me?'

Well not that you are the slightest bit interested, but no I did not. I've had a whale of a time just stuck here in my garage, partying the night away – on my own. 'Good, good, good. Now we must start to think about our trip to France. That's only a few weeks away.' For heaven's sake, she's only just back from one holiday, she's barely unpacked and she's turned her attention to the next.

So here I am, being prepared to go abroad for the first time in my life. But can I rely on Her Ladyship to behave when we get over there? Oh good grief, she's now lurched off again and she's singing *'Day – oh, dayzee – day – yay – yay – oh, Daylight come an' me wan' to go home.'* She's going to embarrass me over there – I just know it!

Now, back to my adventures with Hey Man Dave. Well, from the minute he dropped Richard Benson off at his workplace and again declined the offer of a new battery, he swung me around and we headed south towards Warwick. He was a terrible driver, crashing my gears, shooting out of side roads without stopping to see if the road was clear and never giving any hand signals to tell other motorists where he was planning to go.

We eventually arrived at the university campus office and Hey Man Dave pulled in to a parking space, failed to apply my brakes and shot straight across a manicured lawn and into a beautiful flower bed.

'Oi! You bloody idiot!' It was the gardener who came running towards us, fork in hand and waving threateningly. 'What the 'ell do you think you are doin'? Oi'm sick of you bloody students fooling around. You're new here ain't you?'

Hey Man Dave, somewhat shaken but realising that it was essential that he radiated his cool persona, turned to face the gardener and winced only slightly at the sight of a garden fork being waved in his face.

'Hey Man. Cool it yeah? Brakes aren't as good as they used to be. Okay man?'

The gardener examined the damage to his bed. 'Ruined. Absolutely ruined. Chancellor's wife will be really upset when 'er sees this. What are you doing parking here anyway?'

'Just registering man.' By now a small crowd of students were gathering to see what was going on.

'Well I suggest you move that car bloody quick. You're parked in the chancellor's parking space and when he gets 'ere, he is going to see what you've done to my bed.'

'Look man, just cool it. As soon as I've registered, I and old Daisy here will be gone.' The gardener wandered off mumbling. Not a happy man, I thought to myself.

'Hey man, that's a pretty cool car.' A couple of other students had wandered over to Hey Man Dave; one had an old guitar slung across his shoulders.

'Yeah it is man, isn't it? Old Daisy here has brought me all the way from Northampton. You from far?' Then, spotting the guitar, 'Hey man, do you play that thing?'

'Yes man, I do. Jules and me here are looking to form a group.'

'Hey man, that's really cool. I'm not here five minutes and I've met some cool cats. I play the bass. Take a look on Daisy Girl's back seat.' He gestures towards the wooden tea chest and broom handle. 'Do you need a bass player?'

'Wow man, a tea chest bass. Now that really is cool. Welcome to the Warwick Skiffle Boys. Look, we are renting an old house about a mile away and we have room to spare for someone else. Do you want to share digs with us?'

'You better believe it man. That is a really cool idea. Tell you what? I'll pop in and register and then we can all pile in to Daisy Girl and go to the digs.' A delighted Hey Man Dave leapt up the steps in to the main building.

'Hey man,' the guitar man said to his friend Jules. 'Can you believe that luck? We have found ourselves a bass player and better still transport to take us to our gigs.' I did wonder whether things would get much worse with this trio. And they did.

★★★★★

It was eight hundred and eleven miles – I said – eight hundred and eleven flipping miles. That is what Her Ladyship has expected of me over the past week. It was just too much.

Right up to the last minute, I had hoped that Madam would forget all this nonsense about going to France, but she seemed determined.

'This is a really important preparation for our trip round the world,' she told me. 'There will be more foreign trips, some much longer than this one, but it will all be good experience for both of us. Now let's get you loaded up.'

She started to cram tools, spare parts, a warning triangle, a fire extinguisher and a yellow jacket into every nook and cranny of my interior. The final confirmation that we were going abroad was when she slapped a sticker on my rear end with GB on it.

'Stop being so miserable Old Girl,' she said. 'At least you are able to tell everyone that you are British. That should give you something to be proud of. You won't see many cars over there that can do that.'

It was last Thursday at ten o'clock on the dot that Her Ladyship started me up and steered me out of the drive. Then at eleven o'clock we did exactly the same thing all over again. That was because we'd managed about a mile before I expressed my first objection to this ridiculous trip. I went down to firing on three cylinders, so Madam had to bring me home again to sort me out. For a moment she thought of leaving me behind – I should be so lucky – Then we were off again, heading for Cardiff. What with all the spares and luggage, in addition to the gargantuan form of my driver, I knew I had a bit of a struggle ahead but the sun was shining so for a moment I forgot my objections and started to enjoy the journey.

The next morning, now with Her Ladyship's friend the Nice Miss Clem and her luggage on board, we headed off to meet the entourage of equally crazy owners and relatives who were hell bent on doing the same trip. Now having to carry two rather large backsides and all the bags some one hundred and fifty miles was rather too much and by the time I got to Portsmouth, I was exhausted. Then when Madam drove me on to a ship that evening

I became alarmed. I'd never been on a ship in my life. Had she considered that I might get seasick? No!

Actually, the crossing wasn't too bad. Well, if you are shut up in a very large darkened garage with another five hundred vehicles for company, you are not exactly qualified to make a comment on the trip one way or another. As soon as it was light the next morning, we drove off into a strange land with a strong aroma of Gauloise and garlic. It all felt so different. And what could be more different than being forced to drive on the wrong side of the road? There were signs everywhere telling us to drive on the right. But it wasn't right; it was wrong. I was confused, I've spent my entire life driving on the left, indeed what I would call the right side of the road, so why should I change a habit of a lifetime?

Well, I wasn't going to have it. This was the last straw. How dare she? I had no intention of driving on the wrong side of the road for the next four days. Good God, someone might drive into us. I wanted to go home. I didn't want to move a single inch further into that country. But Madam had quickly manoeuvred me into a queue of cars and I couldn't turn back. Eventually, we arrived at passport control and a French police officer, eyeing the Nice Miss Clem, leaned in through my side screen with a rather lascivious grin on his face. I didn't like his familiarity.

'Bonjour Madame et Madamoiselle. Bienvenue á France. Vos passports s'il vous plait.' The Nice Miss Clem replied with a very polite 'bonjour monsieur' and handed them over.

'Merci Madamoiselle. Vous êtes tres gentil.' He examined the passports and took rather a long look at Her Ladyship. I got the feeling that she had used an old picture in her passport and he couldn't believe that the wrinkled face behind my steering wheel was actually owned by the same person as on the passport. In the end he passed them back, gave the Nice Miss Clem a very warm smile and proffered a 'Bon Journée.'

'Humph,' said Her Ladyship. 'I've heard of the entente cordiale, but the way that chap was leering at you, I think he had a bit too much of the entente and less of the cordiale if you ask me.'

'He was only being polite,' replied the Nice Miss Clem.

Once again, we were rolling forwards, this time towards the exit of the port. I had to think quickly; we were only a few yards away. So I waited until we had stopped right beside the traffic lights at the entrance and I let my engine die…

Gotcha! I thought. Now let's see if the Her Ladyship can get me going again. The trouble was, I had completely forgotten that it wasn't just Her Ladyship; there were all the men driving my relatives on this trip as well. I've noticed before that for many of them, these trips are only fun when one of us breaks down. So there they all were, loaded to the gunwales with spare parts and waiting for any opportunity to fiddle with our engines. I was again reminded of that trip to north Wales two years ago and they were too smart for me then. And they were too smart on this occasion as well.

'It's your petrol pump,' cried the nice Mister John. 'It's completely clogged up with muck.'

Two hours later we were once again on our way with me still on the wrong side of the road. I swung over to the correct side of the road a few times, just to upset Her Ladyship, before settling into the trip. I couldn't understand a word the natives said, but they did seem to be friendly. People would wave at us and when we stopped they would come over to admire us. It all felt rather nice and I could see that my relatives appreciated the attention as well.

There was one thing that really got to me and that was how some of the French cars would come really, really close to my rear end. 'Get away from me you dirty French knicker sniffer,' I would shout in my best French accent. If that didn't work, I would blow out a load of oily smoke at them. Then they either pulled back or went past.

Once we got to the place where we were staying, we were

promised a couple of gentle days touring the Normandy countryside. God help us, Her Ladyship had planned the excursions, and of course it didn't take her very long to get us all lost.

'Follow me very carefully,' she cried out to everyone as we left a museum. 'There's a nasty bit of a road junction we are going on and we don't want to get ourselves onto the Caen Peripherique.' The Peripherique I discovered later is a sort of motorway that the French have built all the way around their big cities so that people do not have to drive through the middle. So off we go, Madam driving with the Nice Miss Clem navigating.

'Keep to the right,' cried the Nice Miss Clem at one point. 'Keep to that road on the right over there. Otherwise you will find yourself on the motorway to Brittany and we really don't want that.'

'No that's wrong,' shouted Her Ladyship. 'That can't be the road; it's just into the suburbs.' Then she embarked on a bizarre driving manoeuvre as she swung from one lane to another. Me? I just went where I was told.

We didn't find ourselves on the Peripherique but we did indeed find ourselves on the motorway to Brittany. The entourage of relatives behind us chose a variety of routes out of this predicament. Some followed us, others headed south on to the Peripherique and the remainder took the correct road. Mobile phones started ringing like mad.

Eventually we found a turn off and sheepishly Madam returned to the confused fold of relatives and their drivers, all of whom had managed to gather themselves together again.

'You should use a Sat-nav,' one of them suggested. 'Look follow me and we won't get lost again.'

Her Ladyship was for once very quiet and we joined the convoy of cars. But let's face it; we all knew that Madam could barely navigate herself out of a glass of wine. I felt quite sorry for the others and had to apologise to my relatives on many an occasion.

Our next port of call was a cider farm and churning up rather a lot of dust, my relatives and I swept into a farmyard where the owners were waiting for us with trays of cider.

'Ooh that's nice,' said Her Ladyship. 'Can I have another?' She didn't wait for permission and downed the second glass in seconds. The Nice Miss Clem looked on disapprovingly.

'What?' Madam had noticed the disapproving look. 'It's not strong. I'll be fine, I was weaned on cider remember. French cider is much weaker than the cider I grew up with. Anyway, we've a big lunch ahead.'

Then they were gone on their tour of the orchards and the cider making process, and to partake of the aforesaid hearty lunch. When they returned they were clutching bottles of various ciders and brandies and were loading them into the safe nooks and crannies of my relatives. They had just started to clamber back in to their cars and prepare themselves for the off when a voice interrupted them.

'Mesdames et messieurs, bienvenue à nos petit village.' All eyes turned in the direction of the voice. There by the entrance to the yard was a small delegation of rather official looking men. Standing at the front was a small man wearing a sash of red, white and blue stripes. The others stood behind him all beaming.

'My God,' said Her Ladyship. 'It's the French mafia.'

'Don't be daft,' said the Nice Miss Clem. 'I'll go and see what they want.'

She went over to the group to talk to them. A few minutes later, she returned.

'It's the mayor and the village council. It seems we've been invited to a reception at the Hotel de Ville. The mayor would like us to partake in some local Normandy fare and, oh yes, to try some more cider. It would be rude to refuse.'

So with the dignitaries filling some of our spare seats and the family who ran the cider farm filling the remainder, we all drove off towards the centre of the village and parked outside the Hotel de

Ville. Everyone trooped in, all were in a good mood, but that was nothing compared to the bonhomie that met my relatives and me when they emerged two hours later. Her Ladyship was arm in arm with the mayor. She was giggling, rather too much if you ask me.

'Ooh Monsieur le Maire, vous êtes très naughty.' He patted her bottom. 'Monsieur le Maire, what do you think I am?' Well he might have not known the answer to that question, but I did. There then followed rather a lot of kissing on the cheeks, something that Madam would never have dreamed of doing when at home.

'Mais Monsieur le Maire, ou est le gendarmerie? Nous sommes un peu tipsy, je croix.' I think Her Ladyship might have been concerned about le breathalyser.

'Je leur ai dit de maintenir à l'écart', the Nice Miss Clem quickly translated. 'It seems he has told them to keep out of the way. Let's get back to the Chateau, before we are all stopped and breathalysed.'

'God I love these people,' cried Her Ladyship. 'They've got their priorities right haven't they?' And we were gone, back towards our hotel. As we drove along, I couldn't help reflecting on how friendly the natives had been; it seemed to me that the officials were much more friendly than at home. And while I don't like having to drive on the wrong side of the road, the French roads are much straighter and easier to navigate. But the most profound difference was Her Ladyship's behaviour. She'd never have been so friendly with a local council official in Britain. She's always complained about one 'officious little prat or another' as she chooses to describe them. 'If those blasted little Hitlers can find a way of being a killjoy or throwing a spanner in the works, they will.'

Our last day in France arrived rather too quickly and it felt as though we had driven all over Normandy. But clearly not everywhere, as Her Ladyship took us all off on a rally as guests of a bunch of French relatives to celebrate the anniversary of VE Day.

'Not far now,' shouted Her Ladyship. 'Well that's what the man said to me.' I was becoming alarmed, this was our last day and here we were, driving further and further away from the ferry port when really I felt that we should be driving closer and closer to it. I was worrying that one of us might break down and none of us would get home.

As it happened, we nearly didn't reach the official starting point and I'll give you one guess whose fault that was. That's right, Her Ladyship's navigating again. The rally was an enjoyable drive as we mingled among our French relatives and we ended up at an enormous chateau with beautiful gardens stretching out below us. Madam pulled up and gracefully accepted a glass of wine and canapés, which were being distributed by some liveried gentlemen. The rally organiser came over to meet us.

'Welcome to Le Chateau D'Angoville,' he said. 'You are welcome to stay here as long as you like. Feel free to park on this slope here, then when you want to leave you can easily get back onto the drive.' He pointed down the slope. 'The gardens down there are really magnificent. The Count has many very rare plants. It's well worth a visit. But make sure your handbrakes are on.'

Madam was taken aback. 'You're English.' She said through a mouthful of tarte tartin.

'Scottish actually, I've lived in Normandy for years. As I said, I do recommend you pay the garden a visit. It's quite sensational. He went off to talk to some of the other owners.

'Come on then.' The Nice Miss Clem was eager to go and have a look and Her Ladyship stuffed one more piece of pastry into her mouth and followed. I simply sat there and enjoyed the view. I imagine that I had been sitting overlooking the garden and chateau for about twenty minutes when two young boys wandered along looking at us all. They were chatting eagerly in French.

'Hey Marcel, regardez cette petite voiture là.' He was pointing straight at me. The boy called Marcel joined his friend and both boys came over to look over me.

'Il est si petit,' said Marcel and he opened my door to get onto the driver's seat, while his companion climbed in my passenger side. As with all young children, it was my steering wheel and gear stick that attracted their immediate attention, and then they found the horn and headlight switch. I looked in vain for Her Ladyship, as I knew it wouldn't be long before they found the handbrake. But she had disappeared somewhere down into the gardens. I felt the brake cables go slack and in spite of being parked on fairly long grass, the slope was just steep enough for me to start rolling forwards. The two boys screamed in unison and baled out and I found myself rolling faster and faster down the slope towards the gardens, my doors flapping like a pair of wings. There were one or two half hearted attempts by other drivers to stop or even slow my progress but it was all in vain and I rolled across the lawn and straight into a rose bed, finally being brought to a stop by a large rose bush in the centre of the bed.

Her Ladyship had finally noticed what was going on and ran in my direction with just about everyone else in tow. At the same time a tall, smartly dressed man appeared at the door of the Chateau and strode over towards me. Madam reached me first, clambering through the flattened rose bushes.

'I hope you aren't up to your old tricks again,' she hissed. 'I haven't forgotten what you did to the Skoda last year.' She closed my doors and examined me for damage. 'Hmph, it could be a lot worse, but look what you've done to these roses.'

The crowd parted to allow the smartly dressed gentleman through. This was a man one rarely sees nowadays; a type we used to describe as 'dapper'. He was wearing a very expensive and beautifully cut suit, highly polished shoes and a cravat held in place with a diamond-studded pin. I couldn't help but be impressed with his style.

'Bonjour Madame. Is this your automobile?' He spoke very good English, with just a hint of a French accent. He barely looked at me; he was surveying with great concern the wreckage of rose bushes I'd left in my trail. Then he spotted the remains of the large bush that had finally stopped my progress.

'Oh non, mon Rosa Gallica. Il a eu cinq cents années.' He turned to Her Ladyship. 'Madame, I am le Compte Henri Montchamps, this is my home, my family have lived here for centuries and this automobile has just destroyed my rose garden. That bush there has been planted here since five hundred years.'

I couldn't really tell whether he was angry or upset. I just sat there willing myself to be back at the top of that slope. Her Ladyship just stood there, her mouth opening and shutting, but no words came out and the Count looked as though he would burst in to tears. Then there was a commotion and the man who had originally welcomed us pushed his way through the crowd, gripping the two boys firmly by their ears.

'Monsieur le Compte, c'était ces deux garçons. Ils jouaient avec la voiture et sauté en tant qu'elle a commencé à se déplacer.' He looked at Her Ladyship, 'It seems that they released the handbrake on your car.' The Count turned angrily to the boys.

'Marcel, Valentin, vous entrerez dans le château maintenant et j'aurai affaire avec vous plus tard.' He turned back to Her Ladyship.

'Madame, please accept my sincere apologies. It was my two sons who have damaged your automobile and my garden. Please dites moi, I mean tell me, if there is any damage done?'

'Well Monsieur le Compte, it is so kind of you to express your concern.' Her Ladyship was managing to suppress her anger remarkably well. With anyone else she would have flipped her lid. This time she was undeniably very happy to be at the centre of attention of a wealthy French count. 'The number plate is little bent back under the radiator, but otherwise I think she just needs a good polish to remove the scratches. But don't worry about the car.' What was she saying now? Not worry about me? 'Your rose bed is ruined. I imagine that Madame le Compte will be very upset about that?' This was said as a question and I was convinced that she was milking for information.

'Ah Madame, quelle domage, ma femme – I mean my wife – she died since a few years. I now bring up Marcel and Valentin on my own.'

'Oh I am so sorry, that must be so difficult for you.' To any casual listener, Her Ladyship was showing concern. To me she was rising to a possible opportunity. Perhaps the count sensed that as well, as he changed the subject back to the matter in hand.

'Madame we must roll your automobile back on to the lawn. Messieurs, s'il vous plait?' Suddenly, I was surrounded by many pairs of hands as I was manoeuvred slowly out of the rose bed. Madam straightened my number plate and removed bits of rose bush from my radiator, wheels and engine compartment.

Brushing the dirt off his hands, the count walked over. 'Madame, as a mark of my apology and respect, I would be honoured if you and your companion would join me in the chateau for dinner tonight.' Now Her Ladyship was in a predicament.

'Well Monsieur le Compte, that is very kind of you.' She looked at the Nice Miss Clem who quickly interjected.

'Yes that is very kind, Monsieur le Compte.' The Nice Miss Clem glared meaningfully at Her Ladyship. 'But we have a ferry to catch tonight.'

'Do we?'

The Nice Miss Clem nodded firmly.

'Oh yes we do, I'd forgotten. I'm sorry Monsieur Le Compte, I am afraid we have to go. Another occasion perhaps.'

Madam was undoubtedly disappointed at this lost opportunity. After the usual goodbyes and more kissing on cheeks, Her Ladyship and the Nice Miss Clem boarded me once more and we headed back to the Caen Ferry Port for the journey across the Channel.

Landing in Britain the next morning, we were still faced with the long drive home. That was two days of gruelling roads packed full of vehicles in the pouring rain. I have to confess that I found myself yearning for the peace and quiet of the roads of Normandy again. I hate driving in the rain. So to express my displeasure, I decided to have a puncture about a mile from home, just too far for Her Ladyship to try to finish the journey on a flat tyre. So she got soaked to the skin changing the wheel. Serves her right for making me work so hard. She who laughs last, laughs longest.

★★★★★

So here I am once more tucked up in my garage, exhausted but at least able to turn my thoughts back to Hey Man Dave and my experiences with him at university. I am really not sure how much time he spent studying, but I don't think it was very much. He was much more interested in playing music with his friends. Mind you, if one considers that strumming a tight piece of string slung between a broom handle and tea chest is actually music, then one needs therapy. It was an awful noise. He went out most nights with his friends and his tea chest to make what they called music in different venues. I'd sit outside patiently waiting and trying not to listen to the cacophony that poured out of the door. I remember one particular occasion when he tumbled out of this pub and manoeuvred the tea chest handle through the now enlarged hole in my roof, I warmed to the thought that we were finally going home. But Hey Man Dave, unpredictable as usual had other ideas.

'Okay Daisy Girl, let's not go home.' He settled into my driving seat, then. 'Hey guys,' he shouted to his musician friends (and I use the term musician lightly). 'It's still early. Let's go on somewhere else.' The friends eagerly piled into me. Then we were off with three passengers and various instruments. We must have looked a sight.

'Where shall we go then, man? The Blue Parrot? Or how about that new coffee bar, what's it called, Antonio's?'

'No way, man. Let's go where we can get a beer or two. I know, let's go to that cellar bar place in Albert Street. Who knows? The owner might let us play for some beers.'

'Do you think so, man? Do you think he would?'

'Well, it's worth a try, isn't it, man?'

We pulled up in a back street and they all got out, grabbed their instruments and headed for a darkened doorway. I heard the distant sound of a bell and eventually a face appeared.

'What do you boys want then? Shouldn't you all be home and tucked up in bed?'

'Hey man,' said Hey Man Dave. 'We wanna come in and play a few numbers for you. Maybe have a beer or two?'

'What do you play then?' The doorman sounded really sceptical. Well he would, wouldn't he, having been confronted by three young students, one carrying a tea chest, another a guitar with only four strings and the third, a jug. I haven't remarked on that phenomena have I? That's right, the man called Jules played an old earthenware jug. Apparently he was supposed to blow across the top of it to get it to make a noise and I can tell you, it wasn't a musical noise.

'Skiffle, man. We play skiffle.' Hey Man Dave seemed quite affronted that the man had even asked the question.

'Skiffle? That's old hat, out of date. It's guitars and drums nowadays. You boys never heard of the Beatles or the Stones?'

Hey Man Dave chose to ignore that question and instead of politely leaving, he and his friends set themselves up and started to strum their instruments and sing on the pavement. At that point, lights started to switch on up and down the street.

'Shut that bloody noise up,' came a voice shouting from the heavens. 'We're trying to sleep up here.'

Hey Man Dave and his friends seemed oblivious to that remark and carried on playing. The doorman, completely lost for words started to back away, back into the safety of the cellar bar. I think he knew what might happen next. A wise man.

'I said, shut that bloody noise up!' There was still no immediate reaction from the tea chest, guitar and jug that is not until the liquid contents of a chamber pot descended at speed upon the assembled company.

'Hey man, what are you doing?' Hey Man Dave stood there, the only sound for a moment was that of dripping liquid falling from his head onto the tea chest, a sort of deep bop, bop, bop. 'You're a square, man. You don't appreciate good music.'

'You call that good music?' The heavenly voice was now bemused. 'God help us, what is the world coming to?' A window slammed shut and the various lights went off one by one.

'People today just don't appreciate good music do they, man?' Hey Man Dave was trying to wipe his face with an old rag he'd found in his pocket.

'Hey man, you pong,' said the four-string guitar.

'Yeah man, you do,' said Jules the jug.

'Yeah man,' said Hey Man Dave, now trying to put the wet tea chest onto my back seat again. 'You guys want a lift back to the digs then?'

'No way man. We'll walk. We need some fresh air.' At that the guitar and Jules the jug walked away.

'Okay Daisy Girl, let's get home. I need a bath.' God he stank. And his wet clothes made me stink as well. It took days to go away.

★★★★★

'Good morning Old Girl.' It's Her Ladyship again. In fact every time I seem to get my teeth into my memoirs, in she bursts and disturbs my whole thought process.

'Good News Old Girl, I've heard from Rick Smales. He is keen to know when we plan to be heading off around the world. Apparently, he thinks he's found some different backing for us, but not enough to fund the whole trip. On top of that he thinks they won't be quite so fussy about the completion insurance. Anyway, I've told him that it won't be for a year or two yet. He's not very happy about that. I think he'd like us to go this year. But I need to feel certain that you are as fit as you can be. But forget the world for a while. We are off to Bryngarw for the national rally now.' So saying she starts to load me up with luggage, spares and a picnic hamper.

'It's a lovely day for a drive. The forecast is good, so I think we'll avoid motorways this weekend,' she announces. 'We'll take the old A48 instead. Bryngarw, here we come.'

I know I am not fond of motorways, but this trip is proving to be a bit of a challenge as we finally reach Swansea. This town seems to suffer from unhinged traffic-light breeding. They've given birth to them every few yards and not only that, every single one of them goes red as we approach. My temperature is starting to rise. More red lights and it's rising higher. Madam is grumbling again.

'Bloody stupid town. Town planners are complete idiots. Why can't they switch them off like they did in that town in Holland? What is it called? Drachten, that's it. They switched them all off and the traffic immediately started flowing a lot better. But not here. Oh no. Let's put up more and more and screw up the traffic flow completely.' I think Her Ladyship's temperature is rising faster than mine. Then she spots a petrol station with a large canopy.

'We'll pop in there Miss D. You need some fuel anyway and I will ask them if we can stop a while for you to cool down.'

A very nice lady ran the garage and she rather fussed over me when Madam explains that I have overheated. I am allowed to sit in the shade and offered a drink of cold water. Twenty minutes pass and we are on our way again.

We reach our destination to find a number of relatives already there. We are guided to our parking spot and Her Ladyship goes off to sign in. She returns with a broad grin on her face.

'Look at this Old Girl,' she thrusts a souvenir mug that they hand out at these events towards me. So? What's so special about this mug?

'Look; look at the car on the mug. It's you. They've used a picture of you on the mug. You're famous Old Girl; you've been glazed onto a souvenir mug.' Well, to be honest I am rather pleased. Immortalised at last.

'Are you camping tonight, Pam?' It's The Nice Mister Arthur, you know the man who fitted my luggage rack.

'You are joking aren't you? The last time I slept in a tent was with the Girl Guides in 1958. Never again… No I am heading back to Pembrokeshire this evening. I have to be back to see someone tomorrow.'

Over the next few hours, Madam comes and goes, we do the driving tests then at the end she returns to me with some trophies.

'There you are Miss D. Top prize for the best car owned by a woman and top prize for the best lady driver in the driving tests. Mind you, I am still the only lady owner and driver.' Somehow I'm not sure that was in the spirit of the competition. She packs everything away and we are off.

We are about halfway home, sailing along the dual carriageway back towards Carmarthen and I do something I haven't done for ages. I quietly spit out one of my core plugs. I cough, splutter and spew out a load of steam. Madam pulls me over into a parking area.

'You've done it again Old Girl, haven't you? It's a blooming core plug isn't it? I thought you had stopped doing this, but no worry, I have a spare one in the glove box.' The cow! Next time I must come up with something she can't fix.

It is interesting though. There was a time when a lady in distress with a broken down car would have had many a 'knight of the road' stopping to offer help. But during the twenty minutes that Madam was fixing me, not one of the dozens of vehicles whizzing past bothered to stop to ask if we were okay. I suppose the days of chivalry have long since passed. Now when we were in France a few months ago, I remember Her Ladyship talking about a 'good samaritan' law over there where drivers are obliged to stop and offer help to those who have broken down. Even in Hey Man Dave's days, people still stopped for those in trouble.

Mind you, Hey Man Dave never did anything to me, no fresh oil, no service, and no checks. Nothing. I was amazed at how I managed to keep going, but I did. We'd been in Warwick, it seemed an age, and I think Hey Man Dave must have been near the end of his time at university. He and his group had got no better, except that the four-string guitar briefly became a six-string guitar until its owner managed to break a string and it became a five-string guitar. During the day, I would just sit there outside the digs and in the evenings, I would be loaded up as usual and hauled off to one musical venue or another.

Then one morning, he came out and started me up. I was surprised, firstly because he never seemed to drive me during the day and secondly, he didn't have his tea chest with him.

'All right Daisy Girl, do you think you could take me to Coventry? I've got a chick to meet there.'

We headed off through Warwick. I can't remember how long it was since I'd seen the place during the day and I couldn't help noticing many road signs I hadn't spotted at night. Hey Man Dave ignored most of them anyway and he was doing just that as we swung round a bend and almost drove in to a little blue car coming towards us with a strange blue beacon on its roof. He slammed on my brakes…

'Hey Man. You're in my way, man. Can you shift yourself?'

'This is a one way street, sir.' A policeman had climbed out of the blue car and was walking slowly towards us. 'You have driven the wrong way down a one-way street. Didn't you see the no entry sign?'

'A what, man? What are you on about? I am on this road, on the left hand side and you coming towards me are on the right.'

'Yes sir, you have observed correctly. Except that you shouldn't be on this road facing in the direction you are. This is a one-way street with two lanes for cars going in the same direction, my direction. You are not allowed to drive down this street in that direction, your direction. Could I see your driving licence please sir?'

'Umm… I don't seem to have it on me, man. It's at home.' The policeman ignored that comment and continued walking towards me.

'This tax disc is out of date sir, two years out of date to be exact. I suppose you have left your insurance documents at home as well?'

'My insurance what, man? What's that for?'

'You are supposed to have a third party insurance for this vehicle sir. You don't have one do you sir?' Hey Man Dave shook his head.

'You don't have a driving licence either do you sir? Please tell me I'm mistaken. I'm off duty in ten minutes and if you are about to say what I think you are going to say, I have a feeling that I am not going to get off duty for rather a long time.'

'Umm. No man. No I don't have a licence. Now could you move your car so that I can get to Coventry?'

'You, young man, are not getting to anywhere except the police station. You wait here a minute.' The policeman headed back to his car and spoke into a telephone receiver. I had the most awful sinking feeling. For the past two years, Hey Man Dave had been driving me with no tax and no insurance and on top of that he didn't have a driving licence either. I had visions of being delivered straight to a scrap yard.

'Right young man, I am arresting you for driving a vehicle that is not taxed or insured and I assume you have no ten year test certificate either do you?'

'Ten year what, man? What's that?'

'It's the new ministry roadworthiness test for cars of ten years old or older. It became law five years ago. Now please correct me if I am wrong, but I think this car is over ten years old, more like thirty if you ask me. I am also arresting you for driving a vehicle while not holding a current driving licence. Translated into language that you understand, "You're nicked, man." Now get into the police car please. I will get a truck to tow this vehicle away.' In due course a truck, also with a blue beacon on top, arrived. I was hitched up to it and then unceremoniously hauled through Warwick. The shame of it. We arrived at the police station and everyone was staring at me, I felt like a criminal.

'Where do you want it?' The driver shouted from his cab to the policeman who originally arrested me.

'Oh stick it over there. Once its driver is convicted, he will either have to sell it or send it to the scrap yard. Mind you, looking at the age of this one a museum might be more appropriate.' I know I'd been described as old, but 'banger' and the suggestion that I might be a suitable museum piece wasn't very nice.

★★★★★

'What a beautiful morning Old Girl. We are off to lunch.' She settles herself in to my driving seat, flicks my engine into life with an efficiency that surprises even me. 'It's a restaurant in the Marina today,' she shouts above the engine noise. 'A perfect venue for my birthday.' Oh, so that is the reason for the good mood. It's her birthday. But her bonhomie is short lived, all because of the zealotry of Pembrokeshire County Council's road engineers.

When we arrived here a year ago, I could count the number of traffic lights in the county on my spark plugs. But today, as we sail through a village towards our lunchtime destination, we are suddenly confronted by a brand new set of lights apparently in the middle of nowhere. They are aided and abetted by at least twelve men in yellow jackets, walking around for no apparent reason.

'Hmmph,' snorts Her Ladyship. 'Another set of bloody traffic lights. The damned things are breeding here now. I expect a county councillor lives down there and he has complained that he cannot get out of this side road in the mornings. So they give him some traffic lights to make him happy. And look at all those men! For Heaven's sake, do they really need quite so many of them to check if the damned things work? Half of them I expect are from Health and Safety. What a state this country is sinking into.' Not content with Madam getting rattled by traffic lights there, as we arrive at the marina, across the road located at suitable distances are the dreaded speed bumps.

Oh God, here we go. There'll be screams and moans about haemorrhoids at any minute. I don't have to wait long. The good people of Milford Haven really do not want to know about the failings of Her Ladyship's lower end anatomy. As usual there isn't a thought for me. No thought about what these bumps might do to my suspension. And it's not nice, I can tell you. Not nice at all. So we slow down to a mile or two an hour to pass over them. I don't know who is wincing the most, Her Ladyship or me.

An hour or so later Madam returns, once again full of bonhomie. A good lunch obviously, but we still have to traverse the speed bumps and the traffic lights to get home. First the bumps and Madam slows right down to her one mile an hour again to allow a gentle and painless progress. Suddenly I am aware of a big vehicle roaring up to my rear end revving his engine as if he is about to start a Formula One car race. I think he's under the misapprehension that I might either get out of his way or go faster. Well, in your dreams sunshine!

He is so close and his car so high, that neither Her Ladyship nor I can make out the driver. Then he leans out of his window to reveal an acne ridden, and baseball be-capped youth blowing his horn and screaming abuse at us.

'Get off the road you old Bag and take that pile of shit with you,' he screams, blowing his horn. Oh-oh, Madam might be full of bonhomie at the moment, but she can also get pretty belligerent when she's like this.

I'm right; she grips my steering wheel as she slams on my brakes. She throws open the door and starts to clamber out to go and give this young whippersnapper a good talking to. He, seeing his opportunity, pulls over to the other side of the road and shoots past us beeping his horn and thrusting a clenched fist out of the window, making a pointing gesture with his middle finger suggesting that there was something for us to look at up in the sky.

'Hello Pam. Nice lunch?' Asks our neighbour as we get home. Her answer is unprintable, save to say she storms into the house.

Anyway where was I with those memoirs? Ah yes, Hey Man Dave arrested and I in fear of my final journey to the scrap yard. I can't remember for quite how long I'd been parked up at the police station when I saw a couple of men walking through the yard. One was a very smart and important looking policeman and the other was an elderly man with a military bearing. He spotted me and started to head in my direction.

'By Jove Charles,' he exclaimed. 'Look at that. I learnt to drive in one of those. Isn't she a beauty?'

'No Humphrey, it is a wreck.' The policeman seemed completely unimpressed; moreover I think he was annoyed that his conversation about some rather important matters had been distracted by me.

'But she's just like that car I had when I was courting Joycie. When was it, twenty three or twenty four? I was still at Sandhurst. This one is not that smart and it could do with a lick of paint. What's it doing here?'

The policeman looked around and spotted a young officer about to get into one of the blue police cars. 'Just a minute constable, can you come over here please?' The other policeman realising who had summoned him came scurrying over. 'Do you know why this old car is here?'

'Yes sir, chief constable sir. I arrested a young student the other day for driving this car while uninsured, taxed or having passed the ten year test. He didn't have a driving licence either. I couldn't leave it where I arrested him in the Castle Way one-way street system. I expect it will have to go and be scrapped. It is a bit of a wreck sir.'

The man called Humphrey interjected. 'Do you think the young fella might sell it, constable? I presume he wouldn't be asking much. If it's cheap, I might be prepared to buy it. It would certainly bring back many happy memories of my younger years.'

The Chief Constable couldn't believe his ears. 'For heaven's sake, Humphrey, you don't want to be bothered with this thing.' But Humphrey appeared to have the bit between his teeth and I was beginning to think that I was about to get a reprieve.

'This would be a perfect project for me now that I am retired, Charles. I'd love to have the opportunity to get this one on the road again. My man Davison could help me. He enjoys doing things like that. Anyway, it can't be that bad and it will be lovely to take Joycie out to lunch and so on. Look, tell you what. If your constable could have a chat with the student and see if he was prepared to sell this car, I'll go and have a chat with Joycie. I'd better get the Memsahib's approval what?'

'Well Humphrey, I think you are losing your mind, but I suppose as we get older we do sometimes try to recapture our youth.

We'll find out if the lad will sell it and I expect he will won't he Constable?' The constable nodded.

'Yes sir, it might be a first offence, but he is still going to have quite a fine to pay.' He saluted the chief constable, turned on his heel and returned to his patrol car.

'Tell him I'll go up to a fiver, constable would you mind?' Humphrey called after the departing policeman.

'That lad's fine will be a lot more than that,' said the Chief Constable. 'Now Humphrey, we were talking about policing numbers. Do you think the Authority will green light the recruitment of another twenty officers?' The men walked slowly off deep in conversation, leaving me to contemplate a sudden possible change in my future.

★★★★★

'How are you feeling today Old Girl?' It's Her Ladyship, yet again distracting me from my reminiscences. Well nice of you to ask, but after that one hundred and twenty mile door to door trip round Pembrokeshire last Sunday, after which I might add, being left out in the rain, it's hardly surprising that I am unwell.

'Good, good, good.' She isn't listening to me is she? 'I have someone to meet you Old Girl. He's come to live with us.' Then I spot it, a strange black creature with white feet, lurking around the door to my home and sniffing at everything. It looks like some sort of malevolent portent from the next world. I hope he is not suggesting that I am on my way to join the invisible traffic jam.

'Miss Daisy,' she says, 'I'd like you to meet Oscar the Asthmatic Barking dog, Oscar, I would like you to meet Miss Daisy, on the shelf spinster of this parish.'

Why on earth would she want me to meet this creature? What has it to do with me and since when was I an on the shelf spinster?

I suppose she is trying to be funny. I peer at him. God, he's ugly. He peers at me and then he moves slowly towards me and sniffs at my wheels. How dare he. Get away from me, you horrible creature; get away! I will not be sniffed at by anyone, least of all you. What's happening now, what are you doing? He lifts his rear leg and widdles onto my front wheel. Ugh, that's horrible. It reminds me of that night with Hey Man Dave.

'Oh dear, it looks as though Oscar has peed on you,' Her Ladyship seems to think that rather funny. Oh Dear? OH DEAR?? It wasn't her he squirted his widdle onto, it was me, and now I smell of something rancid. Can't she control this creature or do I have to endure more of this in the future? I'll tell you what, whatever your name is, get underneath me and I will squirt something on to you that you really won't like.

Her Ladyship washes the widdle from my wheel and tells me that Oscar will really enjoy going for rides in me. Well you can forget that. If you think I am going allow this creature onto my seats, you'd better think again. Anyway, what on earth is this creature doing here in the first place? Why does she need a strange black asthmatic barking dog? What can it do? Can it carry Her Ladyship's rapidly enlarging backside around the place? No. Can it indeed carry up to four people in comfort? No. Can it travel at speeds of up to forty miles an hour? NO! So what on earth is the use of it? What is an Asthmatic Barking Dog anyway? And then he barked. Oh, I understand now.

'Anyway Old Girl, I thought we'd go out later. Let's have a look at why you keep conking out.' I should add here Dear Diary that she has already spent three days trying to find out what's wrong with me. She fiddles with my carburettor, messes around with my petrol pump, pokes a screwdriver at my distributor and achieves absolutely nothing except, if anything, to make me feel even worse. I seriously contemplate giving up completely. No, too cruel. She is going through enough angst and that amuses me enough. In the end she gives up with a 'That's better, I am sure you are feeling better now.' Well kind of you to ask, but no. Then, before I could blink, we are off on our trip with Oscar the Asthmatic Barking Dog stretched out on my rear seat.

She's arranged to meet up with The Nice Mister Terry and The Nice Missus Ruth in a lay-by near Carmarthen, so they could show her the way to our destination.

'Terry, just the person. I'm having a problem with Miss Daisy.' Correction, I think. You are not having a problem with Miss Daisy; Miss Daisy is having a problem with Miss Daisy. 'It's the slow running. She doesn't tick over, her engine just keeps dying.' At this point, we must be reminded that until now the Wrinkled One has taken three days to make a complete mess of fixing me. Well, it takes the Nice Mister Terry exactly three seconds.

'Here's your problem,' he says. 'Look here in the manifold. That hole should be sealed. She's is sucking in too much air.' So that was why I wasn't well. The gallant Mister Terry has come to the rescue. He turns towards the hedgerow and carefully selects a piece of twig. After working it and shaping it with a penknife, he thrusts his twig into the hole and all becomes well with my world.

'Is that all it was?' Her Ladyship was undoubtedly impressed. Mind you, I was too.

Chapter Five

'Pleased to meet you m'dear, Brigadier General Sir Herbert Orsten DSO
and Public Bar at your service.'
I eye him up and down with a look of disdain.

Tuesday 8ᵗʰ January 2008

'Miss Daisy; I'd like you to meet Sir Herbert, Sir Herbert, meet Miss Daisy.' Why is it that Her Ladyship always seems to disturb me when I am enjoying a brief moment of peace? What does she want this time? There is always a bit of a glare when in the mornings the sun shines straight into my headlights. But as I get accustomed to the light this time, there before me stands an old, grey, wreck of a thing. What? WHAT? Get away from here you ghastly thing, whatever you are. First a dog and now this?

'Pleased to meet you m'dear, Brigadier General Sir Herbert Orsten DSO and Public Bar at your service.' I eye him up and down with a look of disdain. Hardly a knight of the realm, I think to myself. He's obviously one of those characters who latch a knighthood or a military rank onto their name and to make matters worse they slap in a few letters afterwards. In this case he's done it all. Anyway, how dare he call me 'm'dear'. Mind you, he looks the worse for wear: terrible complexion, dull paintwork, grey, tarnished chrome and worse still, his headlights are skew whiff. Judging by the way he speaks, I think he's in to petrol additives.

'Driven round the world don't y'know. Mind you, some years ago. Too old for that sort of thing now, far too old.' What a load of rubbish. Him round the world? That wreck? For heaven's sake, he couldn't drive himself around a garage forecourt, let alone the world.

God almighty, am I going to look like that when Her Ladyship has taken me around the world? I certainly hope not. Thankfully the W-word hasn't been mentioned recently. Anyway, Orsten Herbert, whoever you are, I am sure you have something pressing to do. A trip to John O'Groats, or better still another jaunt to Timbuktu perhaps? Don't let me keep you.

'Sir Herbert has come here to live with us,' announces Her Ladyship. 'He's quite a close relative of yours; same birthplace, but three years younger. I thought with your age and your dislike of the winter, I could let you rest during the cold months and take him out and about with me instead.'

I think not, Your Ladyship, definitely not. We don't need him here. I can manage quite well you know, I can do anything he can. Look at him. This Orsten fellow is ugly. And he's grey. Grey, grey, grey. Nothing like my fine lines and well turned rear end. Take him away. I'd rather stare at Dumple Bloody Dale in the rain than have to look at him any longer.

'I think you'll both get on well together don't you?' She's ignoring my feelings again. How many times do I have to say it? No!

'So, I am going to have a shed built for him over there, then he can have his own place to stay. He'll be fine in there and then you can keep your own home. I might need to move you out occasionally when I have to work on him. I am sure you won't mind letting him use your garage when that happens.'

We'll see about that, but at least Her Ladyship is granting me the grace of the seniority of my position. And so it should be. Now please take him away, I want to reminisce and he's ruining my view. He is certainly ruining my concentration and I am trying to remember what happened after being dumped in that police yard.

'Good morning colonel, madam,' it was the policeman who had originally arrested me and Hey Man Dave. He was addressing the man called Humphrey whom I'd met the other day and who now had arrived with his wife. 'I've made those enquiries for you and the young man concerned has accepted your offer of five pounds.'

'Capital, capital, well Joycie Darling, what do you think of her?'

'Humphrey, it's a wreck.' Joycie Darling was completely unimpressed.

'But Joycie, darling, look at her. She's just like that car I had when we were courting. Don't you remember? At Sandhurst? I appreciate that this one is not that smart and it could do with a lick of paint. Look it's only cost a fiver. I thought that when I have smartened it up, it'd bring back many happy memories of our younger years. This would be a perfect project for me now that I am retired, darling. You are always complaining that I spend too much time on the golf course and the County Ground. It can't be that bad and it will be lovely to take her out into the countryside.' My goodness he did try hard to talk her round and it worked.

'Well, I suppose I could put a needle and thread into that hood, darling. Go on then.' Joycie Darling had admitted defeat.

'Well sir.' The policeman felt he should add something to this conversation. 'I suppose it could be made roadworthy. They were sturdy little cars and the chassis will be sound I am sure. But it needs a really good service on top of smartening it up and, don't forget, you must make sure it takes its ten year test this time. And please, make sure it is also taxed and insured before you take it on the road again. We really don't want it back here. You'll be all right taking it home now though. We'll turn a blind eye for that little trip. Good luck with it sir. If you'd like to come in to the station, I have the documents and if you let me have the five pounds, I will make sure that the young man gets his money.' Colonel Humphrey and Joycie Darling headed off into the police station. I was feeling elated. Talk about being saved by the bell. I think Hey Man Dave had washed his hands of me and I would have been on my way to the scrap yard, had not Colonel Humphrey and the chief constable wandered in to the police yard that day.

'Well Old Girl, we need to get you home now,' said Colonel Humphrey on his and Joycie Darling's return. 'Darling, would you drive the Rover home? But please take it very carefully; it is new and we don't want to get it scratched do we?' A flash of anger crossed Joycie Darling's face, but she decided to say nothing. 'You follow me home, I expect this old girl will need some fresh petrol on the way won't you?' He patted my radiator.

'Well,' Joycie Darling addressed the constable. 'I suppose it will keep him off the golf course. That is until he gets bored with it.'

Humphrey Darling bristled slightly. 'Yes, well. Come on, let's get this Old Girl home. Thank you Constable. Thank you for all your help.'

'My pleasure sir. And don't forget, test, insurance and tax.' The policeman smiled and wandered off.

It was a bit of a struggle getting to my new home, but what a home it turned out to be. We arrived at some large wrought iron gates on a road where Warwick started to come to an end and the countryside began. A man ran up to open them up for us.

'Thank you Davison. What do you think of this then? A nice little project for the next few months, what?'

'Err, yes sur, Colonel sur.' Judging by his lack of enthusiasm, this man Davison had obvious doubts.

'Can you clear out one of the old coach houses for this Old Girl? We'll need light, power and a bit of heat, so we can work on her. I'll leave her in front the house for now, and then you can put her away when you've found somewhere for her, what?'

We headed up a long winding gravel drive with Joycie Darling following on behind. Colonel Humphrey pulled up by a large front door to an absolutely enormous house.

'I expect Mrs. Davison will have lunch ready soon, Darling. I'm ready for my Scotch now. G and T?'

'Yes please, Darling.' She turned to the man Davison who had followed on foot up from the gates. 'Hello Davison. Those borders look a lot better now.' Davison touched his forelock briefly. 'What do you think of this then? Do you think the Colonel has finally fallen off his trolley?' Davison laughed nervously.

'Well Ma'am, it'll be an interesting project for 'im this autumn.'

'Us Davison, us. I thought you'd enjoy getting your hands dirty with me, rather than always fussing over that garden for the Memsahib.'

Humphrey and Joycie Darling strode off into the house. Well, talk about moving from the ridiculous to the sublime: a students' back street digs to an almost stately home on the outskirts of Warwick.

'Helloo, Mrs Davison, we're home. Lunch in ten? Is that all right?'

There was a shriek from deep inside the bowels of the house. Davison watched them enter and then started to wander back towards his borders. He was mumbling to himself.

'If I ain't got enough to do with this bloody garden. Now the old bugger wants me to help him with that bloody old banger.' I bristled; 'old banger' indeed. Then he stopped, turned back towards me and started to wander slowly around me. 'Gor you'm a bit of a mess, ain't you? I reckons that the colonel 'as finally lost it. I really 'ave.'

He sauntered off towards the borders again before remembering that he had to find somewhere to put me and he disappeared off behind the big house. For the first time in ages, I felt optimistic about my future.

★★★★★

'Good Morning Old Girl. How are you today? Still feeling grumpy?'

Well yes actually. I cannot understand why you had to go out and buy that grey thing.

'You've really got to get used to the idea that Sir Herbert is here to stay. The season of goodwill to all men might be over, but that is no reason for you to be so bloody minded.'

Well, what could I answer to that? Except that since neither Her Ladyship nor the Grey One are actually men, the season of good will doesn't really apply to them.

Seriously though, where would we all be if I didn't keep Her Ladyship in check? Herbert Orsten, that interloper for her affections, is a different matter. Yesterday for example I had been for a service with the nice Mister Wilson and returned to find that he had moved in to my garage without so much as a 'by your leave' and Her Ladyship plonked me in his shed. She then announced that she was planning to take him to the car club luncheon today, instead of me. 'It'll be a good opportunity to see how well he works,' she said.

She then proceeded to flatten his battery trying to get him to start. So then she plugged him in to the battery charger. And now he still won't start, she's changed his plugs, distributor cap, capacitor and rotor arm. He backfired a few times and that was it.

Time is beginning to run out and she comes over to me. Hopefully, she is going to take me instead. She opens my bonnet and peers into my engine.

'Aha!' She returns to the Grey One. 'I know what's wrong with you. Your plug leads are the wrong way round.' At that she thrusts her hands under his bonnet to fiddle with his connections, 'I really don't understand how this could have happened,' she mutters. 'After all you were fine the other day.'

She looks suspiciously across at me. Why on earth would she look at me like that? Surely she cannot think that I had something to do with it? I mean, how could I? Still if it's any consolation and she is taking the Grey One, the Asthmatic Barking Dog will travel in him instead of me and I don't have to be bothered with dog hairs all over my seats. There is another consolation. Being housed in the garden shed means that I don't have to look at Dumple – bloody – dale anymore and it is quite warm and cosy in here. So having sorted him out she wanders back over to me.

'Miss Daisy, I forgot to tell you; I have some good news and some bad news. First the good news. Sir Herbert is now sorted and running and you can go back into your proper home.'

What a shame, I was beginning to like it here, but I cannot admit that to her. She starts me up and brings me out into the warm sunshine. She pulls out a chamois leather and starts to wipe me down. What's the bad news then? I sense that she was not exactly over the moon with whatever it was.

'Rick Smales called earlier this morning to tell me that the second lot of potential sponsors for the world trip has dropped out. Apparently they don't think the cost of the trip will bring them a decent return on their investment. So they've withdrawn from the project. But not to worry. Rick says there are plenty more fish in the sea. He still seems confident. Anyway, I suppose we could always go without the sponsorship, but it might prove rather expensive.'

I can see that she is disappointed at this news and is doing her best to put a brave face on it. Me? I'm finding it almost impossible to hide my joy. Could it be that sanity is starting to prevail and there is a God up there looking out for me? Now I can settle back and get on with those memoirs.

★★★★★

'There you are Humphrey,' said Joycie Darling as she bit through the last piece of thread. 'That hood should be more waterproof now. But I cannot guarantee it.'

'Thank you m'dear. This old girl is looking a lot better now. Bodywork looks rather splendid now don't you think?' He looked down at a pair of legs sticking out from below my undercarriage.

'How's it going Davison? Have you managed to stop that leak?' A disembodied voice emerged from my nether regions. 'What's that, man? Can't hear you… damned hearing aid.'

Davison emerged, face blackened with oil and grime.

'I think it's sorted now sur, Colonel, sur. It needed a new fibre washer.' I think the man Davison was uncomfortable addressing his employer from beneath his crotch.

'Well done man. Now you'd better get home for your tea or I'll be in trouble yet again with Mrs Davison, what?' Davison scurried away, anxious to escape before the colonel found something else for him to do. 'Well m'dear, let's see if we can get this hood to close properly.' He lifted up the front section from where it was resting and pivoted it over to lock onto my windscreen frame. 'I think that's how this goes. Do you remember that day when I bunked off a lecture and took you out to lunch? Gosh when was that, twenty four? We got caught in that awful rainstorm and were both soaked to the skin before we could close the hood. Don't you remember, Darling?'

'All too well, Darling. And you were worried stiff about bumping in to the commanding officer before you'd had a chance to get yourself cleaned up, weren't you?' Joycie Darling was now helping Humphrey manipulate my hood into its closed position.

'Mind you m'dear, hoods are a lot easier nowadays. Some are even automatic. They emerge from the blasted boot and simply lock themselves in to place. This one's nothing like that. Can you guide it into the hole at your end Darling?'

'I usually do, Humphrey. I usually do. There we are.'

'Capital, capital. Well I think we can try her out in the next few days, just a short trip. Insurance certificate came through this morning. I'll take her over to Jackson's for that test thing and then on the way home, I'll pop into the post office and see if Mrs. Watson can furnish us with a tax disc. We could go to The Plough and Harrow for lunch on Friday. I'll call the Lloyds; see if they'd like to join us. Geoffrey will be so jealous when he sees this old thing.'

'Marvellous, Darling. That would be nice. But don't forget I have the church bazaar committee meeting at three.'

'Of course m'dear, we wouldn't want to blot your copybook with the padre would we?' Joycie Darling wasn't paying attention; she had now been distracted by her roses across from my garage and was dead-heading them with her sewing scissors.

★★★★★

My Garage doors fly open. It's You Know Who again. Well let's be honest it couldn't be anyone else could it?

'Happy Birthday Old Girl. Seventy Four today, how about that then?'

Oh wonderful… Happy Birthday to me… Happy Birthday to me… Never been seventy four before and actually never had the key of the door before either. But here I am, just one year short of my three score years and fifteen and still going strong. The Grey One, he who calls himself Sir Herbert, has gone off to see that nice Mister Wilson now. Apparently there is some important work needing done. Rather a waste of money don't you think? Quite frankly, all he really needs is a car crusher. But it's so nice not to have him around going on, and on, and on about his bloody 'been round the world don't you know'. I mean, he did that years ago when he was barely in to his thirties and he was relatively fit and healthy. I'd like to see him try and do it now. Humph! Probably wouldn't make it to Dover.

I do have some good news though. Her Ladyship has finally replaced my leaking radiator tap. Now I know one should never hurry her. This is Pembrokeshire after all and nothing happens in

Pembrokeshire very quickly. I've been dribbling water for as long as I can remember and she bought the replacement tap three years ago. After I'd made a large puddle of antifreeze on the floor of the new shed, she decided that it was time to do something about it. So I am now relatively happy and am not wetting myself any more.

When I say relatively happy, that is because I'm not so happy about being completely surrounded by potatoes! Why, might one ask, am I surrounded by potatoes? Well, according to Her Ladyship, I have to share my home with these tubers so that they can be 'chitted' whatever that is. So it appears I have now become a gardening accessory!

★★★★★

Where was I, then? Oh yes, that Friday and Colonel Humphrey was going to take Joycie Darling out for lunch. So there I was, sitting proudly outside the big house, new tax disc on display and Davison was busy polishing my bodywork when out came Colonel Humphrey.

'Come along Joycie. Thank you Davison, she's looking quite smart now.' Colonel Humphrey turned briefly and walked a couple of steps back towards the house. 'Oh do hurry up Joycie Darling, the table's booked for twelve thirty and we are meeting the Lloyds. Mustn't be late, what?'

Davison touched his forelock and turned back towards his garden.

'Where are you going Davison? Hop in man, hop in the back. I might need you if this old girl breaks down.' Davison shrugged his shoulders and clambered in onto my rear seat.

'Coming darling. Oh hello Davison, are you coming too?' Joycie Darling having emerged from the house got in while Colonel Humphrey held my passenger door for her.

'Seems so Mum. The colonel wanted me to come along in case this old banger breaks down.' This was said with a distinct lack of enthusiasm, even so his comment went straight over the colonel's head.

'Right Darling, let's go.' The colonel settled into my driving seat, pulled my starter and I burst in to life. 'Gates open Davison?'

'Yes sur.' A murmur emerged from my rear seat, the lack of enthusiasm now sounded like a positive sulk. I imagine that Davison saw this outing as being a complete waste of his time. Colonel Humphrey manoeuvred me along the gravel drive and we were gone, heading out into the countryside for our rendezvous at The Plough and Harrow.

'Happy Darling?'

'Oh Humphrey, this is lovely, just like it was back in your Sandhurst days. It doesn't seem as though we were doing this forty something years ago, does it?'

I was doing nearly thirty five miles an hour and Joycie Darling had to hold her hat in place so it didn't blow away. The Colonel, pipe in mouth and cap firmly pulled down onto his head, was concentrating on the road ahead.

We pulled into a car park and stopped beside a rather posh Jaguar, out of which another couple was emerging.

'Geoffrey, Gwen; what do you think of this then? Pretty smart, what? Five pounds she cost me. Mind you it has cost me another twenty five to put her right, hasn't it, Davison?'

Davison, unsure whether to emerge or to stay put, simply grunted. Colonel Humphrey climbed out and slammed my door, rather too hard I am afraid as one of my headlights swung round.

'You know Davison don't you? Sterling chap, helped me get this old thing sorted out, what? He normally looks after the garden while the stalwart Mrs Davison does the house and cooking. We have to be careful not to upset Mrs Davison don't we, Darling?'

Joycie Darling laughed. 'Yes Humphrey, it would never do to upset Mrs Davison.' Davison nodded in eager agreement to that comment, probably realising he was already in for the high jump for not turning up for his lunch.

Colonel Humphrey undoubtedly realised the same thing at the same time.

'Davison,' he said. 'We're going to be a little while and I've deprived you of one of your good wife's fine lunches. Here, here's four bob, have yourself a pie and a pint on me.'

The man Davison took the four shillings, touched his forelock and headed off towards the public bar, while Humphrey, Joycie and the Lloyds headed towards the restaurant entrance.

Several hours must have passed before the colonel and his party re-emerged.

'Where's Davison?' Joycie Darling was looking around somewhat alarmed. 'How much did you give him darling?'

'Four bob, why?'

'Oh you bloody old fool. You know what he gets like when he's had a few pints of cider. He'll have spent the lot on that stuff and all that on an empty stomach.' Joycie Darling was livid. 'Heavens knows what Mrs Davison is going to say.'

The colonel turned towards the public bar entrance. 'I'll go and get him.'

The pub door opened and out staggered Davison. 'No need, here he comes now.'

The three other sets of eyes turned towards the entrance, Davison was tottering towards them. At the same time he was struggling with the zip in his trousers. Every time he pulled at the zip, he hopped into the air with both feet and then didn't quite manage to land properly, causing him to lurch either to one side or to the other. Geoffrey Lloyd decided that his and Gwen's best course of action now was to bid a hasty retreat.

'Well, we better be off,' said Geoffrey. 'Hop in Gwen.' Gwen obliged, rather too quickly, almost tripping over her coat. 'Bye bye Old Man, excellent lunch, thank you.' He glanced at Davison, then back to the colonel. 'Take care on your way home.' He was into his car and gone long before Davison reached the rest of us. Joycie Darling gave him a look of disgust and got into my passenger seat.

'Good God man, look at you. Stand up straight. And do up that zip.' Colonel Humphrey was reverting to his military persona.

'Sorry Sur, Colonel Sur. Got a little problem downstairs. It'sh shtuck.' He struggled with his zip once again, but to no avail.

'Oh for God's sake man, get in. I dread to think what Mrs Davison will have to say to you.' Davison just groaned. He was not too drunk to realise that he still had to confront his formidable wife.

Colonel Humphrey seemed to have a bit of trouble getting me to start again. 'What do you think Davison? Water in the petrol?' A disjointed mumble returned from my rear seat. Davison, I imagine, was dropping off to sleep. 'Ah that's it.' I decided to fire into life, but only on three cylinders and moments later we staggered out of the car park and onto the lane that would take us home. I have to say that it was a struggle for me and we limped along at no more than twenty miles an hour.

'She's only firing on three cylinders Davison. Any ideas?' There was no answer from the rear sea, just a restless snoring. 'Blast the man. Come along Old Girl. You can do it. Don't let me down, what? It's only a few miles. Sorry about this darling.' Joycie Darling had become tight lipped and kept looking from her watch to her husband and back to her watch again.

'Darling, I really do hope you are not going to make me late for my meeting. You know how the Reverend Pipkin depends on me. Oh do shut up that snoring Davison.' She turned and whacked Davison on his knee with her handbag. He reacted with a few grunts and snorts before resuming his steady snoring.

'I know m'dear, I know. Won't be long now, five – ten minutes at the most.' The Colonel was now gripping my steering wheel very tightly as we arrived at a crossroads. 'Is it clear left, Darling?' Joycie Darling leaned as far forwards as she could and peered through my side screen, while Colonel Humphrey peered to the right.

'All clear left, Darling.' She settled back into her seat again and Colonel Humphrey gingerly rolled me forwards.

It was the blare of the very loud horn that made just about every bolt in my bodywork jump out of its nut and my engine stalled halfway across the road. The Colonel, in shock, tried to swing my steering wheel from left to right, then slammed on my brakes and of course, I didn't stop. Well, not straight away and I found myself buried in a hedge while a very large lorry was snorting and snarling at my side.

'Wha', wha'?' Davison emerged from his self inflicted oblivion. 'Whash happening? Colonel Sur? 'Ave we been ambushed by the Jerries?' The Colonel really wasn't interested in Davison or what he had to say at that moment. It seemed that Joycie Darling was in a state of shock.

'Are you all right m'dear? Are you all right?' Joycie Darling responded with a little moan.

★★★★★

'Wake up m'dear, at least you could say good morning to me.' What? Who's that? That's a different voice. Sorry, where am I? Oh no, not him, please let it not be him. I peer out of the garage. It is him, the Grey One. How dare he? I was having a dream and I wake up to this vision of decrepitude.

'Where have you been for the past week? I was beginning to enjoy your absence.'

'North Wales and Ireland m'dear. The Memsahib decided to take me instead of you. Well, if you think about it, I am the right sort of chap to do a trip like that. Crossed the Wicklow Mountains don't you know.'

'What? She took you? Took you to Ireland? I was supposed to be doing that trip. I always do the abroad trips. She told me that she'd got me ready for it. All part of our training for the round the world run, actually.'

'Well m'dear she took me instead. You were asleep. She probably decided that it was too much for you. Anyway she got me out and loaded me up with all manner of things: spare parts, oil, water, first aid kit, luggage and so on. I thought for a minute that the Mem' was going to take me round the world again. "Don't you get any grand thoughts," she said to me. "We are just off to Anglesey and Ireland. Miss Daisy can have a rest." Well I thought, that's not quite round the world, but I'm certainly the right chap for a trip like this. Now m'dear I know I am getting on, but I'm not as old as you.' The Grey One doesn't half drone on, but I won't rise to that taunt.

'Get on with it you old fool. I want to hear about what should have been my trip to Ireland.' To be honest I am not a little miffed that Her Ladyship had taken him and not me, but I mustn't show it.

'Tell you what, Old Girl, that journey was a lot tougher than I thought it would be. A bit shaky on the old wheels at times don't you know, and that seemed to worry the Memsahib. Then we had barely done Anglesey when we were off to Ireland. Of course almost as soon as we got off the ferry, the Mem got us all lost and before we knew it we were heading towards Belfast on the motorway. Does she lose her way a lot?'

'Oh yes indeed she does. Rather too often.'

'Hmmph, thought so. Anyway Wing Leader, your 'nice Mister Arthur' chap, having decided that we were on the wrong course, banked off and we found ourselves charging headlong into the centre of Dublin. A taxi driver pulled up beside us. "Are you lost then?" he said. The Mem and Wing Leader give him an anxious glance. They should have relied on me. I could have found the hotel. After all I did navigate us out of the Arizona Desert back in seventy four. Well, the taxi driver, he says, "Where you goin' then?" Wing Leader tells him, and then with a 'follow me!' he charges off ahead of us. Mind you, his passenger looked damned worried. The taxi then disappeared in to the distance and we were left to find our own way once again. Not difficult for a chap like me, don't you know. When I reached Australia back in seventy one I had no trouble finding my way through Sydney. Chaps are always better at that sort of thing, don't you know.'

'Oh do get on with it. I haven't got all day.'

'What? Oh yes, Anglesey, Ireland, Dublin. That's it we were in Dublin. Well, we eventually found the hotel and we were unloading the luggage, when up turns the taxi again. "Ah you found it then? I lost you back there." Well of course we bloody found it. Chap like me doesn't get lost for long.'

I bristle as his mind starts to wander yet again, but this time he seems to steer himself back to the story.

'The next day, Wing Leader decided that we should take a trip over the Wicklow Mountains to Kilkenny. I think he must have a very strange sense of humour because we seemed to climb forever. I don't know how far, right up through the clouds though, and I was completely whacked when we reached the top. The road was rough and I got several cases of my shaky wheels again. I think it was a recurrence of the malaria I caught in Malaya. To be honest Old Girl, I needed a rest but the Mem was determined to plough on. She doesn't listen to us does she?'

I shook my headlights, I think I was feeling a bit of empathy with this old bore for once.

'I tried to get her to stop by letting her driver's door fly open a few times. Now she was not only battling with my shaky wheels, but she had to keep reaching out to shut my door. Eventually she stopped to sort me out. What is it about women drivers? They seem to force us chaps on when it's obvious that there is a problem needing sorting. A chap wouldn't drive like that.'

'Shut up you old bore and get on with your story.' For heaven's sake he's going senile, I'm sure of it.

'We made it to Kilkenny, much to my surprise I might add, and then the next day we drove on to Rosslare to catch the ferry home. The Mem worried me rather as she kept asking people where she could buy some poteen, to quote 'for her son-in-law!' She was saying to the others that she could pop the stuff into my second petrol tank. You know, the one that was fitted to give me an extra five hundred miles when I had my little trip round the world.'

'You are drifting off the point again you old fool. Get on with it.'

'What? Yes, well, she went on to say that if it tasted really awful, she could run me on it don't you know. Well she didn't have much joy with the poteen and we boarded the ferry this morning and here we are. None the worse for wear.'

'Excuse me for asking, but shaky wheels and doors that fly open? Is that not worse for wear, you old fool?'

'I got her home, don't you know. I got her home. I expect the Mem will use me in future now. Far more reliable. Well a chap that's gone through Turkey, Syria, Iraq, Iran, Afghanistan and in to India is by far the right choice for the Memsahib.'

'Oh push off you old fool and let me enjoy the view.' Her Ladyship comes out.

'Come on Herbert Orsten, time to get you to bed.' She starts him up and he is taken back to his shed. I am feeling the warmth of the spring sunshine once again on my bodywork and it's making me feel quite sleepy. Her Ladyship comes over to me.

'Hello Old Girl, how are you feeling? A bit peeved that I took

Sir Herbert rather than you I suppose?' I chose not to show any reaction. 'You seem a bit peaky, are you okay? Are you all right Old Girl?' I doze off.

★★★★★

'Are you all right m'dear?'

'It's kind of you to ask, Humphrey, but no. I am not all right.' Joycie Darling sat very, very still. She was shaken, but didn't want to show it, especially in front of Davison.

'Oi!' Another voice disturbed the silence. 'Oi, how the hell didn't you see me?' The owner of the voice was tapping on my side screen. 'God Almighty, my lorry is not that easy to miss. Now get this old jalopy out of the way. I have a deadline to meet.'

Through the foliage of the hedge I deduced that this was the driver of the lorry that nearly drove into the side of us and it seemed he wasn't very happy.

'Come along Davison, give me a hand.' The Colonel got out and held the front seat to allow Davison to get out as well. 'I say sir, I am terribly sorry, I didn't see you. Not very good visibility from this old girl and the hedges could do with a trim. Far too high, what? Just couldn't see you.'

'You shouldn't be out in this old jalopy, it's too dangerous on these modern roads.' He looked directly at me. 'That thing should be in a museum.' The lorry man helped The Colonel to push me out of the way. Davison didn't, he was wandering aimlessly around, examining the hedgerow and gripping his crotch. He was also occasionally hopping up and down on one leg. Very odd behaviour if you ask me.

'Can you steer us into the side, Darling? We need to get out of this chap's way.' Joycie Darling reached across and hoiked my steering wheel so that I could be pulled out of the hedge and then pushed into the side of the road. Judging by the sound of horns emerging from behind the lorry, there was a quite a long queue of vehicles building up.

'There we are, all safe and sound. Thank you sir and again, I'm very sorry. At least there doesn't seem to be any damage to either vehicle and no one is hurt.'

'Well that's as may be,' came the lorry driver's reply. 'But if my load has been damaged you are in for a big bill. I'm carrying sixty cases of brandy so I hope your insurance is in order.'

Davison, suddenly distracted from his examination of the hedgerow, straightened himself up.

'Wha? Whash that? Brandy?'

The Colonel snorted, 'Shut up Davison. I'll speak to you later.' Davison obliged and once again started to peer into the hedgerow before starting to battle with his zip yet again. I think he was eager to dispose of some more of his cider. The lorry driver walked around to the back of his lorry and we heard a door shutter upwards followed a few moments later by it shuttering down again.

'Well, mate,' the lorry driver returned to his cab door. 'You are lucky. A few cases dislodged but no broken bottles. We'll leave it there then.' He got in, started his engine and pulled away. The various horns which had been blowing all stopped simultaneously and the traffic started to move again.

★★★★★

Paarp! Paaarp! 'There you are Old Girl. A nice new horn.' It's Her Ladyship. 'Well not a new one exactly, but an original one. That one you did have, was the wrong one. What do you think?' She presses my horn button again. Paaarp! That was how I used to sound. 'There you are, you've now got you a proper horn ready for the summer. I've got a few friends calling round for a little garden party in a minute, so I thought you'd like to come outside to enjoy the sunshine.'

At that, some of Madam's friends start to arrive. 'Good afternoon Miss Daisy, lovely day isn't it?' Oh it's the nice Mister and Missus Steve. I have to say that I rather do enjoy basking in this summer sunshine. This is the only time of year that I find Dumple-bloody-dale pleasant to look at; that with the sound of bird song mixed with the buzzing of bees around my bodywork and the smell of elderflower wafting on the wind from the field next door; it's bliss, sheer bliss.

Her Ladyship lights the barbeque and now I can hear the sound of corks popping out of bottles.

'Tell you what folks, I'm taking Miss Daisy to the Scolton show in a fortnight and I was wondering if any of you fancied driving Sir Herbert there. It'll be nice for both of them to go.'

Blow me down; she must already be rather tiddled. She never normally allows anyone else to drive us; well she certainly hasn't allowed people to drive me. Perhaps she is bending the rules with the Grey One. Quite frankly I don't know why she would want to take that boring old vestige of the British Empire along when she's got me. He'll only bore everyone to tears.

'It'll be a nice day out,' she says. 'We can take a picnic, and a bottle of wine.' Step forward The Nice Mister Steve.

'I don't mind having a go,' he says.

'Well you'd better come and have a look at him,' she says as she gets up and heads for the Grey One's shed. The Nice Mister Steve follows. She opens up the shed and with a 'Help yourself,' she tosses him the keys and returns to her glass of wine, fearful no doubt that it might get too warm before she can pour it down her throat.

It isn't very long before The Nice Mister Steve returns. He's looking a little pale and addresses Her Ladyship.

'I think you need to come and have a look at this.' Gosh,

hopefully he has found something that is going to cost Her Ladyship a small fortune to put right. Or better still he's found a stash of an illegal substance.

'What is it?' Her Ladyship asks. She sounds annoyed, probably fearing that she is once again about to be parted from her glass of wine.

'There's a wasp nest in the roof lining of the car,' replies The Nice Mister Steve. A wasp's nest? Oh this is brilliant. If this isn't poetic justice, I don't know what is.

'What?' screams the Wrinkled One and up she gets and heads for the shed. Oh wonderful; that is all that crusty old devil is fit for; a home for wayward wasps. But my moment of exhilaration is short lived as Her Ladyship strides into the house and returns with a spray can. She then proceeds to fill Sit Herbert's interior with some noxious chemicals before closing his window.

He is not going to like that, I muse. Still, they did use DDT in the colonies to keep down the mosquitoes, so he must have come across it on his travels. I have a brief sighting of one desperate queen wasp banging herself against the inside of the Grey One's windscreen before she expires and drops from sight. I felt quite sorry for the little thing. She had obviously worked quite hard to build a home for herself and her babies.

I hear the snap of rubber slapping on to bare skin as Her Ladyship reappears wearing a pair of hideously bright pink Marigolds. Has she no shame? She gingerly opens the Grey One's door and picks up the now recently departed queen wasp and flicks her outside. She then removes the half finished nest and flings that onto her compost heap. 'Well that's sorted that little problem,' she announces as she returns to her now warm glass of wine.

'That was a narrow squeak,' mutters a rather shaken Grey One.

'Narrow? Squeak? What are you on about you old fool? You had finally found a use for your miserable life. Your logical next step would have been to become a chicken house. That's just about all you are fit for. '

I didn't realise it until today, but the Colonel and Sir Herbert are alike in so many ways. But the big difference was that Colonel Humphrey was a gentleman while Sir Herbert Bloody Orsten is definitely not. He's just a pompous ass and I still can't understand why Her Ladyship insisted on buying him. So where was I with Colonel Humphrey, Joycie Darling and the man Davison? Oh yes, they had all been rather shaken by their near death experience with that lorry. Well it rather frightened me as well. But it wasn't long before Colonel Humphrey decided to take me out again and this trip turned out to be even more eventful than the last one.

Once again Colonel Humphrey and Joycie Darling had been out for a nice lunch. The man Davison had yet again been dragged unwillingly along, just in case I broke down. But this time under orders from the redoubtable Mrs Davison, as well as The Colonel and Joycie Darling, Davison had ordered a pie and chips and just one pint of cider. Well that was what he was supposed to have had, but he managed to find another couple of sixpences in his pocket to allow him to invest in a second pint of cider. This wasn't enough to get him drunk, but he had a history of trouble with his waterworks; moreover he was still having trouble with his trousers.

I've often wondered when they decided to change the colour of police cars. I always remember those beautiful, sleek, black saloons with a shiny chrome bell at the front and an illuminated police sign on the roof. But by the time I moved in with Colonel Humphrey and Joycie Darling, they had become a pale blue colour with a little spinning blue light on top. The bell had gone, to be replaced by a horn that made them sound like a braying donkey. But I suppose this was the decade of sex, drugs and rock and roll so I could only imagine that this new breed of police car came about as a result of a hallucinogenic experience. They looked terrible. Anyway, one of these silly little things came up behind and was following us.

'Uh oh. Guardians of the law to our stern, Joycie Darling.' Colonel Humphrey was looking nervously into my mirror.

'Well Humphrey, I hope you haven't had too much to drink.' Joycie Darling replied. 'You know what sticklers they are for that sort of thing nowadays.'

It wasn't long before the little blue car overtook us, switched on his spinning blue beacon and pulled up in front of us. Colonel Humphrey slammed on my brakes, but I couldn't stop as fast as the little blue car. Its doors opened and two police constables got out. They simultaneously placed their caps on their heads and walked slowly back towards us, pausing briefly to observe that their rear number plate was now impaled on my starting handle. First Colonel Humphrey and then Davison emerged from my driver's door and the Colonel strode towards the older police constable while Davison walked rather too quickly, and almost suspiciously, around to my rear.

'Good afternoon, sir,' said Constable One, lightly touching the peak on his cap. The second started to walk around me, examining my wheels very carefully. The first policeman was the older one: I sensed a man with a wealth of experience. The other was much younger. Indeed I wondered whether he had even started to shave. He squatted down to examine my nearside headlight.

'Are you having problems with your brakes sir?' Constable One pulled out his notebook, opened it up and licked the tip of his pencil. Meanwhile Constable Two, only half listening to the ensuing conversation, stood up and spotted the man Davison, who was now relieving himself into the hedgerow.

'Well, well, well. What have we here then? A touch of indecent exposure unless I am very much mistaken.' Constable Two eyed Davison's lower anatomy with a degree of disgust. Davison still in the process of relief, tried to stuff the said part of his anatomy back inside his trousers, producing a growing damp patch, which ran down past the knee.

'Hello Officer, just needin' a pee. It's not illegal is it? To pee against the rear nearside wheel of the car?'

'Incorrect, sir, because you are not actually relieving yourself against the rear nearside wheel. You are relieving yourself into a hedge. Under Section Five of the Public Order Act, disorderly conduct causing or likely to cause offence to others is illegal. And unless I am very much mistaken you are relieving yourself in public and that is going to cause offence. Anyway, are you the owner of this vehicle sir?'

'Wha? You've got ter be jokin'. No, it belongs to the colonel sur; over there, talkin' to your mate.' Constable Two glanced over his shoulder then pivoting on his heels he paced deliberately in the direction of his colleague.

'Well I don't think we need to worry about that sir, thank you sir?' Constable One lifted the pencil from the notebook and looked quizzically at the colonel. 'Umm sir? Your name sir?'

'Humphrey Moreton. Colonel Humphrey Moreton… retired. I live at the Larches, just down the road. I play golf with the chief constable every second Tuesday, what?' Constable One raised a knowing eyebrow as Constable Two joined them.

'Is this your, err car sir?' I didn't appreciate the way that 'err' sounded. And before Colonel Humphrey could answer, he added, 'and do you know this man sir?' Constable Two gestured towards Davison who was standing beside me, looking guilty and desperately wanting to get back on to my rear seat.

'Why yes, that's my man Davison. He was my batman during the last conflict. Sterling chap.'

Constable Two seemed to ignore that comment. 'Was he driving this car sir?' Constable One tried desperately to attract his colleague's attention. He didn't like the way the conversation was heading.

'Good God no, constable. He came along in case the car broke down. It's only our second outing, what?'

'I see, sir. You were driving it then?' The colonel nodded. Constable One buried his face behind his hands and turned away. Constable Two got out his own notebook and he too licked the tip of his pencil.

'Well sir, that car didn't stop when we pulled up in front of you, suggesting the brakes don't work properly. Does this car have a Ministry test certificate sir?'

Constable One groaned and wandered away. His years of experience had taught him that there were those to whom a police officer gave an easy time and those to whom one did not. After all, the damage to their number plate could have happened anywhere. More importantly, the colonel played golf with the chief constable and that made him definitely one of the former category. His young partner, with just a couple of years in the police force hadn't a clue. I think it might have occurred to Constable One that both of them might well be heading towards a future career in school patrols.

'Does this car have a test certificate sir?' Constable Two repeated himself, and unaware of the full situation, smelled victory.

'Well actually, yes. She was tested last week and she passed.' Constable Two braced himself for his coup de grace.

'Well they didn't test your brakes very thoroughly, did they sir? Or perhaps your reaction was too slow. Might I enquire whether you have been drinking intoxicating liquor sir?'

'Course I have. Been out to lunch, what?' The colonel was beginning to get annoyed. He'd had enough of this nonsense.

'In which case, perhaps you wouldn't mind undergoing a breathalyser test sir?'

'A what, man? What on earth are you on about?'

'A breathalyser sir, it's a device that will tell us whether or not you have too much alcohol in your blood to drive a motorised vehicle safely. And if it says you have, I will have to ask you to accompany me to the station for a full blood test.'

'Tommy rot! Impudent fellow! Never heard so much nonsense in my life. I'll walk the white line and touch my nose.' He did so. 'There, I'm fine.'

Constable One appeared to want to step in and stop all this. But there was no way he would turn his zealous colleague now. So I think he wanted the road to swallow him up instead.

As he walked past his colleague towards the police car, Constable Two winked and whispered, 'Got him Sid, pompous old bastard.' He re-emerged carrying a small black box with a mouthpiece on it.

'What the hell is this damned thing?' The colonel had gone a deep purple. Well he did have high blood pressure.

'This, sir, is a breathalyser. It's the law now sir, introduced by Mrs Castle to reduce drunken driving on our roads. Now sir, take a deep breath and just blow slowly into this tube.'

A complete silence fell as Joycie Darling, the man Davison, Constable One and I watched the triumphant face of Constable Two as he held the breathalyser for the colonel, who emptied his lungs into the device. When Colonel Humphrey finished, the triumphant look faded as Constable Two stared in amazement at the breathalyser. He then checked the instructions, looked back at the breathalyser and then at the Colonel. Constable One sensing relief, returned to the duo.

'Thank you Colonel. Do we have a problem, Constable Jones?' Constable Two was completely deflated. He was still staring at the crystals.

'I don't understand it, they should have changed colour.'

'I am so sorry to have inconvenienced you, sir.' Constable One re-took command of the situation. 'Would you like to take that thing back to the car, Constable Jones?' He turned again to the Colonel. 'I am so sorry, Sir. These youngsters, they are all so very keen nowadays. I'll put him straight.'

'I don't know, young chaps today, all far too keen to make a name for themselves aren't they? They wouldn't have survived long in the second conflict would they?'

'Indeed no, sir, indeed no. I'll bid you good afternoon, and don't worry about our number plate. I'll tell them that we caught it on a piece of metal when we were turning the car around.'

A disembodied female voice crackled over the radio in the little blue car. Constable One picked up a receiver, 'Three Four receiving, hello, hello.' He shook the receiver, 'hello?'

★★★★★

'Hello… Hello…' Now it's Her Ladyship jolting me out of my memories again. She's on her phone. 'Hello. I can't seem to get an answer. Where the hell is he? He's supposed to be here.' Uh oh, she must be on about The Nice Mister Steve. We are supposed to be going to the Scolton show today.

'What are you going on about, Madam de Mille. I'm here.' The Nice Mister Steve is striding up the drive towards us. He's always called her that. Heavens' knows why.

'Are you ready for Scolton then? I've done us a big picnic and Sir Herbert is primed and ready to go. I'll lead the way.' She opens the door to allow the Asthmatic Barking Dog on to my rear seat. He immediately settles in and lies down. Then it's Her Ladyship's turn to clamber in, start me up and we are off. It's a gloriously sunny day. Even the Grey One, following behind, cannot dampen my good humour. As we shoot along, the dog decides to climb on to the edge of his seat and poke his head over the side of the car. His ears fly back in the slipstream.

'Get back in you stupid dog and lie down.' She turns round and pulls him back on to his seat. With Madam's attention distracted by the dog, I start to swerve over to the wrong side of the road and an approaching car blasts its horn. Her Ladyship curses and swerves back to the right side of the road again. 'Stupid bloody animal. Do you want to get us all killed?' Asthmatic Barking Dog ignores all this and returns to the edge of the car to enjoy the wind again. We get to Scolton Manor and the place is heaving with vehicles of various ages. I think the Grey One and I must have been among the oldest cars there.

'Can you park over there and register please?' One of the marshals directs us to our parking spot. Her Ladyship parks me up and then guides The Nice Mister Steve and the Grey One in to their space, ensuring that there is plenty of room for chairs and a table between us.

'Right, let's get ourselves set up and registered and then we can have a wander.' The Nice Mister Steve agrees that's a good idea and plonks a plaque on the front of the Grey One that says 'The little car that went round the world'.

'Come on Dog, time for you to have a little walk.' Out he leaps and immediately lifts his leg against my back wheel, disgusting creature. Then before Madam can attach a lead to his collar, he gets back onto my rear seat again and settles down to lick his bits. The cheek of it and on top of that, he curls up and starts to snore once more.

'All right then, you can stay here to look after the cars.' Her Ladyship and The Nice Mister Steve wander off, leaving me with the Asthmatic Barking Dog and The Grey One.

I try my best to ignore the creature on my back seat. That's all very well but when someone decides to come over to admire me, 'Arf – Arf – Arf – Arf – Arf,' emanates from my rear. God, I nearly leap out of my tyres. What a noise! The admirer has taken several paces backwards and falls over Madam's picnic basket. Anyway, who does this hound think he is? I decide who can take a look at me, not him. Typical male!

Her Ladyship and The Nice Mister Steve return. 'Hello you two,' she says. 'Enjoying yourselves? Time for lunch I think.' Madam hauls the hamper over to the picnic table and starts to put out sandwiches and titbits. She settles down and they both tuck in. It reminds me of that time when I went to my first rally with Colonel Humphrey and Joycie Darling.

By then, I had enjoyed several very happy years living with them. We only ever went out in the summer months and then it was just for the odd lunch or picnic. Then one day Colonel Humphrey asked Davison to get me out and give me, to quote, a damned good clean. 'I want to be able to see my face reflected in that bonnet, Davison. Are you the man for the job?'

Davison snapped himself to attention as he always did when the colonel switched on his military persona. 'Yes sur. I'll give her a damned good clean sur.'

'Good man, good man.' The colonel marched off humming some military tune to himself. I couldn't help noticing the deep mutual respect that these men held for each other when they were in their military mode. So out came the car polish and I was undergoing a transformation once more.

'Tell you what, Car. I reckons that if I polish you much more, we'll be down to bare metal. I can see your undercoat in places now. I wonder if the colonel would treat you to a new paint job?' He spent most of the day cleaning me up and he put me to bed shining like a new pin.

'Well done, Davison,' the Colonel remarked the next morning. 'A sterling job, absolutely sterling. What do you think Joycie Darling?'

'Do we have to go, Darling? It's such a lovely day and I really could do with a day in the garden.'

'You'll enjoy it m'dear. You've been very busy with your committees and the garden. You deserve a day off. Mrs Davison has made us up a nice picnic and I've packed us a couple of bottles of hock. Come on hop in. We have to be in Banbury by eleven o'clock.'

Joycie Darling was resigned as she climbed on to my passenger seat. Colonel Humphrey closed her door and flicked his handkerchief over the door handle. He then came round and settled himself in to my driver's seat. 'Gates, Davison, please.' And the man Davison literally ran, obviously very relieved that he didn't have to come along as well, to the front gates to let us out and we were away.

It didn't take long to get to Banbury and I had spotted signs guiding us to something called a 'Vintage Transport Extravaganza'. I couldn't help wondering what on earth a vintage transport extravaganza was, but my curiosity was soon resolved as Colonel Humphrey swung us on to a field. There were cars, lorries, motor bikes and even some steam powered traction engines, all moving around.

'What year?' A steward approached us.

'Nineteen thirty four.' Colonel Humphrey replied.

'Ah post vintage. That'll be Class C. If you drive over there, someone will show you exactly where to go.' Two minutes later, we were parked up, Joycie Darling was unloading a rug and the picnic hamper and Colonel Humphrey was flicking a duster over my radiator.

'There you are, Old Girl,' he almost whispered to me. 'You are among your own kind now. Does that make you happy?' Well it did, I was overjoyed. I was surrounded by relatives from my era. It was wonderful, like stepping back in time. 'Can you hold the fort, Joycie Darling? I thought I'd have a wander around before lunch.'

'Off you go, Darling. I'm fine here with my book.' Colonel Humphrey wandered off to look at the other vehicles as a traction engine slowly rolled past me, making the ground shake as it passed. There were people everywhere and I really don't know why my gaze was drawn particularly towards a middle aged couple walking along a couple of rows away. They both looked strangely familiar, but I couldn't quite place them. I knew I'd met them before so I couldn't take my eyes off them. Then they disappeared behind a relative that on reflection looked uncannily like the Grey One. Surely not…

★★★★★

'Morning, m'dear. Lovely day, don't you know.' Oh no, jolted out of my memories yet again.

'What do you want now, you old fool?'

'And good morning to you too, isn't it a lovely day. Just off for my annual check up with the Memsahib don't you know.'

Gosh is it that time of year already? It's not long now before Her Ladyship starts to wrap me up for the long winter and I begin to feel a little low with the dark cold months ahead. But at the moment I am feeling particularly perky. Summer finally arrived after weeks of horrible weather and any plan to put me into hibernation for the winter was postponed. So we have been out and about and it seems that the Grey One is going to have to wait a bit longer before he takes over carrying Her Ladyship around.

'Shouldn't be a problem. Fit as a fiddle don't y'know. The Mem seems quite confident.' Well, after all the work that Her Ladyship and her friends have had to put in to him over the past few months, he should be on top of the world. Good God, this was supposed to be a car that had undergone a restoration not that long ago. But this summer, he had to have his king pins, bushes and track rod ends all done. On top of that his shock absorbers needed serious attention and goodness knows what else. So after all that nonsense, Her Ladyship is going to be pretty unbearable if he fails his annual now.

They've been gone for a couple of hours and I am gazing out on Dumple-bloody-dale when my thoughts are disturbed by the sound of a broken down old banger coughing and spluttering as Guess

177

Who staggers up the drive. My God, he looks absolutely whacked.

'Good news?' I enquire with a barb in my voice. He just limps past without a word, instead concentrating for all he is worth on coming to a safe halt. Her Ladyship gets out with a look like thunder. Oh dear, things haven't gone too well then.

'Sorry Miss Daisy, you are going to have to swap garages for a while,' she says apologetically. 'That pile of scrap iron out there has failed his bloody test. His steering box is badly worn. I've got a fortnight to find another in good condition and sort him out, or he will be going off the road.' And to the rubbish dump? I venture to wonder.

So while I might be relegated to the shed, I don't really mind. That pompous old fool has had his come-uppance and it's worth this little indignity to see to see him brought down to earth. He, mind you, isn't saying a word.

'I suppose I'd better go and phone around to see if I can find you another steering box.' Her Ladyship snaps as she passes him on her way in to the house, leaving the Grey One and myself looking at each other.

'Well?' I enquire. 'What have you to say for yourself?' He says nothing. He's quite deflated and I almost feel sorry for the old fool. It's not polite to knock someone when they are down so I decide to remain silent for now. Madam is back in no time.

'Come on you old pile of scrap, I've found you a replacement box.' Then they are gone, off to somewhere or another, leaving me to my memories again. I was on that field in Banbury wasn't I? Joycie Darling was still buried in her book and there was no sign of Colonel Humphrey. He was obviously enjoying his wanders. Me? I was just loving the sunshine and being among my relatives. It felt reassuring in a funny sort of a way. Then I saw them again, the middle aged couple. They were slowly heading in our direction and I couldn't help noticing that the man seemed unwell. You know, not taking much interest in the proceedings. But he had a limp and

I was sure I recognised that limp. But I couldn't put my wiper blade on where I'd seen that limp before. Then the woman looked up and caught sight of me. She was holding the man's hand quite firmly and with her other hand she pointed at me as she steered the man in my direction. I couldn't hear what she was saying to him, but they were definitely heading my way.

'Eric,' she said. 'It's dear, dear Daisy. I'd recognise that number plate anywhere. Well, after all these years, look Eric, it's Daisy.' By now they were standing beside me and the man didn't seem to understand what she was saying. 'Oh Eric, she is still around after all these years. Surely you remember Daisy. Go on take a good look.'

The man Eric turned his head towards me. At first there were no signs of recognition at all. He looked me over and eventually a sparkle appeared in his eyes.

'Daisy,' he said and he stroked my bonnet. 'Old Daisy.' He smiled happily at his wife. 'Old Daisy.' Now I remembered who they were. It was Eric and Missus Chalk. He was the man who drove me in to a bomb crater, gosh a long time ago now. Eric Chalk continued stroking my bonnet, I imagine he was trying to recall all those trips he used to take me on, but was having trouble.

'Can I help you?' It was Joycie Darling; she'd emerged from her book having been disturbed by Missus Chalk's conversation.

'What? Oh I am so sorry, I didn't see you there. I never dreamed that we would see this car again. She belonged to my husband. Just after the war. He was her second owner. I just can't believe that she is still going strong. Gosh, how old is she? Thirty six years old. I can't believe she hasn't been sent to the scrap yard. Oh please forgive me. I am Patricia Chalk and this is my husband Eric.'

'I am delighted to meet you both. I am Joyce Moreton, my husband Humphrey bought this old car from a young man who had got in to trouble with the police for driving it while uninsured and untaxed. I think he rather needed the money to pay his fine.

We use it for the odd day out. To be honest I thought he had lost the plot when he decided to buy it, but I have to admit it has given him a new lease of life.'

Joycie Darling suddenly paused. 'Oh I'm sorry I didn't mean it like that.'

'Oh that's all right. Eric had an accident at work about five years ago and I am afraid that he doesn't really understand much now. But he's recognised Old Daisy and that is the first time he has recognised anything.'

'Oh I am so very sorry, it must be terribly difficult for you.' Joycie Darling looked up. 'Here's my husband now... Oh Humphrey, darling, you must meet these people. They were the second people to own Daisy here. Just after the war.'

'Hello, I am Patricia Chalk.' She offered her hand to the Colonel. 'And this is my husband Eric. My husband bought Old Daisy here from the wife of one of his comrades who had been killed in North Africa.'

'Oh I'm very pleased to meet you both. I'm Humphrey Moreton.' He looked at Eric. 'Which regiment were you in sir?' Eric looked blankly at Colonel Humphrey.

'Oh, I'm sorry,' said Patricia Chalk. 'I'm afraid that my husband had an accident at work and it left him brain damaged. Until today I thought that his memory had completely gone. But he recognised Old Daisy here. He was in the Oxford and Bucks Light Infantry by the way.'

'I was in the Far East myself.' Colonel Humphrey didn't know what else to say. Then, 'Well, I am glad that Daisy has helped him remember something.' Eric Chalk had moved round to look in to my interior.

'It's Daisy,' he looked directly at his wife. 'It's Daisy.'

'Yes dear, that's right. It's Daisy.' She replied walking round to take his hand again. 'So, you call her Daisy as well?'

'Yes, we do. It seems that the last owner called her that and we, well we just adopted that name. Suits her, what?'

'Yes, when my husband bought her after the war she was called Daisy then. Silly name really. But since the Johnstons, they were her first owners, called her that, the name sort of stuck with her.'

'Well if I hadn't bought her, she'd be scrap iron by now, what? We have a lot of fun with Daisy don't we Joycie Darling?'

'If you call breaking down regularly, driving in to the hedge and being stopped by the police, fun, I suppose I would agree.' I didn't know whether or not to be offended by that remark.

'Well it is so good to see her now. And to see that look on Eric's face, that look of recognition, well that really has made my day and of course it has made his day as well.'

★★★★★

'Away in the land of nod are we Old Girl?' Oh pook, Her Ladyship, yet again. She must have managed to sort out the Grey One. She stands there with a triumphant look on her face. 'Now you old fool, if you don't pass this time, you're heading for the car crusher,' she shouts as she heads into the house. She's heading for the gin bottle, I think to myself; I've seen that look before. He's still very subdued though. It must have been her mention of the car crusher that shook him. Do you know, in the thirty years since I underwent my restoration I have never failed my yearly health check. Yet the Grey One, barely a year into this family has. He'll never live this one down. Now where was I?

Oh yes just outside Banbury, in a field. Patricia Chalk was still gazing at me and I did wonder what was going through the mind of her husband Eric. Was he remembering those times when I seemed the only form of escape from his harridan of a wife and mother in law? I remember she had changed after her mother died. But now she is totally devoted to her husband. I was most impressed and it made me realise how easy it is to misjudge people.

Colonel Humphrey was finding it difficult to know what to say next. A physical injury he could deal with, but a mental one made him very uncomfortable. Anyway he had remembered that there were a couple of bottles of his favourite hock to quaff and he was keen to make a start on his lunch.

Patricia Chalk, whether she was sensing this or not, decided that perhaps they should move on. 'Well I suppose we had better get on, hadn't we Eric?' She turned to Joycie Darling and Colonel Humphrey. 'Thank you so much for allowing us to see dear old Daisy again. It has not only made my day, it has worked wonders for Eric.'

'I am so sorry, my dear, it must be a terrible trial for you.' Joycie Darling who had been on the sidelines of the conversation took Patricia's free hand and held it tightly for several seconds and quietly thanked God that her husband hadn't ever suffered anything like that. Patricia Chalk forced a smile, pulled her hand free and with her husband Eric, finally walked out of my life.

'Well m'dear, now isn't that quite extraordinary. The Old Girl's second owners, just out of the blue, what? But poor woman, what a bloody awful thing to have to look after a husband in that state of repair, what?'

'There but for the grace of God go we, Humphrey. Come on, let's have this picnic.' Joycie Darling opened up the hamper. At that prompt, Colonel Humphrey pulled a bottle of hock out of the cold box and resolutely withdrew the cork. 'I think I need this. Can I pour you one as well darling? We should drink a toast to Daisy, What?'

'I think we should add Patricia Chalk to that toast Humphrey, don't you?'

★★★★★

'Good Morning Miss Daisy,' Her Ladyship has barged in with a determined look on her face 'I've got you an early Christmas present. I saw it in the shops and it's perfect for you, especially as you always seem to get us lost. Well NO MORE!' She brandishes a box at me. 'No more getting lost,' she cries as she wheels me out into the sunlight, 'because this is going to ensure that we never get lost again.' At this, she proceeds to unpack the box like an excited child opening a birthday present. Bits of the wrapping fly everywhere as she eventually retrieves a little black box with a screen on it.

'It's called a satellite navigation thingy. Now what we do is we stick this bit onto your windscreen and we plug that lead into your electricity. Then all I have to do is to enter our destination and the little black box will tell us how to get there without so much as a how do you do. What could be simpler than that?'

A map, perhaps? No electricity, no satellite and no ugly little black box stuck to my windscreen. They have been used pretty successfully for centuries. In fact any idiot can use one. Ah, that's not true... I've seen her... map in hand, turning it round and round, tongue firmly pressed into the side of her cheek, not only trying to figure out exactly where to go, but also trying to work out where she is at the moment. No, there are those who can navigate and those who cannot. And we all know into which category Her Ladyship places herself.

It was on the Caen Peripherique – remember? That was perhaps her most spectacular navigation disaster ever. There, at the head of fifteen relatives heading west, she took the wrong road and we found ourselves on the *Payage* to Brest, while others were driving towards Le Mans and the remainder heading back the way we came.

'It's brilliant Miss Daisy,' she cries, poking her finger at the screen. 'Look. I can play Sudoku on it when we are stuck in traffic jams. And wow, yes. It even tells me when we are approaching a speed camera. Hang on,' she cries. 'According to this we are approaching one now! It can't be, we're not moving.'

That, dear confused old friend, is because Pembrokeshire's finest have set up a speed trap just outside our front gate. Now Dear Diary, do you understand what I have to live with?

Chapter Six

'Let me in,' she cries through the firmly locked door.
'Let me in. You've got champagne in there, I know it.
I want to be a luvvie like you.'

Saturday 3rd January 2009

It was a few months ago now that Her Ladyship flung open my door. She seemed terribly excited. 'Guess what?' she screamed. A relative has driven on the moon, I wondered. What a daft question to throw at me first thing in the morning. How would I know what to guess, especially as she comes up with some pretty weird ideas most of the time?

'We're going to be on the wireless,' she cried out. 'I've fixed it with someone from the BBC. We'll be famous and it will be really good publicity when we eventually go round the world!'

Correction, *you* are going to be on the wireless and I am going to have nothing to do with it. You have to understand that this is a woman who has spent a lifetime working in the media and complaining about having to work with publicity-seeking, second-rate celebrities and now she was getting terribly animated about going on the wireless herself. What on earth was she thinking?

I then forgot all about this little outburst until one morning she walked in with a strange woman holding a furry thing. This was immediately thrust at my radiator; I couldn't think why.

'Miss Daisy, I would like you to meet Sylvia From The BBC.' She leant towards me as if to flick a duster on my bonnet and she then whispered quietly so that Sylvia From The BBC couldn't hear her. 'I know that you aren't interested in being on the wireless. But

I am, so just behave yourself okay?'

Moi? Where on earth did she get an idea like that? I was happy to take them for a run, but that was all.

'We will need lots of sound effects,' remarked Sylvia From The BBC. Then, 'Gosh do you have to wind that handle thing to start her up?'

Oh good grief. Handle thing indeed. No dear lady, that handle thing as you call it is to wind me up so I can play the Blue Danube waltz on my horn. Of course it's for starting me up. Isn't that what they're for on all cars?

'You better start behaving Miss D, I know what you're thinking,' hissed Her Ladyship through clenched teeth as she tweaked my petrol pump. 'Otherwise you'll be shut up in the Argos shed, before you can dip your headlights. All right?'

Madam turned to Sylvia From The BBC, 'Yes it is, but she does have an electric starter as well. I have a feeling that this Old Girl is in a bit of a bad mood at the moment. I do hope she'll behave for you.'

Cheek! I wasn't in a bad mood; I just didn't want to partake in this degrading session of self-seeking publicity. Her Ladyship rolled me out and took down the hood. She then opened the door to allow the Asthmatic Barking Dog on to my rear seat and then climbed in herself. The furry thing was being waved all over the place and I did wonder if Sylvia From The BBC was going to clean me with it. We started up and headed off towards Haverfordwest.

'There are some interesting hills and bends in the town. You'll get some nice effects here,' cried Her Ladyship above my engine noise. I had a feeling that Sylvia From The BBC, upon discovering that I didn't have seat belts, had become rather nervous. Well it's hardly surprising, the way Madam drives. Then, having toured the town, Madam turned me round and headed for home.

'Can we stop somewhere for me to get out so I can record you driving by?'

Madam pulled me over in to a parking area to allow Sylvia From The BBC to get out. The Asthmatic Barking Dog had obviously decided that it was time for him to abandon ship as well and he leapt out to join her. Then to annoy Her Ladyship, he refused to get back in again, so Madam had to get out, pick him up and dump him on my rear seat. If the truth be known, I think it was because he had realised what I already knew. Her Ladyship was showing off and it was embarrassing him as well.

We got back home, none the worse for wear. 'I've got plenty of effects now,' said Sylvia From The BBC. 'We need to record your voice piece now.'

'I'll get my script.' Her Ladyship started to get out.

'Perhaps we should record this in the car,' said Sylvia From The BBC. 'The acoustics will be right and it'll help you get into the mood of the piece.' Well, what a load of rubbish that was. The hood was down for goodness sake, what acoustics were there to think about? Her Ladyship nodded sagely pretending to understand. She grabbed her script and got back in.

'I've written about seven minutes' worth, is that okay?'

'Perfect,' said Sylvia From The BBC. Exactly forty three minutes later, Her Ladyship had finished her script. That turned out to be forty three minutes of fluffs and retakes. Those poor people at the BBC were going to be working on this one until the next millennium, just trying to make sense of it, let alone being creative with it.

We didn't hear anymore of Sylvia From The BBC and indeed I'd thought that with the Christmas break and copious supplies of her favourite Christmas tipple, Madam had forgotten about it all as well. But no, she's just thrown open my garage doors and burst in carrying a mug of coffee.

'We're on the wireless any minute now.' She switches on the wireless set she keeps in the garage and settles down with her coffee.

The trouble with this wireless is that it takes about half a minute to warm up. So we miss the start and before I can blink, it's over. Her Ladyship looks at me thoughtfully.

'Well what did you think? You're famous now.' Does she want a truthful answer or a polite one? 'Come on Old Girl,' she says. 'Let's go for a drive. I want to try out that Satellite Thingy.' Thanks for reminding me, I'd forgotten about the weird thing she keeps sticking onto my windscreen. It ruins my looks and has knocked my credibility for six! How can I face my relatives?

'So you need that to navigate yourself out of the garage, do you Old Girl?' The Grey One had remarked with a chuckle the other day. Oh the shame of it. Why doesn't Her Ladyship stick it on him instead?

She twiddles with my petrol pump, turns over my starting handle a few times, then she climbs in to start my engine. Yes, that's how it's done.

'It may be a bit chilly,' she says. 'But it's a lovely sunny day and you need a bit of fresh air running through your radiator. No good just sitting in here moping, is it? I will programme in a destination and we can test this thing to make sure it knows how to get us there. I know, let's ask it to take us to Solva.'

So with tongue firmly set into her right cheek, she punches at the Thingy's little screen and then we are off into the bright blue yonder. She's right. It is a chilly morning and the frost is still glistening on the hedgerows and grass verges.

'Turn right in one hundred yards.' An unfamiliar voice makes me jump, then I realise it's that Satellite Thingy and as Her Ladyship obeys, it continues to speak. 'Proceed along this road for four miles.'

Oh God, I wondered. Is this going to be the future of our journeys together? This disembowelled voice telling me what to do. I really didn't think that it would be as bad as this. I suppose that the next development will be that Madam doesn't have to drive me anymore. She'll just sit back and enjoy the trip while I do all the work by obeying every command from that plastic voice and screen!

'At the roundabout, take the second exit.' Her Ladyship obeys and we are climbing a hill into Haverfordwest.

'Follow the road for half a mile and then turn left.' Her Ladyship complies. 'At the next junction turn right.' Her Ladyship thrusts out her right arm to tell the car behind what she is up to and Thingy falls off the windscreen, tangling its cable around her legs and my gear stick. Her one word comment is unprintable but it was preceded by an 'Oh'… Anyway, she manages to manoeuvre me safely in to the side of the road.

'If I didn't know you better Miss Daisy, I might have thought you did that deliberately,' she mutters as she untangles the cable. Why does she always blame me? I mean, would I do a thing like that? Indeed, how could I do a thing like that? With Thingy once again fixed to the windscreen, she switches it on again and we have barely moved off when. 'Make a U turn if possible and take a left turn after fifty yards.' Now that wasn't a very sensible thing for Thingy to say.

'What? Turn round? No! That's wrong. We are going the right way! What do you mean, make a U turn? Idiot!' A brief silence is followed by, 'Make a U turn if possible and turn left after two hundred yards.'

'No, no, no, I want you to take us to Solva, not Milford bloody Haven!'

'Make a U turn if possible and turn left after three hundred…' That, thankfully, was the last I heard from the voice on this occasion as The Wrinkled One, now losing her presence of mind, knocks Thingy onto the floor and we continue our journey in a way that I have managed perfectly well all my life. Somehow I have a funny feeling that Her Ladyship is wondering who of her friends might like a Satellite Thingy next Christmas, only slightly used. I don't know, all these modern computerised toys that people buy nowadays. I wonder what Colonel Humphrey would have thought of such things. Little devices like Thingy that talk to satellites, telephones that humans can use anywhere. Good heavens, they don't even have go to the cinema anymore to see a film. Instead they put the cinema in their living room.

No, the Colonel, as he would say, would have no truck with such damned nonsense. I remember that time when his brand new Rover broke down and he decided to use me instead to take Joycie Darling to Warwick for a concert at St. Mary's Church. This was a man who was uncomfortable with the modern world and was struggling to come to terms with the fact that his beloved country had just elected a woman prime minister. Little did I realise at the time that this journey was going to trigger yet another change in my life.

'Sorry about this, Joycie Darling. Not very nice for your birthday, I'm afraid. Brand new Rover, you wouldn't believe it would you? They just don't make cars properly any more do they? They're too obsessed with all those damned luxury bits, I think they call them bolt on goodies. I ask you, heaters, and seat belts. Can you imagine anything more ridiculous than a seat belt? What if you want to bale out quickly? Now just about every new car comes with a radio and on top of that many have a cassette tape player built in as well. Mind you, I think windscreen washers are a good idea, but there are just too many things to go wrong. Not like old Daisy here. No nonsense with her. She may break down occasionally – well she is nearly fifty after all. She would never have given any trouble back when she was new.'

'Oh do shut up, Humphrey. Think of your blood pressure. Come on, or we'll be late for the concert.' Joycie Darling got in and after a harrumph, Colonel Humphrey closed her door, walked round the back of me and climbed in as well. We head off into Warwick. 'You really mustn't get yourself into such high dudgeons. You know what Doctor Glover said.'

Colonel Humphrey, once settled behind my steering wheel, calmed down. 'You see Joycie Darling? This old girl doesn't let us down.' He paused. 'Do you think this Thatcher woman will sort out the bloody mess this country is in? I mean, women have only had the vote for fifty years.'

'Just stop worrying about it Darling, let's enjoy the evening.' After one more harrumph, Colonel Humphrey concentrated on our journey to Warwick.

We parked up not far from a church and Colonel Humphrey got out. 'Come on Joycie Darling, we don't want to be late do we? Oh… oh… oooh… oh my God!' At that the colonel sat back heavily on my running board. Joycie Darling came running round.

'Humphrey! Humphrey Darling are you all right? My God, you're as white as a sheet. Humphrey, Humphrey, Darling? Can you hear me?'

'What? What? Joycie? What happened? I suddenly felt really odd. Had to sit down, what? I'll be all right in a moment.'

'Humphrey, I think we should go home. Let's give the concert a miss. I'll call Doctor Glover and get him to come over and have a look at you. I really think you would be better off in bed.'

'I'll be fine Old Girl. Feeling a lot better already, what? Come on, let's go and enjoy some Mozart.' Colonel Humphrey got to his feet and a little unsteadily they headed off into the church.

It was getting late and I was becoming a bit worried about having to go home in the dark. Colonel Humphrey had never driven me at night before. But the sound of a two tone horn a few streets away and approaching fast caught my attention. I noticed that the horn was attached to an ambulance as it swung around a corner and pulled up in front of the church. Two men got out, opened up the back and pulled out a stretcher, which they took into the church. A few moments later they returned with someone on the stretcher and my heart sank when I spotted Joycie Darling coming out holding the hand of whoever was lying on the stretcher. It had to be the colonel and I realised that something awful had happened. Joycie Darling joined Colonel Humphrey in the back and the ambulance drove off blowing its horn again, leaving me in that car park wondering what was going to happen next. Poor Joycie Darling, what a way to spend her birthday.

★★★★★

Her Ladyship bursts in to my garage. She's got some birthday cards in her hand. Oh God, she is going to sing!

'Happy Birthday to you. Happy birthday to you. Happy birthday Miss Daisy, happy birthday to you.' She starts to open the cards. I imagine they're all from her. No I'm wrong, there's one from the Asthmatic Barking Dog and one from The Grey One. Oh gosh, is it March already? Of course. The fifteenth of March and my seventy fifth birthday – my diamond or is it platinum jubilee? And look outside, spring is bursting out, daffodils are blooming and I am feeling as good as I felt on that Thursday afternoon in 1934 when I first rolled out of the factory.

Gosh 75 years. So much has changed in the world since I was born. A human walked on the moon when I was 34 and has barely done so since. Roads are designed so that modern cars can drive along them at a hundred miles an hour, but no one is allowed to drive on them at more than seventy. When I was young, if a car could go more than seventy miles an hour and there weren't many that could, it did. Everything has gone topsy turvy. Nowadays when children behave like hooligans, they aren't given a clip around the ear like they were when I was young; we are told instead that it's not their fault, nor that of their parents. It's the system that has let them down.

Her Ladyship was moaning about all this to a friend the other day. She was complaining about the way that the politically correct brigade and the health and safety mob now seem to rule our lives.

'They are just like George Orwell's Thought Police. The world has gone bloody mad. I'm not even allowed to say what my favourite cuddly toy was except that it was the 'G' word and it had a black face. I loved that toy so much, but now it offends people. What is happening to this crazy world?'

But we mustn't moan on. I've made it to seventy five and I won't forget that there are many of my relatives that didn't. They have long since languished into dust and rust on some ancient scrap heap. I wonder what celebration Her Ladyship has in store for me. Hopefully, she will not embarrass me by doing something of which I would disapprove. I'll tell you what I would like; I would like a nice meander through leafy lanes, perhaps stopping for a breather at a little roadside café or thatched country pub, just like I used to with Oh David and Don't Worry Beatrice.

'Guess what Old Girl? Guess what I am treating you to, for your seventy fifth birthday? Well, we are going to France again and I know how much you enjoyed yourself last time?'

Enjoyed myself? That land of the garlic eating, Gauloise smoking Fr... whoops sorry – I can't say that, can I? Got to be politically correct now haven't we? I think not!

'I know what you're thinking. But not many more long foreign runs now, then we can make a start on our trip round the world. I've been looking at the route that Sir Herbert took in the 1970s and while Iran, Iraq and Afghanistan are out of the question, we could go through southern Russia and then turn south through Mongolia, China, Thailand and into Malaysia. That'll be the safest route to take. What do you think?'

I will treat that remark with the contempt it deserves. Read my radiator... I am not going!

'Now, we'd better get you ready for your North Wales Run.' Oh God do you have to? Can't you take the Grey One instead?

'I am not sure that Sir Herbert will be up to it, to be honest. He did struggle through Ireland last year. Anyway it isn't as far as usual. Just to Barmouth, and I don't want to tire you out if we are going to Normandy in September. I'll get you ready now and then we shall be off on Friday.'

I can't win can I? Now where was I? Oh yes, Colonel Humphrey had been rushed into hospital.

I remained stuck in that car park for several days, then one morning a truck arrived and Davison hopped out of the passenger door.

'This is it, this old jalopy here. Mrs Moreton wants me to get it back home.' I was hauled up on to the rear of the truck and we headed back to the Larches. As we went up the drive, I noticed that all the curtains were drawn and the place was so quiet. I was taken round the back and unloaded in to my warm stable block. The man Davison flicked a duster over my bodywork. He was quite subdued.

'Well Daisy Car, I dunno what'll 'appen to you now. Now that the Colonel's dead. I mean, it looks as though the Missus is goin' to have to sell up and move somewhere smaller. She won't like that. She loves them gardens. But this house is just too damned big for 'er on 'er own. I dunno what'll 'appen to me and Mavis'. We've 'ad that cottage down the lane there since the Colonel and I was demobbed. 'E bought 'un when 'e bought this place. Gawd knows what'll 'appen to us.'

I've had my differences with him, but now I felt rather sorry for poor old Davison. He'd given his life to Colonel Humphrey and now he seemed so lost without his commanding officer. Davison carried on polishing me, seemingly not knowing what to do next.

★★★★★

'Oh do come on Old Girl. Do snap out of it! We've got a drive to Barmouth to get done today.' Her Ladyship tosses her luggage on to my rear seat. I can't help noticing that she has plonked that damned Satellite Thingy on my windscreen again. Surely she knows how to get to Barmouth, especially as we are joining some of my relatives en route. How can we get lost?

We make it as far as Aberaeron, where we stop for a break and to meet up with the others. Her Ladyship gets bored waiting for them and starts to play with the Satellite Thingy. I wonder how long it will be before the inevitable happens.

'What? No! That's wrong. How can we be in bloody Frankfurt? We are just outside the town of Aberaeron. Stupid thing.'

My relatives arrive and Madam plants us firmly in the middle of the group as we continue north. She keeps poking at the Satellite Thingy, which suggests that that we are actually located in different parts of Europe, none of which happen to be in north west Wales.

We reach our hotel and it's a perfect early spring evening. The hotel overlooks the sea and I am able to watch the sun slowly set, growing larger and turning redder the closer it gets to disappearing over the horizon. Just before she gets out and takes her luggage into the hotel, Her Ladyship has another stab at the Satellite Thingy.

'Now it seems we are in Madrid. Bloody useless piece of rubbish.' She whips it off the windscreen and disappears through the entrance door.

The next morning after a night of tolerating seagulls relieving themselves on various parts of my and my relatives' anatomies, our owners join us. The Nice Mister John is our Wing Leader this weekend.

'Right, we have a big tour today. Does anyone need fuel?' A few owners nod their heads, but not Madam. She is keen to find out where the Satellite Thingy thinks we are now.

'Oh I see,' she says. 'Wenceslas Square in Prague are we? Useless pile of junk!' Then we are off again. The weather is not as good as yesterday, it's raining, but it is still a nice drive and we arrive at the edge of the Tal-y-Llin Lake, by a pub where they all decide to take luncheon and once again Madam returns to me with a not insignificant degree of bonhomie. She's been sitting in there, in the warm. Enjoying a nice meal, while I am out here in the cold and rain. We head back to our hotel in Barmouth and before Her Ladyship gets out she takes another poke at the screen of the Satellite Thingy.

'Oh, that's interesting,' she says. 'We've made it to Berlin now, the Brandenburg Gate to be exact. I wonder when it will decide to invade Poland. We haven't been there yet!' She heads into the hotel, again taking the Thingy with her and giving me some peace. It isn't long before a seagull lands on my roof. They really are ugly close up aren't they, and of course we all know what it is going to do don't we? Uurgh, Madam will be pleased. He flies off.

'Good morning Old Girl. Sleep well?'

If you care to examine my roof, you will see not!

'Oh dear you've been splatted by a few seagulls, haven't you?' She pulls out an old rag and does her best to wipe me off. 'Right, I let the Satellite Thing's battery go completely flat last night. And now we shall plug in to your electricity and hopefully it will work properly.' She fiddles with my battery compartment and returns the Thingy to my windscreen.

'Well that wasn't worth the effort. Ah! It seems we are now in Bordeaux. It's going back when we get home! We are going to have some fun today, we are going to climb up Bwlch y Groes.' What's that tongue twister when it's at home? 'I'm told it's a two mile long hill that starts gently and gets steeper and steeper. It seems that this hill was used by Austins back in the nineteen twenties and thirties to test their cars and that's where we're heading this morning.'

The Nice Mister John arrives in the car park along with everyone else, gives his instructions and we are off into the great unknown.

It doesn't take us long to reach the foot of the hill and we start to climb. This is easy, we are in third gear and I'm having no trouble at all. Whoops! Sharp bend ahead. Oooh very sharp bend, now I am down into second. I can't enjoy the view as this is beginning to be really hard work. On top of that, in my imagination I can hear the Grey One ranting on about his 'bin round the world don't you know' and comparing this to climbing in the Andes. It gets steeper and steeper and I can see the summit. Some of my relatives have already given up and conked out. I'm nearly boiling myself, but I think I can make it. What's that? Get out of the way you modern pile of rubbish. There is a flashy modern coming towards me and there isn't room for both of us on this road. Get out of my way! Her Ladyship keeps me climbing, she isn't going to give way and he's getting closer.

Oh blast and bother, at the last minute she pulls me over and slams on my brakes. No thank you from the other driver. Well, he is wearing a baseball cap and that says everything doesn't it? Her Ladyship starts to pull me out again, but I am now boiling. She switches me off and rolls back in to the little lay by we'd been forced into. 'You would have made this hill if it wasn't for that ignorant twit. Doesn't he know that those coming down a hill should give way to those going up?'

After about ten minutes, I have cooled enough for Madam to open my radiator cap to top me up with water and we comfortably reach the summit. Out of the twelve of us who started up this hill, only two made it unscathed. The Nice Mister John allows us all a rest to enjoy the view before we move on towards Lake Vyrnwy and then back to Barmouth. I cannot help thinking that drivers are much more selfish nowadays. That incident would never have happened thirty odd years ago. Even in Colonel Humphrey's day, people were still polite. Ah yes, Colonel Humphrey, or I should say The Late Colonel Humphrey.

Well it seemed that I was cocooned up in that stable for weeks. Then one morning Davison came in.

'Well Daisy car, you belong to me now. The Colonel's left you to me in his will. I was hopin' to keep you yur, but the Missus has sold the house and is moving somewhere smaller, so I have to take you 'ome with me. Trouble is, I only have a motorcycle licence. So's officially I can't drive you, but since I'm only round the corner… well, yur goes.' He got in, I started straight away and we headed off down the Colonel's drive for the last time.

The Davison's cottage wasn't far, only half a mile. It was a little red brick, semi detached, two up and two down with an enormous garden. The back was mainly down to vegetables and there was a small flock of chickens in one corner. Davison's wife came out of the front door as we arrived, rubbing her flour covered hands in her apron. In the eight years I had lived at The Larches, I had never seen her. I'd heard her a lot, but never actually seen her. She was a large woman. One of those well built countrywomen with bright ruddy cheeks. She appeared to have a kind face, but even so I got the impression that it was she who ruled that roost. Well let's face it, she had also ruled Colonel Humphrey and Joycie Darling's roost as well, judging by how highly they thought of her.

'You shouldn't 'ave driven that old car 'ome, Sidney.'

'T'isn't far. Thought I'd risk it. Come on Mavis, give me a hand getting it into the back garden.'

'What are you goin' to do with it then?'

'Dunno. Might learn to drive. Can't be that difficult.'

'You'd be better spending your time finding a new job. Colonel Moreton might have left us a bit, but that should stay as our nest egg.' She opened the gates to the cottage garden and Davison manoeuvred me round to the back.

''Ave you an old sheet or blanket Mavis? I ought to cover this car with something.'

'I'm not throwing out any of my sheets or blankets for you, certainly not for that old jalopy.'

'Well, it'll 'ave to sit out in the open for now then.' Davison followed his wife into the cottage. Judging by the flour on her hands he guessed – correctly – that it was steak and kidney pie for dinner.

★★★★★

I'm still absolutely pooped from that trip to Barmouth. That was a steep hill and if it hadn't been for that baseball becapped BMW I am sure I would have made it unscathed. Her Ladyship waltzes in.

'If we are going to France later this year Old Girl, I've decided to go on a diet, I want to lose a couple of stone. The question is, do I have the will power to keep at it?'

Your problem, Your Ladyship, is not will power. It's more your won't power that you will have to worry about. I give you a week and you'll be back to your normal self.

'Now Old Girl, you've been thinking that the trip to France is going to be your seventy fifth birthday present, don't you?'

Well to be honest, Your Ladyship, I rather think you had made that fact perfectly clear a little while ago and I have been somewhat underwhelmed with the whole thing. She has a broad grin on her face and I am worried.

'In actual fact Old Girl, I'm taking you off for your birthday present right now.' In she gets, starts me up and we are off, I haven't a clue to where, especially as the Asthmatic Barking Dog bas been left behind.

'You're going to enjoy this, Old Girl,' she says as she swings me into a building. It was a large, warm and empty grey room with rather too much dust around for my liking. We pull up.

'So this is Miss Daisy,' says this man as he comes in through a grey door set in one of the grey walls. I couldn't help thinking that a room this colour would be so suitable for that Orston fellow. He'd disappear into the greyness and a jolly good job too.

'Miss Daisy, this is Ray the Spray,' interjects the Wrinkled One. 'He is going to make you look beautiful.' Well, I thought I looked pretty good already. A few dents and scratches here and there, but wouldn't you expect that from anyone my age? Both of them start to wander around looking closely at me. I feel quite uncomfortable. You know, as if I was being eyed up for some surgical procedure.

'That's right,' says the man Her Ladyship had introduced as Ray the Spray. 'I'm going to give you a face lift.'

Excuse me, sir, that procedure may be suitable – no necessary – for the average American matron, but we British septuagenarians need not, and I emphasise not, indulge in such extravagancies. We may grow old either gracefully or disgracefully, but whatever route we take, facelifts are unnecessary.

Then getting into a friend's car Madam has gone, leaving me in the hands of the man called Ray the Spray to respray my wings and bonnet. I have to confess that perhaps I am going to rather enjoy this attention. Well, it isn't actually a face lift is it? It's more a case of a bit of beauty treatment... isn't it?

This wasn't the case with Sidney and Mavis Davison. She seemed to resent me being there in her back garden, just standing there doing nothing. I could often hear her demanding of her husband a decision on what he was going to do with me. He would insist that he was going to pass his driving test and then get me back on the road. I've never ceased to be amazed at the power of Mavis Davison's voice. It was at a pitch that appeared to gather the attention of everyone within half a mile and I reckon it could break glass at less than fifty paces. Poor Sidney Davison just crumbled when she shouted. He'd usually go and hide somewhere. He'd given up standing up to her.

'Driving test?' she shouted at him on this occasion. 'Driving test? Whether you pass that driving test or not, there is no way that you'm getting me in to that old eye-sore.'

All I could think on that occasion was that it was a good job too. I might have described Mavis Davison as one of those 'ample' countrywomen. Well, ample was putting it far too kindly. She had a shape not unlike that of The Wrinkled One, but she was much, much larger and with a voice like a high pitched foghorn, she was quite terrifying. Poor old Sidney Davison was as thin as a rake, he just wanted a quiet life, but remarkably he always put up with Mavis Davison's diatribes – perhaps because her cooking was second to none.

★★★★★

I think I have been with Ray The Spray for about a week and Madam is back. Judging by the look on Her Ladyship's face she's obviously delighted with the way I look.

'Gosh Old Girl, you look like new! What a fantastic job. Thank you Ray, she looks a million dollars.'

Pounds please. Let's not compare me to the currency of an old colony. She settles her bill, an act involving handing over money, indeed an act with which she is always very uncomfortable. So with me feeling like a new pin, Her Ladyship takes me home. At least I'm not dumped in a garden like I was with the Davisons. I remember when the grass and weeds had grown up to my doors, Davison would use me as one of his hiding places. One afternoon, he clambered into me and lay down on my rear seat.

'Don't make a sound car. I'm in trouble with the Missus again. I pretended to go for a job interview when she wanted me to do some weeding. Instead I went to the pub and she smelt the cider on my breath.' He suddenly ducked his head.

'Sidney Davison, you come back in here now, or there will be no cottage pie for you for tea.' Davison decided to continue lying low. Even the temptation of cottage pie couldn't draw him in to the open this time. Then it started to rain heavily. The years had taken their toll on my hood in spite of Joycie Darling's handiwork and as a result, poor old Davison got very wet.

★★★★★

Have you noticed that as soon as that nice weather forecasting team says we can expect a hotter than usual summer this year, it starts to blow and rain as if there were no tomorrow? But it's not the weather that has preoccupied Her Ladyship recently, well not much anyway. It all started with the doors flying open this morning. My little adventures with this woman usually do involve doors flying open.

'Right Miss Daisy,' she cries. Oh God, she's got that look in her eye again. 'I have a surprise for you!' Another one? 'I'm going to put electricity into your garage,' she adds. 'And it's not going to cost us a penny.' What? Are you going to steal it then? 'I've bought a solar panel and a control box. Once I've set it all up, we can have electricity in here completely free of charge.' I cannot help wondering just how much all this nonsense cost her to buy. Free electricity indeed.

Then out comes a ladder, Madam's tongue plants itself firmly in her right cheek and she's clambering up the ladder with the solar panel under her arm. I can't hear everything that's going on, but I do hear the occasional expletives and comments coming down from the roof. 'Well if I'm supposed to screw this bloody thing into the roofing felt, the bloody place will leak. Oh sod the thing, dropped it now. Ouch – damned thing! This is ridiculous. That won't fit.' She finally descends the ladder with a length of cable in her teeth. Then she's busying herself with all things technical, fitting more wires, switches, lights and plugs.

'Right Old Girl, here we go. Roll of drums please.' She's losing it; she's really losing it. 'I hereby declare this electrical supply well

and truly open. May God bless all who use it and benefit from it.'
She throws a switch. There's a fizz, a pop and some smoke, all
followed by an awful smell.

'Well, maybe not! I think I might have done something wrong,'
a sheepish voice declares from the darkness.

★★★★★

It was a pretty dark and grey morning when Sidney Davison came
out to me clutching a couple of square white cards, each with a big
red L painted on it.

'Well car, you'm and I are 'aving our driving test today. My mate
Ted 'as agreed to sit with me while I get the feel of you before the test.'

He attached one of the cards to my radiator and the other to the
spare wheel and as it started to get lighter, he cleaned the muck and
dust off me that had been building up over the last few months.
You see, I was parked right at the back of the garden and too close
to the field behind the house. The farmer had chosen to plough
and harrow the field when the wind was blowing in my direction.
He always chose a windy day to work on that field and when he
decided to use his muck spreader… well! You can guess which way
the wind was blowing. Sidney Davison cleaned the last bits of muck
off my bonnet and went in for his breakfast. He might have been
the target of Mavis Davison's barbed tongue, but she always fed
him well.

As he came out of the back door with his friend Ted, I briefly
caught the end of one of Mavis Davison's diatribes. '… and don't
think you can bring that old jalopy back here if you fail your test,
Sidney Davison.'

'No dear. Come on Ted, let's get the 'ell out of here, quick.'

'Gor blimey Sidney, what the hell is that pong?' Ted climbed
into my passenger seat.

'Oh, old Tom Rogers was muck spreading last week and some of it was blown in our direction. Gawd it was funny.'

'Funny? This car right stinks.'

'The Missus 'ad put her washing out an' then 'ad to do it all over again. Laugh? I thought I were goin' to 'ave a corona, it was so funny. She didn't though, an' I 'ad to come and hide in this old car till she got over it. C'mon let's get into town.' He started me up and we manoeuvred ourselves out of the gates and into the lane.

'You sure the examiner is going to be happy with this pong, Sidney?'

'E's not testing me on 'ow this car smells. E's testing my driving. Tell you what though, if I fail, I ain't taking this old girl to the scrappie.'

On the subject of scrappies, that reminds me of something really funny that happened yesterday. I couldn't contain myself. I thought that my headlights would fall off, I was laughing so much. There I was sitting in the doorway to my garage, enjoying the sunshine while watching Her Ladyship and her friend, the Nice Mister Ed attempting to refit the wings onto The Grey One. The wings that The Nice Mister Ed had repaired and repainted by the way. When I say Her Ladyship was helping, well, she was more standing around and looking helpless while The Nice Mister Ed did all the work.

Then just as I was beginning to bore of the situation, preferring to watch a snail meander across the drive, a beaten up old truck pulled up at the bottom, loaded to the gunwales with old metalwork. It was being driven by a gentleman of unshaven complexion and rather too many gold teeth.

'Any scrap Missus?' he shouted up the drive, eyeing the Grey One with an uncanny greed. Her Ladyship looked from the gold teeth to the Grey One and back to the gold teeth again.

'What?' she cried out, as if she had been hit by a thunderbolt. 'Do you mean this?' She was gesturing at an equally horrified Grey

One. Then recovering her composure, she politely declined Gold Tooth's request. It was the look on the Grey One's face that did for me. Mind you the look on the face of Davison's driving test examiner was something to behold.

'Mister Davison?' A man had appeared from the driving test centre carrying a clipboard. He was looking around at all the expectant examinees.

'Tha's me sur,' Sidney Davison announced as his friend Ted wandered off to the pub. 'Over here.' The examiner strode over and on seeing me, stopped dead.

'You are taking your test in that thing?' He asked incredulously. 'That, that old jalopy?'

Sidney Davison was perturbed. 'Yessur. Is that a problem?'

'Well, yes it is actually. We've stopped requiring drivers to use hand signals and your car doesn't have any indicators. I suppose I can bend the rules and let you use hand signals. I presume that this car does stop when you apply the brakes?'

'She passed 'er ministry test nine months ago. She's fine. I've got my L-plates, see?'

'Yes… well I suppose we'd better make a start.' Both men climbed in and I got the feeling that I was going to be more under test than Sidney Davison. 'God in heaven, what on earth is that awful smell?'

'Farmer was muck spreading in the next field lars' week Sur. Wind blew 'un all over the car. Thought I'd cleaned it all off, see?'

'Yes, well I suppose I will have to put up with it.' He opened my side screen and took a deep breath. 'Now, I want you to start the car, pull away and turn right as you leave the driving test centre.'

'Yessur, no problem.' Sidney Davison started me up.

★★★★★

This is always a busy time of the year for me with lots of car runs and rallies and I have to confess that at my age, I do rather prefer the static events to the long runs. I like to sit in the sun being admired by the public rather than hauling Her Ladyship around the countryside on what is often a pointless journey. 'This'll be a good preparation for our run round the world,' she always says. I had hoped that ridiculous idea had been forgotten, but no.

There was one summer event this year that really took the biscuit. It was our annual Summer Rally at Bryngarw when, accompanied by her grandson, Her Ladyship decided to camp. 'He'll enjoy that,' she said to his mother. So this year's trip required me to carry a load of camping equipment as well as the usual picnic hamper and luggage. What a disaster it was. She brought the tent, she brought sleeping bags, but she forgot to pack any sleeping mats. As a result she had to borrow some from The Nice Mister Arthur and they were painfully thin.

'Actually they are deceptively comfortable,' said the Nice Mister Arthur. 'As you unroll them they draw in air.' Madam didn't seem convinced.

What a disastrous night. 'Gran I can't get to sleep,' said the boy at regular intervals and at first Madam made conciliatory remarks, but as the night wore on she got quite irritable, as she was unable to get comfortable enough to drop off herself. Meanwhile I sat by their tent with the Asthmatic Barking Dog snoring and breaking a particularly unsavoury wind from my back seat – well, he had been given rather too much of the unwanted barbequed burgers the night before.

The next morning two bleary-eyed humans emerged from the tent as soon as it was dawn. The boy announced that he was hungry, but Madam had forgotten to pack any equipment to cook breakfast. 'You will have to have a bit of our picnic lunch until the others wake up,' she said. But both of them were ravenous and there was little left for lunch. The boy didn't mind. He made up for it with bacon butties provided by the nice Missus Pat and ice cream, reluctantly paid for by Her Ladyship.

'Your mother will kill me', she muttered as she handed over yet another two pound coin. 'Get me one as well.' That's right, that diet... Well the won't power rather than the will power won didn't it?

Then it was time for the driving tests, which the Nice Mister Arthur organises every year, and we joined the queue to take part. But I was talking about that other driving test, wasn't I? The one that became the harbinger of my near demise.

'Right,' said the examiner. 'I want you to turn left up ahead and then to park the car just around the corner on the left hand side.' Sidney Davison obliged and I was rather surprised at the panache with which he manoeuvred me into position.

'Good,' said the examiner. 'Now I want you to reverse back around the corner and park tidily beside the kerb when you have done so.'

It was here that our problems started. I didn't have a tight enough lock to get into position correctly, so Sidney Davison had to move me backwards and forwards to get close enough to the kerb. Then he made me mount the pavement.

'Hmmm.' The examiner wrote something onto his pad. 'Okay, now I want you to pull out again, turn left into the road we were in before, drive up a bit and park again in a place where you can complete a three point turn.'

'Mirror, signal, handbrake and pull out,' Sidney Davison muttered to himself, but although he must have seen the car coming up behind us, he didn't wait. BLAAAAAH went the other car's horn as we pulled out in front of it. The car swerved and the examiner proceeded to write even more on his pad, this time rather vigorously.

'Whoops, sorry,' said Sidney Davison, now becoming quite flustered.

The three point turn didn't go that well either. Well it wasn't exactly a three point turn, more a seven point turn, as he chose a point where there was another vehicle parked at the side of the road. If only he had driven a few yards further, he would have had the room. So I think he had already failed his driving test long before we actually came to the emergency stop. He should have reminded the examiner that my cable brakes are just not as good as those on modern cars. So after we had smacked into the back of the delivery van and proffered our apologies, the examiner asked Sidney Davison to drive him directly back to the driving test centre.

'Well Mister Davison, I imagine that you have gathered that you have failed. You failed on failing to use your mirror correctly, failing to complete a three point turn and failing the emergency stop. If it's any consolation, you did pass on your use of hand signals.'

'Ah yes, well I 'ave a motorbike see. Trouble is that the Missus won't go in the side-car anymore, so I'm wanting to pass this test and use the car.'

'That's as may be Mister Davison, but I would strongly advise that when you come for your next test, that you come in a more modern car. Goodbye.' He handed over a sheet of paper explaining where we had failed and walked quickly back in to the test centre, as if not wanting to prolong our embarrassment any further.

'You what?' Mavis Davison screamed when we got home. 'You failed and you 'ad the nerve to bring that old jalopy back 'ome?' Sidney Davison was very quiet; he looked around for an escape route. He had hoped so much that he could have come back with a pass. 'I don't want that thing dumped in my back garden again.'

'I'll try to sell 'un, Mavis. I'll try to sell 'un.'

'Well if you've got to put it somewhere, put it over by the chickens. It'll be out of my sight and they might find it comfortable.'

*****

'Good morning Miss Daisy,' Madam cries as she bursts in. 'I have decided that the time has come to fit you up with indicators. Once this is done, I will be able to tell other vehicles and their drivers whether I am turning left or right by the flick of a switch. It will be much safer when we are in France.'

WHY? Will someone please explain to me why, when for the past seventy five years my drivers have quite successfully been able to proffer that information by using hand signals? Why now, after so long, should I have to provide that information with some ghastly flashing amber lights?

'The thing is Old Girl, modern drivers do not understand what the hand signals mean anymore.' Oh for heaven's sake why not? Surely drivers and cars today understand such simple indications of our intent. I mean, we all know when following a horse drawn carriage, that if the driver holds his whip vertically in the air, that he is going to stop, don't we? But it seems that I will have to demonstrate my turning intentions with the aid of an electrical device. Anyway, these indicator things would have been no help the other day when Madam was heading for one of her events. We were tootling happily along a rather pretty little lane and approaching a double bend when a very large lorry with Polish number plates careered round and hurtled towards us on my side of the road.

Her Ladyship, who like me had been rather enjoying the scenery rammed her right foot onto the brake pedal and grabbed the hand brake with her left hand. She slowly pivoted vertically as she pressed on the first and pulled on the second. Out of her mouth came 'What the f......' The full word was drowned by the sound of my four tyres skidding along the road and I continued to skid as she directed me towards a bank and out of the lorry's path.

It was to no avail I am afraid, as a rather nasty grinding noise confirmed that I had grazed myself against the high stone bank and we came to a standstill. Madam then pushed me into reverse to get out of the lorry's way. This action was accompanied by more grinding. It seemed that he wasn't going to stop for anyone. We tucked into a small area so that the lorry could get through. Her Ladyship, still shaken, didn't have the presence of mind to take the lorry's number and by the time she had collected herself, it had ploughed on, doubtless intent on scattering other vehicles in its wake.

The result of this little escapade was a bill for a hundred and fifty pounds, me no further prepared for the trip abroad and Her Ladyship wondering what had happened to the old knights of the road.

When I came into the world way back when, it was intended that we would carry people on trips a few miles into the countryside. I think of the Johnstons and the Colonel and Joycie Darling. They would find a nice place to stop, lay a rug on the ground, open a hamper and eat wafer thin cucumber sandwiches and cherry cake and that would be all washed down with a nice cup of tea. Then as the sun started to touch the tops of the hills in the west, they would pack everything up and head back into the town from whence they'd come. A picture of bliss don't you think?

Then why the hell does Her Ladyship insist on loading me up with just about every spare part she has, piles of luggage, her damnable Satellite Thingy and this year, with her grandson squeezed in as well, choose to haul us all off to the land of Johnny Foreigner? Every time we do one of these trips it is accompanied with her usual mantra, 'all part of our preparation for our little trip round the world, Old Girl.' So now I am sitting in a motorway services just outside Cardiff. Before we left Pembrokeshire, The Grey One had already made obscene references to my indicators, likening me to one of those dirty old men in grubby raincoats who flash at unsuspecting people in the park. I had to be rid of them.

Then miraculously, as we approach this part of our destination, the flashers fail. I am delighted. Madam isn't.

'Damned bloody things,' she cries. 'Barely a week old and they fail. Back to hand signals then.' We finish our journey to Cardiff with Her Ladyship thrusting her right hand out of her window to make right turns and The Boy thrusting his hand out to tell people that we are turning left.

'We can sort that out when we are in France,' Her Ladyship announces as she unloads their luggage. 'But we'd better take the rotor arm out. If we don't, some little creep in a hoodie or a baseball cap is bound to try to steal the Old Girl and take her for a joy ride. Can't see the joy in it myself though.'

Madam opens my bonnet, flicks open the distributor and removes the rotor arm.

'During the war, it was illegal not to remove rotor arms from stationary vehicles,' she explains to The Boy in her history teacher mode. 'If you parked a vehicle up anywhere and were leaving it unattended, you had to immobilise it. So people removed the rotor arm.' The Boy couldn't be less interested. He had seen the sign for Burger King.

'Good morning Old Girl. Sleep well? We did.' Her Ladyship loads up their luggage, she and The Boy climb in, she switches me on and pulls the starter button. Wurr-ur-ur-ur-ur-urrr, wurr-ur-ur-ur-ur-urrr... 'What the hell is wrong with you now? You drove us up here perfectly yesterday...'

Wurr-ur-ur-ur-ur-urrr, wurr-ur-ur-ur-ur-urrr...

'Oh for God's sake... Don't do this to me now!'

The Boy interjects, 'Gran you've forgotten to put the rotor thingy back in.'

'What? What do you mean? Oh yes, of course,' she mumbles to herself as she gets out to remedy the problem. Oh dear, we are barely a hundred miles into this trip and she is messing things up. We meet up with the others who are joining us and leave in a small convoy for Portsmouth. I have to chuckle when the Satellite Thingy decides to take us on a tour of Warminster.

'What the hell is it doing now?' Her Ladyship starts to tap it.

'Don't do that Gran, you'll mess it up,' The Boy ventures to suggest.

'Don't be ridiculous, these pieces of technology always benefit from a good wallop'. At that point the screen goes blank. The Boy gives Her Ladyship a knowing look and all she can do is harrumph!

It is pitch black when we arrive in France the next morning. Six of us drive off the ferry. Then as soon as we leave the port, the others all disappear.

'Where the hell have they all gone now? They are supposed to stick to me like glue while I find the coast road!' Madam seems a little annoyed. 'Anyway, where the hell are we? This isn't the road we want. Let's switch on the sat nav.' I am surprised at her renewed faith in that thing.

We all gather together again and head along the coast road towards Arromanches.

'Have you done World War Two at school?' Her Ladyship asks of her grandson.

'Yes Gran, why?'

'Well, you see the beaches to the right of this road?' The Boy nods. 'It was all along here that the allies landed when they started to liberate Europe. The British and Canadians landed on that beach over there. Hundreds of thousands of them, there were French and American soldiers as well. If you keep your eyes peeled, you will see the odd tank or field gun mounted on plinths as memorials.'

We get safely to Arromanches and after a good lunch, Her Ladyship's mood has significantly improved. Dare I suggest that this was down to a glass or two of house wine in that restaurant?

'Right, I think we'll all go and find the Chateau now,' and we are off. Two of my relatives immediately lose their way and we pull into a lay by while one of us goes back to look for them. Eventually the missing two turn up, but the relative who went in search of them has now gone missing. I don't know, plonk humans in cars in a foreign country and they keep getting lost. I wonder if it is because we have to drive on the wrong side of the road and get disorientated. It would be far better if we British kept to our side of the road and they kept to theirs. I am sure that my French relatives with their knowledge of these roads could avoid us. I just hope that there won't be any Polish lorries coming towards us. They don't seem to know what side of the road they should be on.

Next morning, Her Ladyship blast her, manages to repair my flashers. But it seems that now some of my relatives are having problems as well. The youngest, an MG that had encountered petrol pump problems yesterday, has started to indicate right when her driver signals left. Another is having battery problems and won't start. Eventually we are all up and running again and we head off to a museum. But you know humans! Always open for a distraction.

'There's a nice little Bistro over there where we can have lunch,' says a voice. We finally reach our museum, which is barely thirty minutes from the chateau, four hours after we were supposed to.

'Morning Old Girl. I have a nice day for you today. We are not going anywhere save to park up in the village. We've been invited to a special feast as guests of Monsieur le Maire. It's something to do with their National Heritage Day.'

We all parade to the centre of the village where they have stretched tables right down the street. It seems as though the entire population sit down to lunch together here. It seems that my family and I are on show and I have to confess that I am enjoying all this attention. After too much wine and far too much food, Her

Ladyship offers Monsieur Le Maire a drive around his village. But first he has to make a speech. I can't understand a word, nor can The Boy and if the truth be known, neither can Her Ladyship, but she still nods her head at appropriate moments to pretend that she does. Speech over, Madam then persuades the others to join in by taking one or two other villagers for a ride as well.

Suddenly the entire population of this little French village decide that they want to have a ride and we end up doing trip after trip after trip. Every time we return to the centre of the village, the queue seems longer and it isn't long before the children work out that if on a return from one trip they go to the back of the queue, the odds are pretty high that they will get another ride in a different relative. Some of us get wise to this and dump our passengers at the bottom of the street then, before anyone else can get in, they high tail it back to the Chateau. Not Madam though, we just keep going on until everyone has gone home.

The next day Her Ladyship announces that we are going on a tour of a cider farm; we'll sample some cider perhaps and have some lunch there. Oh my God, more food? She's already getting heavier and I'm the poor soul that has to carry her enlarging bottom around. She's conveniently forgotten about that diet hasn't she? At this rate, instead of losing her two stone, she will end up as large as Mavis Davison. Now if that isn't a portent of disaster for the Round the World Trip, then what is? Several hours later she lurches out of the restaurant, full of bonhomie and clutching three bottles.

'Don't worry Miss D,' she says noticing my disapproval. 'These aren't for me. These are gifts for friends at home.'

We finally make our way to the ferry port and twenty four hours later I drive into my garage. I'm completely exhausted, but I have made it. I have carried Her Ladyship and her grandson on an eight hundred mile round trip through France without a major hitch. Then as she closes the door, 'You've been brilliant Miss Daisy. A fantastic trip. I am very proud of you. You've definitely earned a number of Brownie points ready for our trip round the world. I think we can go for a really big one next year. How about Spain or Portugal? That could be rather nice.'

You cannot be serious. Please say you are joking! But she's not here to hear me. She never listens anyway. There are times when I rather wish that I had been left out with Sidney Davison's chickens. Oooh yes, those chickens.

I don't remember how long I was stuck out in Mavis Davison's chicken run, but it seemed an eternity. No one seemed to want me and Sidney Davison had even given up trying to sell me. My only friends were the chickens who rather liked to lay their eggs on my seats and all I ever saw of either of the Davisons was when they came out to collect the eggs. With no one to look after me properly and only chickens for company, I just sat there rotting away. It was the gale that really finished me off. It battered me all night, and what was left of Joycie Darling's handiwork was completely destroyed as the hood pulled itself away from its mountings, and even my side screens were ripped apart by the winds. The next morning I looked terrible and since I no longer had a hood, even the chickens lost interest in me. So I sat there for weeks – months – to be honest it seemed years.

Then one afternoon a car pulled up in front of the house and a man got out. He came through the gates and wandered across to me.

'My, you are in a state aren't you? What are you?' He wanders around to my front, pulls out a rag and wipes my radiator cowl. 'Austin eh? Austin Seven and a Tourer at that. How old are you? Nineteen thirty three?'

'Nineteen thirty four actually. Can I 'elp you?' Sidney Davison had come out to see what this man wanted.

He turned to meet my owner. 'Oh hello, I am sorry to barge in like this, but I noticed this car parked up here when I drove past

217

this morning and I wanted to take a look when I came back. She's a bit of a beauty isn't she? My name is Roger Armstrong, by the way. I buy and sell vintage cars.'

'Are you now?' Sidney Davison didn't know what to make of this visitor, except that he had a brand new Jaguar parked outside in the road.

'Is this one for sale?'

'It might be. I have other people interested in buying it. I just haven't decided who to sell it to.'

'I'll give you fifty pounds for it.'

Sidney Davison tried to hide a cough of surprise. I think he was expecting an offer of about five pounds at the most. Roger Armstrong silently cursed himself when he realised that Sidney had no idea what I might be worth. Personally, I couldn't believe I was worth that much either. For heaven's sake, the colonel only paid five pounds for me and that was over ten years ago.

'Umm.' Sidney, having quickly recovered from the shock of this high offer, tried to push the price higher. 'She's a good little car. 'Ow about sixty pound?'

'I am sorry Mister, umm, Mister?'

'It's Davison. My name's Sidney Davison.'

'Well Mister Davison, I don't horse trade. I offer what I think a car is worth. To me this little one is worth fifty pounds, not a penny more. That's my offer. If you don't want to accept it, then you still have your car and I still have my money. It's up to you.'

'Fifty five?'

'I said fifty pounds Mister Davison. That's my offer.'

'Oh all right then, I'll accept fifty.' Sidney Davison was finding it hard to control his excitement at getting fifty pounds for me. Mind you I was too. Only ten minutes before, I was expecting to quietly rot away in that chicken run.

'Good. I will give you ten pounds as a deposit and I have a sale agreement in my car that I want you to sign on receipt of the deposit. Is that all right with you?'

'Yup, fine.' Sidney Davison followed Roger Armstrong to his car. He signed the sale document and accepted a ten pound note.

'I'll send someone along to pick up this car and its documents and pay you the remaining forty pounds in the next few days. Will you be around?'

'Yessur, I'll be here.'

'Good, good. Well thank you Mister Davison. It's good doing business with you. Hopefully I can find someone who will give that old car a new lease of life.' As the Jaguar drove off, Sidney Davison ran in to the house. He couldn't wait to give Mavis the good news. It wasn't long before a shriek emerged from the house, but for once it was a happy shriek.

Two days later, I was manoeuvred out of the chicken run and onto a car transporter. My last sight of Sidney and Mavis Davison was of them standing at their front door watching me being driven away. Sidney Davison was kissing the four ten pound notes, when Mavis Davison whipped them out of his grasp and placed them in the pocket of her apron.

We arrived at a large, modern, barn-like building on the outskirts of Leamington Spa. I was rolled off the transporter and into this building where there were dozens of ancestors, relatives and siblings of all shapes and sizes. Some were in a sorry state like me, while others looked immaculate.

'What do you reckon on this one Frank? I got her for fifty; bargain huh? She's one year short of being fifty years old, a nineteen thirty four Tourer and a very nice little restoration project for someone. Put her round the back with the other restoration projects. I have a feeling that she won't be here for very long. Oh and give her a bit of a clean up. She'll sell a lot quicker once all that chicken shit has been washed off.'

'Okay guv.' Frank wheeled me away, picked up a bucket of water and a sponge and cleaned me up.

The Guv was right, I was only there a few weeks. People came and went, most of them were after the fully restored cars at the front, but occasionally someone would wander back to look at the 'restoration projects' as we were called. Then one day a young man came to have a look at us and his attention was immediately drawn to me.

'Well, well, well, what have we here? You are a bit of a beauty aren't you?'

'Can I help you sir?' It was The Guv.

'Yes, you can actually. What do you know about this one then?'

'Not much to be honest. She's a nineteen thirty four Austin Seven, four-seat Tourer. I don't know if the engine works, the battery is shot, but it does turn over when you try the crank. The wheels all turn and the handbrake and steering seem to work as well. That's all I know.'

'How much are you asking?'

'Four hundred pounds sir.' The young man swallowed hard, but that was nothing like my reaction. Four hundred pounds? Has the world gone mad? That is nearly four times what I cost new.

The young man turned away to look at another relative. 'I'm sorry, I haven't got that much. Would you accept three hundred pounds?'

'Tell you what, you obviously like this little old thing, three hundred and fifty pounds and I will even deliver her to you. How about that?'

'I think you have a deal. Will you take a cheque?'

'Certainly sir.' As they walk off I hear The Guv ask, 'Is this your first restoration sir?'

'Yes it is actually. I've been wanting to have a go at getting a vintage car on the road for a while now and my father told me that he drove one of these when he was a student in the sixties.'

★★★★★

'Good afternoon Old Girl.' Madam appears with a determined look on her face. She's looking rather smart. 'Guess what Old Girl? I've been invited to an art exhibition in Newport and it says I can bring a guest, so I thought I'd take you.'

Correction oh Wrinkled One. It's a nice sunny day and you'd like to go in me so that you can show off in front of your arty friends. Anyway, I have a funny feeling they won't let me in. She flaps the invitation at me and prepares to get my engine started. The Asthmatic Barking Dog, sensing that something might be about to happen without him, flops down in front of my front wheels and drops off to sleep.

'Out of the way Dog,' she cries, flapping the invitation in his face. He slowly lifts his head, opens a blood shot eye, takes a look at her and then me before settling down again and dozing off to sleep.

'Oh all right then, I'll get your blanket.' He leaps up with a 'now you're talking' look on his face and while she pops into the house for his travel blanket, he jumps in through my opened door and settles onto my rear seat.

'Out, out, out,' screams Madam upon her return. 'I need to put your blanket on the seat.' But he's not going to move. I think he suspects that she will drive off without him if he moved, so Her Ladyship has to heave his blanket under his reclining body and tuck it in. He offers no help whatsoever and by the time she finishes, she's looking quite flustered.

'Right, let's go,' she cries and I shoot out of the garage door onto the drive, at which point she slams on my brakes. 'Oh pook. I've forgotten to open the gates.' Out she gets to resolve that little issue and off we go. It's a lovely sunny day, tree blossom in full bloom and the grass in the fields is radiating a lush rich green. It takes us nearly an hour to get to Newport.

We stop by a shop. Madam pulls out a map, turns it in several directions before shoving it unfolded back into my passenger foot well.

'Excuse me,' she asks a passer by. 'Can you direct me to St Mary's Hall? It's an Art Exhibition.'

'Je ne comprends pas Madame. Je ne parle pas anglais.'

'Blooming foreigner, you'd think he would know his way around, wouldn't you Old Girl? Ah, here's someone else. Excuse me… can you direct me to St. Mary's Hall? They have an art exhibition there.'

'Sorry love,' comes the reply. 'We're only here on holiday.' A harrumph emanates from Her Ladyship and that is followed by 'Bloody tourists. What's the point of coming here and not knowing where you are going?' Several enquiries later, we find St. Mary's Hall and we park outside.

'That's strange,' Madam mutters. 'The place seems locked up. Where are all the luvvies?' She clambers out of me and tries the door. It's firmly shut and locked. The Asthmatic Barking Dog, having snored all the way here, starts to take an interest in what's going on.

'Let me in,' she cries through the locked door. 'Let me in. You've got champagne in there, I know it. I've come all this way. Here's my invitation, look!' She tries to shove it under the door.

'Can I help you?' A voice from behind me turns out to be that of a clergyman. Oh God, what is she going to say now? But Madam collects herself as she struggles in an ungamely fashion back on to her feet and brushes herself down.

'The art exhibition,' she mutters almost apologetically. 'I have an invitation to the art exhibition.'

'Oh no, no, no. That's not today, that's next Thursday,' the clergyman replies. 'Oh yes, next Thursday, indeed. Good afternoon.' He touches his hat and walks away speeding up as he goes, obviously deciding that the best solution in this situation is to achieve the greatest possible distance between him and this mad and probably alcoholic woman. He steers himself in through a garden gate, hoping that on the other side of that door sits a cup of tea and a slice of Mrs Blakethorpe's really nice lemon drizzle cake.

Madam proceeds to look from her invitation to the locked door, then to the disappearing clergyman, back to me and finally back to the locked door again. She clambers back into the driving seat.

'Well Old Girl,' she announces, trying to hide her embarrassment. 'Next Thursday it is then. That's what we'll do; we'll come back next Thursday. Now let's go. The Asthmatic Barking Dog decides that there has been far too much excitement for him for one day and settles back to his snoring as Her Ladyship starts me up and heads for home.

'Actually Old Girl, I've got a brilliant idea,' Her Ladyship announces as we bounce along. 'There is one more thing I want to do before we go home. Let's go and find a police speed trap. I want to ask them a favour.' Her Ladyship swings me off the main road. 'I think I know where we can find one.'

She addresses that last remark to The Asthmatic Barking Dog on the back seat. He ignores her completely, now tired of sleeping and preferring to stand with his front paws on the wheel arch and leaning out over my side so that the wind blows into his mouth and eyes. His ears fly out backwards, making a flapping noise should he turn his head one way or the other, an act he tries to avoid as it undoubtedly hurts him.

We tootle along and as we go round a bend, Madam notices a white van parked in a lay by with an image of a camera and the word 'Think' emblazoned on its rear door.

'That's what I was looking for.' She cries and without slowing down, she swings into a layby and pulls up in front of the van. I'm confused, what the hell is she going to do now? She hops out and proceeds to knock on a rear door of the van.

'Helloo anybody there?'

A man appears. 'May I help you madam?'

'Umm, yes you can actually. I need your help.'

'Yes madam?' He sounds a tad irritated.

'I need your help because when my speedometer tells me that I am doing thirty miles an hour, my Satellite Navigation Thingy says I am only doing twenty five. I was wondering; if I went back up that road and came back towards you doing what my speedometer tells me is thirty, well I wonder if you could confirm exactly what speed I am doing? You see, I am planning to drive this old car round the world and I would like to know how accurate the speedometer is.'

I can't believe what I am hearing. What on earth does this woman think she is doing? This is so embarrassing.

'I am sorry madam, no. We have a job to do here and it's not calibrating the speedometers of elderly cars, whether, indeed, they plan to go round the world or not!'

'But, but, but...' The door of the van slams shut, leaving Madam's last 'but' hanging in thin air. 'Well,' she snorts, 'he wasn't very helpful was he?'

Of course he wasn't helpful, you silly woman. He's there to catch people speeding and not helping some dotty old dear check her speedometer! God give me strength. Now take me home, I have my memoirs to finish.

So, where was I? Yes, I was delivered to my new home as promised and my new owner, a man called James Peters, pushed me in to this old garage. His wife joined us.

'So this is the new project is it? It's a pretty little thing but it's in a terrible state. Are you sure you are up to it?' She wanders around me looking closely at me. 'There's a lot of rust down here.'

'I know,' he said. 'It is in one hell of a state Bea. I don't know how long it's going to take, but the next time it rolls out on that road it will be like a brand new car. What time's lunch?'

'About an hour and a half, why?'

'Well I thought I would make a start pulling her to pieces now, if that's okay.' I was taken aback. Why would he want to take me to pieces?

'Why not? But lunch at one, no later. I'm on shift this afternoon and we have a new consultant starting. I mustn't give him a bad impression.' She pecked him on the cheek and headed back into the house.

James Peters grabbed his toolbox and put it on the floor beside me. 'Well Car, here goes.' He started by removing what was left of my hood, seats and trim. 'We won't need any of these things for a while. I'll put them in the roof; they'll be safe up there. Wait a minute, what's this? That's a clever place to put a tool kit, tucked away under the seat like that. So what tools have you got here then? An old fan belt, well that's no good anymore, it's rotten. Gosh, that's an ancient jack and an even older puncture kit. Probably no good anymore either. Ah some spare bulbs, always useful. No, they all appear to be blown.' He tossed them into the bin. 'Three spanners and a screw driver. Hardly a treasure trove and here's a damp old piece of matting in the bottom. I suppose someone put that there to stop the tools clattering about. Well we'll get rid of that. What the hell?'

He produced a very stained brown envelope, which was half stuck to the matting. 'It's very damp.' He opened the envelope very carefully and withdrew an equally stained and damp piece of paper. 'Well at least the writer used a pencil. It's dated 14th November 1939.'

To whom it may concern. My name is David Johnston; I live in Oxford with my wife Beatrice and my two year old son, Albert. I normally work at Nuffield College, but now I have been called up and am about to join my regiment. I don't know what will happen to me but hopefully I will make it

*home to my family when this is all over, but who knows. Your reading this
letter means that I haven't made it and I thought I would tell you a little bit
about this car.*

*I bought Daisy on 19ᵗʰ March 1934. She was brand new and I bought
her before they introduced the driving test because I wasn't sure I would pass.
My wife Beatrice and I would drive out into the country every weekend and
Daisy even rushed us to hospital so that my son could be born. Daisy has
been very special to us all and I hope when this war is over, she will continue
to be so. If you are her new owner, please look after her. She's a wonderful
little car.*

'Good heaven's, so your name is Daisy is it? Well Daisy, I
promise you that I will look after you. Bea will be interested in this
letter though. Gosh, yes. That's odd isn't it? David Johnston's wife
was called Beatrice as well. I think that when I have finished with
you, not only will I put this letter back at the bottom of the toolbox,
but I will write another one to put in as well and I will write it
exactly fifty years to the day after David Johnston wrote his. That
means I have ten and a half months to get you on the road again.
But now I must go and show Bea this letter. It must be lunchtime
anyway...'

Chapter Seven

Pretending to be blind, she pokes her walking stick around as if looking for the edge of the pavement. The scene before us becomes like a frozen film frame as the traffic stops dead and a man in the car nearest to her gets out, takes her arm and starts to escort her over the road.

Monday 11th January 2010

A sardine can? He called me a blooming SARDINE CAN? The cheek of the man. How dare he? He, by the way is – or should I say was until quite recently – a friend of Her Ladyship's who happened to ask after my health, using the said pseudonym in his description of me. How dare he? Indeed, it may appear to be a bit cosy when two people sit inside me, but sardine can I am not. Mind you, my annoyance at these remarks were as nothing to that of Her Ladyship's. She threw open my doors this morning without so much as a 'Good morning Old Girl. Doesn't Dumpledale look nice this morning?' I could see that she was not expressing her usual early morning bonhomie. In fact she was… well, she was, I suppose you could call it, snorting. Her nostrils were expanding and contracting rather like a horse back from a long gallop. She paced around the garage for a while and then she told me what had been said. Well, if I'd had nostrils like hers I would have done exactly the same. But there was something else worrying her and looking outside, I assumed it was the seven or eight inches of snow outside my garage. Madam followed my gaze.

'Yes,' she said, 'they told me that it never snows in Pembrokeshire. Look at it. Look at that damned stuff. We've got to get you down on to that road. Mister Chris will be here soon to take you on his trailer to see Mister Arthur. And then on top of all that old girl, while you are away, I have to have that toenail surgery done.' She goes on to describe what she is having done and really, such detail is best left unsaid.

The thing is, and I am not exaggerating, Her Ladyship can lay claim to being one of this world's worst hypochondriacs. You know the sort of person. You never ask them how they are feeling, unless of course you've got an hour or two to spare. She was working on me the other day when the telephone rang. Whoever called must have asked that fateful question. I knew immediately, judging by her reply.

'Well, not too bad considering...' Then, 'Apart from a chesty cough and my having to go in for some toenail surgery, I am having the most awful pains in my lower back. To be honest, at the moment I am hardly ever without pain.'

Oh for heaven's sake. This woman seems to revel in her illnesses. If they ever created a Hypochondriacs' Anonymous, then the Wrinkled One would be up for the post of World President. Mind you the person who called obviously also wished to discuss her own illnesses.

'How are you?' She ventured and then mouthed at me that she shouldn't have asked that question as she settled herself on my driving seat, phone clamped to her ear. Her side of the conversation went something like this:

'Yes... Oh dear... Oh I see... Mmmm... Oh... Poor you... Oh I know... Did you say enema? Well they are very good with these special cameras nowadays... It'll certainly show if there are any problems down there... Oh, they can't do it until they've relieved the Haemorrhoids? You don't have to tell me about Haemorrhoids... I am a martyr to them, especially when driving Miss Daisy over speed humps.'

That's right. Blame me... They're agony for me too you know.

'Well, Old Girl, let's get you down to the road. Mister Chris will be here in a minute and I want you ready to load up. Ah here he is now.'

Have you ever watched one of those period films when someone, well wrapped against the elements, climbs up onto the top of a stagecoach as it heads off across some cold snowy landscape, with a coachman blasting his coaching horn right beside that person's ear? And have you ever wondered what it might have been like to sit on top of that same stagecoach for what seems like hours with snow and mud being thrown at you with wild abandon?

Well I can tell you exactly what it is like because I am having to do exactly that. The only difference is that my stagecoach is The Nice Mister Chris's car trailer. We've been barely on the road fifteen minutes and I've been screaming at them to stop, I'm being splashed with snow, mud and something they wouldn't have had to suffer in the 18th century – salt. But does anyone take any notice? No, of course not! They're chatting away in the cosy cab of The Nice Mister Chris's car without a care in the world.

We reach our destination and I am covered in the stuff. I imagine that you might be wondering why I've been pretending to be an extra in *Pride and Prejudice*. Well, Her Ladyship has brought me up to see The Nice Mister Arthur. You remember him don't you? He fitted me up with a luggage rack, gosh, five or six years ago now. Well this time I've come here so that The Nice Mister Arthur can do something to my engine. Apparently I am burning a bit of oil and he has very kindly offered to replace my valve guides for her. Well for me actually. It's got nothing to do with her. At least I can have a quiet week in The Nice Mister Arthur's garage and ponder my past.

I've often wondered why that man James Peters paid three hundred and fifty pounds for me. Can you believe that? Three hundred and fifty pounds, nearly fifty years after I cost just one hundred and six pounds and I was then brand new. I have also wondered what exactly he did to me after he started to pull me to pieces, but my memory of what he might or might not have done is a complete blank. Then why would I remember? I have since heard that he pulled me to pieces. Every nut, bolt, spring and bearing. You name it, he removed it, cleaned it up or replaced it with a new bit and then labelled it for when he started to put me back together again. I suppose you could say that I was the Humpty Dumpty that could be put back together again.

★★★★★

'Hello Old Girl. Are you feeling better now? No more nasty burning oil I hope?' Her Ladyship disturbs my reverie once more. Gosh those few days have gone quickly. 'Well I think we must get you home now.'

I peer out of the Nice Mister Arthur's workshop and am pleased to see that the snow is all gone and the sun is shining; and thank God, she's arrived without that trailer. Instead she came by train and apparently she couldn't even get that right. She got lost at the local railway station when she arrived, if that is at all possible at a station with just two platforms, poor dear, I really should be concerned for her. But no, I don't think so. We head for home, filling up with some petrol on the way and I feel remarkably well. I don't know what valve guides are, but we are home in no time at all.

'Well, Miss D,' she says as she picks up a clipboard and crosses something out with a felt tip pen. 'That's one job done and dusted ready for your run to Spain.'

What? Excuse me, what was that? Spain? When you mentioned it last year, I thought you were joking.

She seems to be ignoring me. With her tongue firmly in her cheek, she is closely examining her clipboard.

'Mmmm what? Now Old Girl, Spain will be your last big trip before we head off round the world and we have to make sure you are absolutely fit for this particular trip. After all, it's all the way down through France and turns right at the Pyrenees and in to

Spain, some two thousand miles. How are you at bull fighting by the way? Oh yes, I suppose I will have to get you a sombrero and some castanets.' At that point she wanders out of the garage chuckling to herself. I can't think why.

★★★★★

As I've said, my memory of my first nine months with James Peters was pretty well blank. But I do remember waking up in his garage as he tightened a connection on my battery. I felt different, but I couldn't tell exactly why I felt different.

'There you are Daisy, you have electricity again. We still need to get your trim and hood done, but you're looking great.' The garage door opened and Bea came in. 'Well what do you think then Bea? She's nearly finished. Actually can you give me a hand? I need to check that her lights are working.'

'She's looking super,' said Bea. 'That's a lovely colour. Tail lights? Yes they're working. And the brakes. Yes. Where have you put the indicators?'

'I haven't,' said James Peters. 'She didn't have indicators before, so I don't think she needs them now. Headlights? Main? Yes? Dipped? Good, that all works then. All being well, as soon as she gets back from the trimmers, she can go for her MOT. Then she will be back on the road for the first time in goodness knows how long.'

I once overheard Her Ladyship discussing what was the most annoying thing about modern driving. Well, just about all of it actually, it's so different now. These modern tin and plastic monstrosities that loosely pretend to be motorcars are perhaps my greatest hate, especially when there are sticky faced children pulling faces at me out of the rear window. They are too fast, their drivers are inconsiderate of us oldies and let's face it, they really are ugly, aren't they? There is no grace to them. Not like me.

Now it seems that Madam has found a renewed cause to condemn modern drivers and their cars. It happened like this. She had marched off on her morning hike with the Asthmatic Barking Dog a bit earlier than usual, head held high, walking stick attacking every weed at the roadside. In fact this all happened during what humans call the school run, a time when parents choose to race their brats to school by car rather than making them walk. It seems she was walking up a hill in the middle of the village when she was brushed on the arm by a car driving past. Apparently it was too close.

'You should have seen the damned thing Old Girl,' she cried when she came home rubbing her elbow. 'It was one of those Chelsea tractor things; far too large for the blasted yummy mummy at the wheel. She was racing to school, too damned fast because she was late. There was I enjoying the morning air and this monstrosity catches its wing mirror on my arm. I cried out but the damnable woman didn't stop.' I think Her Ladyship is getting rather worked up about all this. Then she is off again.

'I mean… They've put in a bloody twenty mile an hour limit through this village so that the little darlings can be walked safely to school. Do they bother with that? Do they hell! These blasted people pile their kids into their awful machines and race to the school just in time for the nine o'clock bell, ploughing down any decent pedestrians along the way. I don't know; we're breeding a human species that won't need their legs before very long. It's laziness, sheer bloody laziness.'

My goodness, she really is getting worse as she gets older. A real grumpy old woman. But I do see her point. People used to walk or cycle in my day. But now they all just pile into a car to go anywhere more than a few hundred yards. There's another menace though; these blooming modern things are getting bigger and bigger. Not satisfied with their own motorised monstrosity, these people spot that their neighbour has bought an even larger vehicle than theirs and suddenly it's 'Oh dear, I don't feel safe driving this tiny little car anymore, perhaps I ought to buy a bigger one, just like the Jones's. It'll be much safer.' And so it goes on. Perhaps they should just bypass the car completely and buy themselves a Churchill tank.

Of course the Grey One, Brigadier General Sir Herbert Orsten DSO and Public Bar of this parish had to express his opinion when he heard what happened. 'Trouble is m'dear, women simply can't drive. Should never be allowed to if I had my way. It's all about – I think they call it spatial awareness – and that is something that the female of the human species has absolutely no idea about.'

Well of course, he would know wouldn't he? Our tame smarty pants who has "been round the world don't you know." Well if the dents and bends in his bumpers are anything to go by, I don't think he has much spatial awareness either. Pompous old fool.

I suppose I should have some sympathy for Her Ladyship's injury. But somehow, knowing that hypochondria rules her life, I just can't. In addition to her hypochondria, she continues to embarrass me and as she gets older she's getting worse. It seems as though she's the one who ought to be MOT tested, not me. In my younger days they used to called it the Ten Year Test, although by the time that James Peters took me for mine after the big rebuild, the test then applied to all cars over three years old. I had hoped that since I was as good as being brand new, the test wouldn't apply to me. But apparently that wasn't the case and James Peters climbed in and gingerly drove me to the garage.

'Hello, my name is Peters. I've booked this in for its MOT.' The garage man looked me over.

'Very nice,' he said. 'She looks very nice indeed. If the brakes, steering and lights work as well as she looks, then it won't be a problem. I've just got to finish seeing to that gentleman over there, then I'll get on with yours. Would you like to come back in an hour?'

'Actually, do you mind if I watch?' I had a feeling that James

Peters just didn't want to leave me with a stranger, especially after all the work he had put in to me.

'That's absolutely fine, actually it might be helpful. I've never tested a car quite as old as this one.' The garage man went over to finish his other job, while the man who had been standing beside that car came over to look at me.

'What a beautiful little Austin that is. Yours I presume?' James Peters, now showing a little nervousness at the upcoming test, nodded his head.

'It's her first test since her restoration. To be honest I'm a little anxious. You know, worrying that I've done something wrong.'

'Oh Bob's good. He's very understanding. Unless it's actually dangerous, he will give it the nod. How long have you had the car?'

'Barely a year actually. I bought her as a wreck. She had been a chicken house in the Warwickshire countryside before that.'

'Look, this might just be the car I am looking for…'

'Oh! I'm very sorry, she's not for sale.' James Peters responded quickly.

'No, no, I don't want to buy her. I'm a television producer; it's just that we've managed to lay our hands on an old Austin tour guide of the Cotswolds and Shakespeare country. It was published in 1934 and we've been thinking of making a little film with the book. You know, comparing motoring today to what it was like fifty years ago.'

'Oh? This car was fifty years old last month. March nineteen thirty four. That was when she was first registered.'

'Fantastic, perfect. Look here's my card, give me a call when you get back home, if you are interested.' He walked back to his own car with a bounce in his step.

'Well Daisy, it looks as though as long as you pass your MOT, you're going to be a film star.' Yes, I liked that idea.

*****

'God, am I pleased to see you…' It is Her Ladyship disturbing me once more. 'I've been up to London. What a ghastly place, too many people, full of foreigners and everyone seems to be rushing everywhere. And the hotel, God it was awful. Eight pounds for a glass of wine! Can you believe it? Eight Pounds? You can buy a whole bottle for that. The TV in my room kept on promoting films with titles like "Lesbian Love Triangle" and "Bisexual Girls Holiday Romp". Is everyone who stays there a deviant pervert? On top of that, breakfast was like walking into the tower of Babel. Japanese to the left of me, Russian to the right, Singhalese behind me and German to the front. It was a flipping nightmare. But I did see an Arab gentleman helping himself to some bacon and a sausage. I am sure they're not supposed to do that. Made me chuckle. So yes, I am very pleased to be home. I thought we'd go for a drive to return me to sanity. Fancy a bank holiday weekend trip to the shops?'

We pull into the supermarket car park. The place is heaving. 'Bloody grockels,' mutters Her Ladyship. 'Blooming four by fours everywhere, taking up all the spaces. Ah there's one.' At which she slams her foot on my accelerator and we race towards the space that Madam has spotted, briefly in her rush separating a woman from her very full trolley.

'Sorreee!' Her Ladyship cries out, her eyes focussed on our parking space. But we aren't the only ones heading for it. There's a four by four racing towards it from the other direction. We're nearer though and Madam swings in, a whisper ahead of the monster car. But that car's driver is not happy. 'Excuse me. That is my parking space,' says a voice out of an open crack in the heavily tinted window.

Madam gets out, walks up to the tinted monster, checks its number plate, and then walks all around me looking at the ground. 'Oh I'm sorry,' she says eventually. I can't see your number written on this space anywhere.' She's asking for trouble here. Then, 'You own this spot then, do you?' At this point the driver of the other car starts to get out. I choose to look the other way. I don't like violence. But then his companion restrains him.

'You bloody people,' he shouts. 'You should be in a home and that old banger on the scrap heap.' His four by four obviously agrees with him, as it seems to growl as it drives away. Well really, these people do get themselves upset. In a home indeed. Old banger? Scrap heap? Cheeky sod!

★★★★★

I did pass that MOT by the way and as James Peters drove me home, we were both feeling on top of the world. In addition, it looked as though I was going to be a television star. Bea came out of the house as we got home. 'How did it go then?'

'We passed with flying colours and… well, you really aren't going to believe this.' James Peters was really excited. 'We arrived for the test and we had to wait a bit. I got talking to this bloke who it turned out is a television producer. Look, here's his card. He wants to make a film with old Daisy here, something about comparing motoring fifty years ago to what it's like today. He asked me to phone him if I was interested. At the time I was so anxious about the test, I didn't agree to it. But now, well now I'd better go and give him a call.'

A few months later, I had earned James Peters five hundred pounds. That is what they paid for a week of filming with me. Mind you, he had already spent that on buying a car trailer to move me around from location to location. The film was about a man and his wife who hadn't driven on the road since nineteen thirty four and they kept getting into trouble with the police because the law and driving conditions had changed. In the last bit, we were caught speeding through a village and the police ended up towing us home.

Oh yes, talking of speeding, I haven't laughed so much in years.

This morning, Her Ladyship stormed out of her house and headed for The Grey One's shed. She was fuming and waving a piece of paper.

'Now look what you've gone and done,' cried Her Ladyship as she waved the piece of paper at his windscreen. 'Thirty six miles an hour. You're going to get me fined now you Bloody Old Fool.' Then she stormed back into the house, leaving a somewhat shocked looking Grey One staring blankly across the yard.

Curiosity overtook me and I enquired what happened. 'Well M'dear, it was after that Rally. Few weeks back don't you know…' I nod. 'The Memsahib had arranged for me to be left with your Mister Arthur in Pontarddulais. A few days later she came back to drive me home. Now, there's this very steep hill out of that town and we had to climb that, but for a chap like me who has been over the Andes, don't you know…'

'Yes, yes, yes. Forget your blooming "driven round the world and crossed the Andes don't you know" and get on with it. What about your speeding?'

'Well M'dear, we reached the top of the hill, a steep one don't you know and I had started to speed up, when the Memsahib noticed this speed van. She checks my speedo and says, "We're okay Sir H. We're only a couple of miles over the limit. They won't do us for that." Well, the rest as they say appears to have been history and this morning the Mem gets the summons. Didn't know I still had a bit of lead in my pencil and now I'm in trouble.'

'You? Done for speeding?' I could feel the laughter welling up inside me and seeing his crestfallen look I tried to suppress it. I really tried. But then it all burst forth and I haven't stopped laughing since. Every time I see him, I start all over again. He keeps telling me that he can't see what is so damned funny and that just makes me worse. At least the only time I was caught speeding, was for a film.

It was a couple of years after that little filming escapade that we all moved to Bristol. James Peters had been offered promotion. He came out to me one morning. 'Someone is coming to value you today, it's for the insurance cover for your move.' The man duly arrived, examined every nook and cranny of me and took photographs.

'Well,' he said. I will send you a letter for the insurers, but off the top of my head, I would say that this car is worth about two and a half thousand pounds? TWO THOUSAND FIVE HUNDRED POUNDS? I was astonished enough when James Peters paid three hundred and fifty pounds for me, but now several years since my restoration, I was being valued at two thousand five hundred pounds. The world was really going mad.

★★★★★

'This trip to Spain is going to be jolly good fun,' Her Ladyship announces as she gives me a good wash and a polish. 'Sun, sangria and sex. Well maybe not the sex. Too old for that now, I think more siesta than sex at my age, don't you?' Well, jolly, good and fun it may be for her. But for me it will be a 1,500 mile haul up and down the Cantabrian Mountains and on top of that, I am told that the Spanish, like the French, drive on the wrong side of the road. I do sometimes wonder why these continentals insist on doing that. Maybe it's because it's called the right side. I mean it's the wrong side. It's all so confusing.

'Got to make sure you're fit for Spain,' shouts Her Ladyship as we drive into the Pembrokeshire countryside. 'Remember, this Spanish trip will be your very last big one before we head off round the world next spring. Oh I haven't told you have I? Still no joy from that Smales man. Wasted promises if you ask me. Sponsorship indeed. Anyway, I've decided that we'll do it without his help.'

It is the middle of August, the sun is shining and the roads are crowded. Her Ladyship is out for lunch with her friend, The Nice

Mister Chris. By some bizarre arrangement, they are both out for their respective birthday lunches and he is supposed to be getting a chance to drive me before we go to Spain, but she still has her hands firmly on my steering wheel and if you ask me, has no intention of letting him have a go. Uh, oh, she's checking her speedometer again. She's been doing this rather a lot recently. Ever since The Grey One roared past that speed camera at thirty six miles an hour, Her Ladyship has become overly nervous of being caught again.

'Do you think I should pull in to let all these cars past?'

'Good God no,' ventures The Nice Mister Chris. 'My dear girl, let them wait. These roads are not safe enough for a car to go any faster.' Madam is now anxiously looking in her mirror.

'My God, there's a Chelsea tractor racing up on the outside and overtaking everyone.'

'Stupid idiot,' remarks The Nice Mister Chris turning round to take a look.

The Chelsea tractor is forced by an approaching car to swing in behind us and then gets as close as he can to my rear end. Madam has clenched her teeth meaning she's not pulling over. We hear shouting. 'Get out of the bloody way. Bloody move over.'

Madam clenches her teeth even more and keeps me firmly on the road. There's nowhere to pull over even if she wanted to and the Chelsea tractor gets even closer and starts to blow its horn. I can feel the heat of his engine.

'Hold steady Old Girl,' says The Nice Mister Chris. 'Don't be bullied by this twit.' We swing around a bend and there is a straight road ahead of us; it's clear and the Chelsea tractor lurches across to the wrong side of the road and roars past us, making that two finger gesture that suggests that he finds fault with Her Ladyship's driving.

'Hmmph,' she snorts. 'No sign of the bloody police when some idiot like that drives like a hooligan.'

'Let's find a place to lunch,' says The Nice Mister Chris.

'Good idea' she agrees. And I have to say that I go along with that idea as well. I need to recover.

★★★★★

Life with James Peters became rather boring after we moved to Bristol. We did go to the odd car show and on the odd run, but he had become obsessed with the restoration bug and was spending most of his time restoring other beaten up old relatives. But these he would sell on as soon as he finished them. He would drive them for a few weeks just to make sure they were working properly and then they were gone. That done, he turned his attention to his next project. For some reason he always hung on to me. I found that strange. So did Bea.

'Why don't you get rid of Daisy?' she asked one morning as he was removing the engine from his latest restoration project. 'It would give you a lot more room in the garage.'

'I don't know, but somehow I want to hang on to her. She was my first restoration and I suppose that makes her rather special. I suppose I should take her out more, but when I get my teeth into a new project, I become a bit blinkered about it and I want to get that job finished. Tell you what, why don't we take her out on Sunday? The children would love a day out.'

'Oh, you've remembered that you have children then.' That was rather barbed, especially from Bea. She was normally a quiet and gentle woman who wouldn't say boo to a goose, but I had noticed that she had been a bit cold towards James Peters for a while.

'Come on Bea.' He stepped back from his latest project and looked at her. 'That's not fair.'

'It's very fair actually. We hardly see you nowadays. You're doing longer hours at work since we moved down from the Midlands and then, when you come home you get straight into your overalls and play with your cars. You seem to have no time for me and the kids anymore.' She marched out of the garage back in to the house. She was right, I might have been under covers, but I think I saw more of him than anyone else did.

★★★★★

'Good morning Miss Daisy'. Her Ladyship cries as she flings open the garage door. 'It's a nice day for the Round Pembrokeshire Run.' Oh how I hate it when she is in one of her bright and breezy moods. She's got that needle sharp look in her eye again. There's no point arguing with her. On these occasions she is right, always right and even if you can prove she's wrong… she's still right.

'Anyway, we are only three weeks away from the Spanish trip, so we are going to treat today as our final test run. It's going to be a hundred miles and since that is what I shall be expecting of you every day when we head off to the land of flamenco, castanets and Boleros, this will be good for you.'

How do you respond to that? Quite simply you can't, and within minutes I'm out of the garage and waiting expectantly in the hazy morning sunshine.

'Now,' she says, 'I'm going to fit you up with the Sat Nav. I need to be sure it's working properly for Spain. I didn't have time when I cleaned your brakes the other day.' How could I forget the day she tried to clean my brakes with a high speed wire brush indeed? They've not felt right since. But you, Madam, wouldn't know that would you? Why couldn't you have just left me alone? My brakes were working perfectly well. But no. Someone just has to fiddle.

Then we're off to the start of the run. There may only be a week or so to go before the Spanish trip, but Madam's fiddling with my brakes might just save me from having to go at all. I mean, if my brakes are still playing up, I imagine she will have to take the Grey One instead? Old 'been round the world don't you know' is far more used to journeys like that and if I'm lucky, he'll break down and have to be left there. I am sure he could be cut up and used in the foundations of a new Spanish motorway or something.

We arrive at the starting point but every time she applies my brakes, I feel a terrible cramp in my wheels and I sound worse than Her Ladyship breaking wind; far worse. God it's painful and it's really noisy, every rivet, nut and bolt in my body vibrate every time she touches the brake pedal. On the odd occasion I thought I was going to fall to pieces. But Madam ploughs on regardless.

We are barely half way round the tour and Her Ladyship decides that we should withdraw from the run and head for home. I can tell that she is upset at having to make this decision, but with my brakes as they are, even she cannot insist that we continue like this.

But by the time we get home, Madam is undaunted. 'I am not going to let this go Miss Daisy,' and she's on the phone to The Nice Mr Arthur. 'Bring her over,' he says, 'we can sort out this little problem. It won't take long.'

Blast. Foiled again! Who will save me from this meddlesome woman? Now where have I heard that said before?

★★★★★

The relationship between James and Bea Peters got progressively worse. Mind you, I thought she had the patience of a saint with him. He was still spending just about every spare minute in the garage with his latest project. I lost count of just how many. Then on a few occasions each year, I would be hauled out for some trip or another with Bea and the children. But on every trip you could cut the atmosphere with a knife. Bea only appeared to agree to come along for the sake of the children who loved having rides in me.

But James Peters wasn't looking after me properly either. I was beginning to feel weak on these runs and there seemed to be a problem with my engine that he hadn't spotted when he originally stripped it down. Now though, he just couldn't be bothered to investigate. With my bad engine, he gradually lost interest in taking me out anymore. I had lived with him for seventeen years and for the last four of those I sat in his garage under a dustsheet. That was until one morning six years ago.

'Hello Daisy,' he said as he came in to my garage and whipped my covers off one morning. 'I'm afraid that I'm going to have to let you go. Bea and I are getting a divorce and I shall be moving to Norwich. I won't have a garage at the new place, so I am afraid you can't come with me. I was talking to a lady from Cardiff last night and she has offered me three thousand five hundred pounds for you. You're worth more than that, but I think that's the best price I can get at short notice and especially with your engine like it is. She's a bit eccentric, but I'm sure you'll like her.'

I had hardly listened to him. I still couldn't get used to the fact that the older I got, the more I became worth and it seemed that it no longer mattered what state I was in.

A few days later, on my seventieth birthday, I was rolled out of James Peters' garage for the last time and got ready for the gruelling drive to Cardiff. A friend of James Peters followed in a modern car and I couldn't help noticing him put a rope in its boot just along with a spare can of oil just before we left.

'It's just in case, Daisy,' he said. 'I'm sure you'll manage this journey on your own, but if we do break down, we can still get you to your destination.'

Well it was a horrible drive. I was making horrible noises and for some reason I couldn't do much more than thirty miles an hour.

As soon as we crossed the Severn Bridge, James Peters pulled me off the motorway and we continued on to Cardiff on the ordinary roads. 'You can do it Daisy, come on, you can do it. Come on Old Girl, nearly there.' It took us over three hours to get to the home of my new owner and that, dear friends, is how Her Ladyship came into my life with her host of barmy schemes that have brought me to this point in my life. After seven years with her, I still haven't had a chance to write my memoirs.

'So, here we are,' says Her Ladyship as she loads me up with everything but the kitchen sink. 'Spain today, tomorrow the world. Tell you what though; I'm taking no chances, so we are loading you up with plenty of spares. I think we'll be covered for just about any normal breakdown. I'll put in a couple of fire extinguishers as well. Well, you never know.'

Fire extinguishers? What the hell does she think is going to happen? Are we going to be torched by rioting Spaniards?

'Oh yes, there's something else. I've had to have you revalued for the insurance cover in Spain. It seems that you are worth seven and a half thousand pounds now. Can you imagine it?'

Well to be honest, nothing surprises me any more. Seven years with Her Ladyship has taught me never to be surprised. But to be valued as being worth what seventy five of me would have been worth when I was born is just ridiculous.

'Oh, and there's another thing. You know Chris don't you?' Ah yes, The Nice Mister Chris. He always drives me so carefully. 'I'm afraid that he won't be coming with us now. He's been taken ill. So you're going to have to put up with just me. If it's any consolation, you won't have to carry his luggage as well as mine.'

Now that is a shame, The Nice Mister Chris not coming with us. He would have made the journey so much more enjoyable. Anyway we can be pretty sure that she will have packed enough luggage for more than one person.

It's early on Thursday when we leave Pembrokeshire. Her

Ladyship fills me up with petrol and we start east, briefly pausing at the motorway services for The Lady to join us. It's good to see The Lady again; indeed it's good to see The Nice Mister Mike and Missus Sue. I haven't seen them since we all trotted off to Normandy last year. I like The Lady, but she isn't quite one of us. She's American you see, a child of Detroit. But I won't hold that against her. I usually get on quite well with foreigners, but that is still no reason to drag me off to foreign parts.

Anyway, before I can blink, we're off again, this time heading for Portsmouth. 'Don't worry Old Girl,' shouts Her Ladyship as we trot up the motorway. 'Only a hundred and fifty miles to go. After this one, it'll be much shorter hops each day.'

Only a hundred and fifty miles indeed, we've already done seventy five. That's two hundred and twenty five if my sums are correct. That is a ridiculous amount of mileage to try to complete in one day. Gosh, back with the Johnstons, a round trip of fifty miles was quite enough. Her Ladyship promised 'we definitely won't do more than a hundred and fifty miles a day Old Girl'. Well so much for her promise and, indeed, her mathematics.

We are driving past Bath when my first little incident happens. Her Ladyship slows down and pulls me over into a parking area. The Lady pulls in closely behind us.

'It looks as though Miss Daisy has stopped charging her battery,' Her Ladyship shouts towards The Nice Mister Mike. 'The red light is on. I will have a quick look-see, but it shouldn't be a problem. I packed a battery charger actually.' Blast the woman, she thinks of everything doesn't she?

Madam spends about ten minutes fiddling and poking her finger, then a cloth, into my dynamo. 'It's your pacemaker Old Girl,' she says. 'You're not pumping electricity around your system. No matter, we'll carry on.' She climbs back in and we drive on to Portsmouth.

The rest of our party join us the next morning. The Nice Mister and Missus Richard, I've not met them before, arrive in a relative that looks rather like me, except she has no doors. Mind you, judging by the way they have equipped themselves, what with all the canvas bags, tents, pots and pans, I get the feeling that they have done trips like this before. Anyway, I hope I can be parked close to this cousin. It wouldn't be polite if I didn't have a chat with her.

Are my eyes deceiving me? Oh joy of joys, that's The Nice Mister Arthur and his family arriving in their Land Rover. 'Where's Ruby then?' Her Ladyship seems a bit concerned.

'Too small for the four of us,' replies The Nice Mister Arthur. 'All this camping gear, it would have required two Sevens. This is more convenient. Anyway, one of you is bound to need a tow before long.' The sight of The Nice Mister Arthur's family cheer me up no end, as it's usually The Nice Mister Arthur who has sorted me out when Her Ladyship messes me up. He's much more sensible, more down to earth. Now I know that he's on this run with us, perhaps I might get back from Spain alive.

I've done ferry crossings before and to be honest, they really are not much fun for us motor cars. You sit on this damp deck for heaven knows how long in close proximity to one another, while our drivers are up above, thoroughly enjoying themselves, eating and drinking the night away. Although in fairness Madam does pop down just before we sail.

'Hello Old Girl. Are you okay? Comfy? I've had a look around; it's a rather smart ship you know. They even have a swimming pool and a promenade deck with comfy wicker chairs to sit in to watch the sunset. It reminds me rather of that film about the Titanic. They had wicker chairs on the promenade deck as well.' That is all I want to hear. I suppose now we are going to collide with an iceberg and sink in the Bay of Biscay.

As it happens, I cannot sleep. Not only is it rather choppy, I am spending the entire journey with my nose stuck up the bottom of a Chelsea tractor, complete with spray-on mud. But worst of all, these damned vehicles keep letting their alarms go off. Parked next to me though is The Nice Mister and Missus Richard's car. So at least I can pass some of this awful journey in conversation with her.

'Hello,' say I. 'What's your name?'

'Don't have a name. Don't need a name,' comes the brief reply.

'What do you mean? All my relatives have names. Even The Grey One back home. He's called Sir Herbert. You've got to have a name.'

'Well I don't.'

'So have you done trips like this before?'

'Yup.'

'Well, where have you been?'

'Oh, Crossed the Andes, done Corsica and we did Route Sixty Six.'

'You've been down Route Sixty Six?' I have to sound impressed, although for the life of me I've never heard of it and I think any talk of the Andes will bring thoughts of old 'Don't You Know' to my mind and I certainly don't want to dwell on that.

'Yup.'

'What was it like?'

'Hot, flat and straight.'

'Gosh that must have been interesting.'

'Nope.'

'You are not one for using words are you?'

'Nope.' And that is it, my entire conversation for the whole trip with this relative, who I think I'll christen Grumpy.

When Madam returns the next morning, she looks a bit peaky. 'Well that was a crossing and a half,' she mutters as she lowers her frame gently onto my driving seat. Then as she sets The Satellite Thingy and we drive off the ferry, she starts to mutter to herself,

'Keep to the right, keep to the right, drive on the right.' We pass two grinning policemen who seem more interested in a couple of young women than Her Ladyship's passport and before we know it, we are out of the port and into the town. My first experience of the land of castanets is that it seems rather like France. Everyone as expected is driving on the wrong side of the road again, but the locals do seem to be a bit more excitable than the French. Perhaps it's the heat. For example, here we are, all in a tidy convoy and as we pass down the main street suddenly, what had hitherto been a quiet shopping centre, turns into bedlam. People spill out of the cafés and shops to look at us. Some applaud us, some even cheer us on; others wander into the road to take our pictures. How friendly these strange people are. Is the whole trip going to be like this? Hopefully if it isn't that gruelling, I might enjoy myself. Then everything is ruined by the voice of the Satellite Thingy. 'Make a U Turn if possible and take the first left.' I'm quickly brought down to earth as I realise that we've taken a wrong turn and since Her Ladyship cannot navigate herself out of a circus ring even with the help of The Satellite Thingy, we are about to become lost. Oh brilliant, we've completed just two miles and we still have another thousand to go.

We arrive at the campsite and out of the reception wanders an elderly man. 'Hola,' says Her Ladyship. I never realised she could speak Spanish. Well it quickly transpires that I was right. She can't…

'Hola Señor. You haff zee bungalows reservée pour us?'

'Moment señora. Sophia! Sophia!' A young woman appears from another office. 'Señora, ésta es mi esposa. Thees ees my wife. She is Sophia. I am José, si?' We all stare from José to Sophia and back again. José must have been in his seventies and his wife barely into her twenties. On top of that Sophia has a baby in a pram and a toddler at her side.

'My goodness, I've seen some child brides in my time,' Her Ladyship says to the others as she parks me up beside the chalet a few moments later. 'But this one takes the biscuit. Do you think it's Spain's several hundred ways of cooking octopus that's putting lead into his pencil? Because I'm really impressed. Now let's get the old girl plugged in and we can charge up her battery. Then I'm off to the restaurant for supper. Anyone care to join me?' Everyone decides that is a good idea.

Her Ladyship is the last to return that evening and without doubt she is the worse for wear. 'Hello Old Girl,' she slurs. 'Whoops! Shhh.' She puts her finger to her lips. 'Shhhh. Quiet Old Girl. Quiet. Our friend José was in the bar with the Child Bride. It's all his fault that I'm a bit tiddly. He kept plying me glasses of white port. "Eet's from my private supply, eet comes from Portugal", he kept saying to me as he poured yet another glass. Shhh, Old Girl. Don't make so much noise. You'll wake everyone up. And another thing, I met a really charming man called Alfonso. He was there with José and the way the Child Bride was looking at him you would think that he was the father of her children. He's younger than José you know; much younger. Anyway, he thinks you are a very nice car. A very, very nice car. So what do you think of that?'

Look at me. Do I look as though I care whether he thinks I am 'a very nice car' or not? She ignores me.

'Yes he's really charming. Whoops, who put that cable there? Oh it was me wasn't it?'

Go to bed woman, you are embarrassing me and I'm tired. Anyway, was he trying to seduce you? Or you, him?

The next morning she rushes out of the chalet scratching her arms. 'Little bastards, little effing bastards. Look at me; I'm covered in mosquito bites.

'Well,' said The Nice Missus Sue, who is always really sensible in these matters. 'If you insist on leaving your window wide open when we're only feet from a stagnant swimming pool, what do you expect?'

Her Ladyship harrumphs and proceeds to unplug me from the mains. So, no hangover here then?

We have barely waved goodbye to the Child Bride and hit the road to our next destination when Madam pulls me over.

'There's something wrong with the brake lights,' she calls out to The Nice Mister Arthur. 'They seem to be on all the time.' Well to be honest they aren't exactly that. They are on when she's driving along and they go off when she puts her foot on the brakes. The Nice Mister Arthur clambers underneath me to fiddle with my nether regions.

'Try that', he calls out. 'No? How about this?' and 'Try it now'.

'Still not right,' cries Her Ladyship. The Nice Mister Arthur decides to set them so they don't come on at all.

'It'll save your battery,' he says. 'We'll have a proper go at them later. Hang on a mo.' He fiddles with something in another part of my anatomy and the brake lights start to work properly. Well, for some of the time anyway!

Then we are off again, on the first stage of what over the next six days is supposed to be a series of easy trips of, what was it she said again? Oh yes… no more than a hundred and fifty miles a day. What she failed to mention at the time was that we have to cross the Cantabrian Mountain range to get to Santiago de Compostela and that means we are going to have to cover as many miles up and down as we will endeavour to achieve horizontally. We haul ourselves up a mountain and then roll down the other side, not once, but on about four occasions every blooming day and these are not pretty little mountain passes with a café on top. Oh no, we are driving up through the clouds where the vegetation seems to disappear and that which does thrive grows horizontally.

'Blow me, this one is over a thousand feet higher than Snowdon,' she announces as we pull over on to some hard standing. 'Well done Old Girl. Now you've climbed this one, you can climb anything.' I just don't want to think about it, I'm just glad of the opportunity to have a rest and now I think I am suffering from altitude sickness, although I am not absolutely sure what that is. Put it like this, after fifteen minutes, Madam decides it's time to leave, but my engine won't start. So what does she do? She asks the others to give me a shove and we roll down the other side of the mountain.

'Air's a bit thin up here. We've plenty of time to get you started again,' Madam shouts as we head downward going faster and faster. 'Oooh hell, that bend was rather sharp… God here's another one. Brakes, Old Girl, brakes. Oooooooh, that was close.' I feel that in the interests of my own safety and I suppose that of my occupant, it is time to let my engine start again. Two cylinders, then the third and finally the fourth. 'Well done Old Girl,' Her Ladyship shouts. 'I knew you'd get going again eventually.'

We finally arrive at our next stopover, a place called Gijon. Well that is how it is spelt, but everyone seems to call it 'Hihon'. Strange language these Spaniards have. As Madam parks me up and plugs me in to the battery charger again, The Nice Mister Arthur wanders over to ask after my health, specifically the state of my pacemaker and to add that he was following us earlier and my brake lights were still misbehaving. At that he clambers underneath my undercarriage and fiddles with the same thing he had fiddled with earlier.

'That should be all right now,' he says wiping the oil off his hands. Madam thanks him graciously, adding that if he is now happy and doesn't need her assistance any further she is going to go for a swim.

I find it nearly impossible to describe the sight that passes before me five minutes after that announcement. An apparition appears in a shocking pink swimsuit and wrapped in a towel.

'There's no need to look at me like that Old Girl. I enjoy the occasional swim, seriously, I do. It may be nearly October, but it's a lovely warm and sunny day and we are much further south than the UK.'

Consider this. Her Ladyship is not gone for very long. It should have taken her about five minutes to reach the swimming pool and five minutes to get back. So when she returns barely fifteen minutes later wrapped in her wet towel and shivering, I am not surprised. Madam is not one for jumping into a pool and immediately swimming ten lengths. She is one of those people who take an absolute age to get in, slowly allowing the water to work its way up her body. So I imagine that it took her several minutes to get in and having decided it was far too damned cold, she got straight out again and returned to the warmth of her bungalow.

'I feel much better for that Old Girl. A few lengths… excellent for one's health.' And she's gone inside, into the warm. You can draw your own conclusion, but I don't think she quite adopted the spirit of Dunkirk on this occasion.

We all have the next day off. I sit happily in the sunshine plugged into my battery charger again and it really feels good as the volts trickle in to brighten me up. Her Ladyship and her friends decide to head into 'Hihon' on a bus. Madam apparently tries to flash her pensioner's bus pass at the driver, he in turn gives her a blank look and she has to cough up a couple of Euros to pay for her ticket. When she returns later she is still muttering something about typical blasted foreigners, fleecing poor British pensioners.

We are on our way again the next morning, more mountains and indeed our next stopover is to be a little place called A Fonsagrada, a village so high up in the mountains that the clouds will be several hundred feet below us. This time Her Ladyship sets The Satellite Thingy to avoid motorways and also to take the shortest possible route and bugger the consequences. I don't think this is a very good idea, especially in rural Spain. The 'shortest possible route' seems to mean that we can travel on anything that could loosely describe itself as a road and on several occasions we find ourselves turning off onto what are really no more than dirt tracks, in fact tracks that wind themselves up and down mountain sides with sheer rock towering up above us to one side and sheer drops of several hundred feet to the other side of us. Then to top it all, I find myself scattering chickens as we hurtle through what seems to be somebody's farmyard. So when we finally pull up at our campsite in A Fonsagrada, Her Ladyship is the recipient of many a black look from the others. She does her best to blame The Satellite Thingy with a shrug of her shoulders.

The following morning, I am just sitting there enjoying the warmth of the rising sun when someone releases my handbrake and starts to roll me away. What? What's going on here? Am I being car-napped? But no, it's The Nice Mister Arthur, puffing and panting as he pushes me towards his Landrover. Her Ladyship appears in a state of semi undress. 'We're going to change over this dynamo,' he announces. It seems to me that The Nice Mister Arthur is never happier than when he is plunging his hands into an engine compartment like mine. I think it must be a man thing, I find that most of them like doing that. Not Her Ladyship though. She touches something oily and immediately has to find a cloth with which to wipe her hands clean again. Still, two hours later, I feel brilliant again and I can feel the life blood passing through my own wires once more.

'There you are Old Girl,' she says. 'Your pacemaker is working again. We can put the battery charger away now.'

But no sooner have they fixed my pacemaker when The Lady complains about not feeling well. 'Her dynamo has stopped charging now,' announces The Nice Mister Mike.

'Must be catching,' adds Her Ladyship chuckling. No one else thought that was very funny.

So with The Lady now suffering from a lack of volts, we embark on our last hop to Santiago de Compostela. 'Just one hundred and forty three miles to go Old Girl, then we'll have made it.' Her

Ladyship appears triumphant as she presses the buttons on The Satellite Thingy. 'Let's see where this will take us today.'

Well, it all goes really well until, that is, we are within spitting distance of Santiago. We arrive at what appears to be a very new roundabout. 'At the roundabout, take the first exit,' barks the Satellite Thingy.

'What? But the sign says Santiago is the second exit, straight ahead. What's this damned thing trying to do?' Madam is quite flustered and for some bizarre reason she's tapping the screen, then at the last minute she decides to follow the command. This turns out to be a rather bad decision as we are suddenly taken on a twelve mile journey through a forest and narrow lanes before being dumped at a junction by a major road with so much traffic on it I cannot move forwards nor, as it transpires, can I move backwards. The Lady is stopped directly behind me. Her battery is completely flat. She cannot even produce enough electricity for a spark. An audience of local Spaniards quickly gather around us. They appear to be highly amused by our predicament. Then The Nice Mister Arthur announces that he has an idea that should get The Lady going again.

But first I have to get out of the way, so with a lot of hand waving and smiling at the traffic racing in both directions in front of us, Her Ladyship manages to manoeuvre me out onto the main road, point me in the direction of Santiago and park me at the side of the road. In the meantime, The Nice Mister Arthur puts his finishing touches with The Lady into effect and then everyone, including the locals, pushes her a little way back up the hill from whence we had come so she can roll forwards for a jump start.

'Now we do have a problem,' The Nice Mister Arthur explains. 'Once we are back in our vehicles, we'll have no one to stop the traffic for us. Somehow I don't think we'll get the locals to understand what we want to do.'

'No problem, I've got an idea to get you all out,' Her Ladyship announces. 'I'll go and use that pedestrian crossing up there and I'll take my time crossing the road. Then when the traffic stops, you can all pull out. How about that?'

'Well I suppose it is worth a try. At this stage quite frankly anything is worth a try,' says The Nice Mister Richard climbing back into Grumpy. How naïve of Her Ladyship. How naïve she is to assume that Spanish drivers will stop for her to cross the road. She tries a few times but every time she ventures a foot on to the road, they completely ignore her and continue to roar past in both directions. Then she has another idea and she trots back towards me. She grabs her walking stick and a pair of dark sunglasses before returning to the crossing.

'Watch this,' she shouts to the others. 'This should work.' To everyone's astonishment she dons the dark glasses and pretending to be blind, she pokes her stick around as if looking for the edge of the pavement. The scene before us becomes like a frozen film frame as the traffic stops dead and a man in the car nearest to her gets out, takes her arm and starts to escort her over the road. 'Go, go, go,' she shouts to the others. 'Get those cars behind Miss Daisy.' To my profound amazement, and I have to admit a degree of admiration, the others are all able to pull out of the side road and park behind me.

'Mucho gracias Señor, mucho gracias.' The man nods his head, makes sure that Madam is safely perched on the pavement again and goes back to his car.

'How about that then folks? I got you all out.' Madam has a broad grin on her face as she whips off her sunglasses and waves her walking stick in the air. Unfortunately the man who had helped her across the road, realises that he has been duped and what he shouts before he gets back into his car and drive off is probably unrepeatable, but since I don't understand Spanish I suppose it doesn't really matter. Now we have just one more very small problem. We, the humans and cars, are sitting in a lay by on one side of the road facing Santiago de Compostela and Her Ladyship is stranded on the other side. Somehow, I'm not surprised that the Spanish traffic does not seem that keen on letting her cross again.

We finally limp into the campsite in Santiago and The Lady is manoeuvred into a parking space beside our bungalow. Her Ladyship produces my battery charger, not for me this time, but for The Lady.

'Right Old Girl,' Her Ladyship says as she settles me in for the night. 'Early start tomorrow. Photo call at eight in the morning, in front of the Cathedral.' Photo call? I know nothing about a photo call. Get me cleaned up woman, give me a wash and a polish. I can't do a photo call in this state.

At that point, she is distracted by the sound of the pop of a cork being extracted from a wine bottle by The Nice Missus Sue and any thought of cleaning me disappears along with the sunset. It reminds me of the Asthmatic Barking Dog responding to the sound of his food being served. Her ears prick up and almost miraculously she manages to produce a glass from nowhere and plunges it towards the neck of the open bottle and that is the last I see of her.

True to form at eight o'clock the next morning we are all lined up on the square in front of Santiago's cathedral.

'Hurry up everyone,' cries Her Ladyship. 'The authorities say that we have to be out of here by five past.' Unfortunately there is one tiny little snag. It's still dark, in fact it's pitch black, apart from the small pools of yellow light under each street lamp and the cathedral itself being illuminated by floodlights. So Madam wanders round smiling at the local Civil Guard and occasionally staring skywards, trying to will God to turn the sun on.

'Do you think I should go and talk to the police to see if they'll let us stay a little longer, at least until the light improves?' The others shake their heads.

'Leave it,' says The Nice Mister Richard. 'They'll tell us to move on when they're ready. Keep taking pictures and hopefully we'll get a decent one before they move us on.'

With photographs taken we leave the square. Suddenly I don't feel very well. I have no energy to climb the hill back to the campsite. 'What's up Old Girl?' Her Ladyship appears concerned. Well I am hardly surprised, here we are, as far as we can be from home, I am unwell and I think that Madam is worried that she might have to call the rescue service to trailer me home. I am allowed to rest for the remainder of the day. I think Her Ladyship thinks that a day's rest will bring back my strength.

Next morning she is loading me up again.

'We're going north today Old Girl, up to the coast. No more mountains to climb now. Well no high ones. We'll start on our journey home now. I've set the Sat Nav to avoid motorways, but to take the quickest rather than the shortest route, so no more farmyards or chickens either. That should be a lot easier for you.' She shouts across at the others.

'We'll head north east on the N634 to Ribadeo and all being well, we should reach the coast some time after lunch.' She manoeuvres her frame into my driving seat and we are off.

At first the road signs seem to agree with what The Satellite Thingy tells her, but then we stumble across a roundabout that isn't supposed to be there. It thinks we are still on the N634. But this rather new roundabout has one exit leading to a motorway and the other exit is unmarked.

'Where do we go now?' Madam shouts at The Satellite Thingy. 'Where the hell do we go now? We don't want to go to A Coruna on the motorway, we want the blooming six three four to Ribadeo!'

So Madam decides to circumnavigate the roundabout a couple of times before finally heading me out onto the unmarked road.

'This is the way,' she shouts triumphantly at no one in particular.

'This is the way. Look even the sat nav agrees.' I'm not so sure, mainly because when she's that sure she's right, she is usually wrong. The road becomes a narrow lane and to our right a high barbed wire fence looms over us. We pass a sort of watchtower with a notice suggesting that we are entering a secure area and worse than that, I spot a sign that suggests we are driving beside a Spanish Air Force base.

'Oh dear, I wonder if we should be here?' Madam is suddenly subdued; the earlier spark of confidence has disappeared. Then up ahead I spot a vehicle with blue lights on top and a sign on the back saying they are the Civil Guard and from the rear seats two men are watching us following along behind them.

Her Ladyship spots them as well.

'I really don't think we should be on this road. Oh God we're heading for twenty years in a Spanish prison for spying and there is nowhere to turn round. Tell you what Old Girl, act innocent. They'll probably leave us alone then.'

The vehicle ahead pulls up and four uniformed men, all wearing sunglasses get out and line themselves up across the road, their right hands gripping their gun holsters and awaiting our approach. Madam applies my brakes; The Lady pulls up behind us, Grumpy behind her and The Nice Mister Arthur's Land Rover behind them. Her Ladyship gets out and gestures to the others to stay where they are.

'I'll handle this,' she calls to them. 'It'll be absolutely fine'. She then mutters, 'Well, I hope it will be fine.' She turns to the Civil Guard. 'Good Morning Constables. I mean Bueno Dias Señors.' She smiles nervously.

One of the uniformed men unclips his holster and starts to finger his pistol. 'Hola señora, puede usted decirme lo que usted está haciendo aquí?'

'Umm what? Sorry, No comprende, no speakie Espagnol. Speakie English?' One of the men curls his lip and flicks his head skywards in acknowledgment. 'Oh Good, I'll take that as a yes then.

Well we thought we were on the N364, you know? The road to Ribadeo? Well that's the road the Satellite Navigation said we were on. You are welcome to take a look inside my car. Sorry are we in a restricted area? Oh God, now what?'

The man with the curled lip speaks to his comrades.

'La vaca vieja dice que están perdidos. Han tomado una vuelta incorrecta. ¿Dios que ella es fea es ella no?' They all burst out laughing and somehow I don't think what he said was exactly complimentary about Her Ladyship. Doesn't vaca mean cow?

'Don't worry señora, we will show you the way back to the road you want.'

'Oh, thank you, thank you, thank you. We are so grateful.' What a creep she is. I wonder if there has ever been a female version of Uriah Heep.

'Follow us señora. Eet's not far.' They get back into their vehicle and head on up the track.

'It's all okay,' she shouts back to the others. 'I've sorted it with these chaps. We are to follow them.' Then in she hops, starts me up and off we go, the Spanish Civil Guard followed by three vintage cars and a Land Rover. We must be a sight as we weave our way along what is by now no more than a grass track. Eventually the Civil Guard pulls over and one of them gets out and gestures us to follow the track a bit further where I presume we will find the road we want. We eventually arrive at a brand new stretch of road. Unfortunately there is no actual road junction from our track on to the new road, no simple way for us to just hop onto it. There is about five feet of very rough ground between us and the road we want. Where the rough ground comes to an end we have to climb about five inches over some hard core before we can reach the tarmac of the new road. This might be all very well if the carriageway we want was on our side. But no, we now have to wait for a gap in the traffic to drive across that carriageway to join the northbound one.

'Well Old Girl, at least there is no central barrier. Road's clear, so here goes…' She manoeuvres me over the rough ground and, checking there are no cars coming either way, we shoot across to the carriageway. I will never know, but I bet she shut her eyes for that manoeuvre. The others follow anxiously, then we are on our way north again.

'Whew,' mutters Her Ladyship. 'That was a close one. Come on Old Girl let's get on home.'

We are nearly at the north coast when Her Ladyship swings me into a café car park.

'How about here for a picnic lunch?' She shouts to the others as they pull up beside her.

The Nice Missus Sue isn't so sure.

'Don't you think the café owner might take offence if we picnic out here in his car park?'

'Good God no. I am sure they will be delighted that we are gracing them with our presence.' I do sometimes wonder whether Her Ladyship is on the same planet as the rest of us. 'Anyway, I need to use their loo.' At this point she marches in to the café. The conversation of the occupants of the café that has until now been so vociferously spilling out of the entrance suddenly goes very quiet. Everyone who is outside with me, look towards the entrance.

'Bonjour, I mean bueno dias Señor. I need to use your toilet Si?' The silence is deafening. Is this astonishment or has she interrupted a secret meeting of a branch of the Spanish Fascist party? I glance through the window at Her Ladyship and to my bewilderment she starts to smack her bottom, bending forwards slightly to stretch her jeans tightly over her anatomy.

'Sittee vous Señor, sittee vous.'

The barman and all his customers are, to a man, staring open mouthed at this vision of an elderly British woman now slapping her backside with renewed vigour. This apparition lasts several seconds before one of the customers gets the message. Unfortunately it's the wrong message as he jumps off his stool and leads Madam by the arm to a chair.

'No, no, no,' she cries, leaping to her feet again. 'I need to use the Señoras – the toilet, la toilette, toiletten, las damas.'

'Ah, si, si,' acknowledges the barman and with a broad grin crossing his face, he points to a door in the corner of the room. Her Ladyship disappears behind the door to peals of laughter from everyone present, then a few minutes later she returns, completely oblivious to the ribaldry that is now following her every move.

'Gracias Señor, mucho gracias.' The café owner says something that is followed by another great peal of laughter.

'Well that was easy. It's amazing how simple it is to communicate with these people when you can't speak their language.'

I have a feeling that those in our group are not very convinced; they're looking at her with expressions of total bewilderment.

'Anyway, I'm hungry, let's get on with our lunch, I am sure they won't mind.'

I think the café owner had decided that it is far better for 'Los locos Inglesis' to be outside having their picnic than causing chaos in his café. When the others feel brave enough, they too venture in to use the loo. This time the barman just shrugs his shoulders and points to the door in the corner.

'Come on, let's go,' Her Ladyship shouts after packing the picnic hamper away and easing herself back onto my driving seat. 'Not far to the camp site now. The Satellite Navigation has it all in hand.'

By now The Nice Missus Sue has given the Satellite Thingy the nickname Flora Dora. Quite frankly I think that 'Flipping Dumb' is a more appropriate epithet because a couple of miles before we reach our destination, the screen goes blank.

'What? What the hell is happening now? Where's it gone?

Where's the Sat Nav gone? Screen's gone blank. Switched itself off! Hellooo, anyone in there?'

She swings me into a service station and the others all obediently pull in behind us.

'I hope you haven't done this on purpose,' she snarls at me as she gets out. 'I know you don't approve of the thing, so you might think it funny, but I am not impressed.' Why is it always my fault when things go wrong?

'Sorry folks, we have a problem. The Sat Nav has given up the will to live. We'll have to try to find the place on a map.' The Nice Mister Arthur steps forward.

'Not to worry, ours knows where to go. We'll take the lead now.' So after a little shuffle around of cars, we are on our way again and moments later we reach our next destination.

It seems that The Nice Mister Mike is still having trouble with The Lady's dynamo. I feel sorry for her, but at least she is in his good hands. Unlike Her Ladyship, he knows what to do and within minutes he has whipped the dynamo out, stripped it down and is fixing it. Now why can't Madam do things like that?

After another day off in which Her Ladyship gives me a clean, tops up my oil and spends the rest of the day on the beach, we are once again on our way back towards the ferry, but we still have two more days of driving ahead of us and to be honest, I'm getting really fed up with it all. I'm still unwell; in fact I haven't felt right since we left Santiago. Everything seems to be a bit of a strain.

'You really are struggling this morning Old Girl, aren't you?' Oh finally, Her Ladyship has noticed and she pulls me over. She could have sorted this all out yesterday. But no, she was far too busy sunning herself on the beach. Everyone else pulls over behind me and as always when I have a problem, all the men in the party come over and poke their heads into my engine compartment. Her Ladyship moves around behind them like an anxious mother hen trying to peer over their shoulders to see what they are up to.

'Is the fuel coming through?' One of them, I couldn't see who, suddenly gropes down beside my engine. Excuse me but that tickles. 'Nope, there's plenty of fuel pumping through.'

'Is she sparking?' says another. 'Let's check the points.'

'They seem okay. Let's take a plug out and see if she's actually sparking? Anyone got a plug spanner?'

'I have.' It's Her Ladyship, suddenly pleased that she can contribute to my cure. 'Here it is.'

'God, look at the carbon on that.' The Nice Mister Arthur flashes my plug at the others. 'They're completely oiled up as well.' He turns to Madam. 'I'm surprised this car would even start. Don't you ever clean them?'

'I've got some spares. New ones.' Her Ladyship is burrowing under my passenger seat. 'Here they are.'

'Okay let's change them all.' There's more activity in my engine compartment, followed by, 'Right, let's try that.' Well that is much better, I feel a lot brighter. Madam packs up my tool kit and before I know it, we are on our way again.

'Only two hundred and fifty miles to go to the ferry now,' shouts Her Ladyship. 'Soon be home.'

After two more days of driving, we finally make it to the ferry port. Madam pulls us back into the same campsite from where we had started this journey nearly two weeks ago.

'Now where is everyone?' The place seems deserted. 'Helloo… hellooo… Anyone here?'

'Look at your watch. I reckon they are having a siesta,' says The Nice Mister Mike.

'Look, the bar's open,' says Her Ladyship. 'I'll see if anyone's in there.' She returns moments later with dear old José. He seems a little tired and emotional.

'¿Sophia, donde es usted? ¿Sophia?' He's looking vainly around, but Sophia is nowhere to be seen. He totters up the steps to the reception office.

'It seems that our friend has made an early start on his supply especial.' Her Ladyship grins to the others. 'I wonder where the Child Bride has got to. Isn't that Alfonso's car over there? Are you guys thinking what I'm thinking?'

José calls out again. 'Sophia?' No answer. 'I weel haf to check you een myself.' He heads behind the reception counter, trips over a mat and falls with a crash to the floor. 'Cójalo. Cójalo, cójalo, cójalo.' He clambers to his feet again. 'One bungalow? Numero uno.'

'Si.' Her Ladyship nods her head as he hands her the key. 'Is – that – the – same – one – as – last – time?' She speaks very slowly and deliberately as if she thinks he will understand her better.

'¿Qué?'

'Theee – bungalooow. Ees – eet – el – same – as – el last – time?' God give me strength, what is she trying to say?

'¿Qué?'

'Thank you, we'll find it.' Madam, having realised that further conversation is pointless leaves the reception with a 'See you tonight…' and dear old José totters back towards his white Port, which in his opinion has been interrupted for far too long.

'Didn't understand a word he said,' Her Ladyship announces. 'But it says Cabin Number One on the key fob.' She clambers in to me. 'Let's get you parked up Old Girl. We go back home on the ferry tomorrow afternoon.'

It is so nice to be back in Britain and what a lovely sunny morning greets me as I drive off the ferry. Madam is not in the best of moods.

'Big meal last night Old Girl, stuffed myself, couldn't get to sleep. Had a rough night.'

Harrumph, it was all right for you, I had to sit through a fifteen hour concert played on a cacophony of car alarms and now I am faced with a two hundred and fifty mile trip to get us both home. And what will you be doing your Ladyship? Let me see now... oh yes, sitting comfortably in the driving seat pointing me in the right direction. She swings me towards immigration and passport control.

'Had a good trip madam?' says the man at passport control with a smile. 'Did that old car get you to where you wanted to go?'

'Well, yes actually. She did brilliantly, I'm really proud of her. We had a few problems, but for a seventy six year old car, I'm just delighted that we've made it this far. Twelve hundred and fifty miles down and just two hundred and fifty miles to go.'

Am I hearing right? Is that Her Ladyship singing my praises? Surely not.

'Have you anything to declare madam?' We've reached the customs area and two bored customs officers are walking around and looking us over.

'Well yes actually. I have a fuel tank full of Spanish Brandy because Spanish petrol is such rubbish.' She thinks she is joking. Well she was joking, but obviously no one had told her that these two British customs officers who have had to get up really early to greet a ferry, tend to be seriously lacking in the sense of humour front. The looks of boredom vanish as fast as you can click your fingers.

'Would you get out of the car please, madam? Could you tell us where you have been please?'

Uh oh, here we go. I've heard that you never joke at customs officers, unless you want your car to be completely stripped.

'Thank you. Would you please stand over there?'

'It was only a joke. Umm there is a group of us and we've driven to Santiago de Compostela and back. Actually there really is petrol in the tank and I have just a bottle of brandy on the back seat. There, between those two cases.'

They aren't listening to her and they start to unload me. Cases, bags, coats, the fire extinguishers, the tool kits...

'And what do we have here?' They had removed my rear seat to reveal some packages.

'They are just the spare parts, I packed them in there before we left. There's a carburettor in there and a petrol pump, spare gaskets, ignition coil, distributor, that sort of thing. Nothing illegal, I assure you.'

I'm standing here with both my doors wide open and my entire contents spread all around me. Madam just stands there with her mouth moving as though she is trying to speak, but by now, nothing is coming out.

'I think we'd better do a strip search.' The senior man turns to his female colleague. 'Don't you agree Miss Simpson?' Did I detect a hint of a grin at that point? No... they wouldn't... these officers of Her Majesty's Customs and Excise would never... would they? Miss Simpson nods her head, looks very seriously at Her Ladyship and goes to open the door into their office.

The colour has completely drained from Madam's face.

'But, but, but...'

The male officer just couldn't control his grin anymore.

'You can load up your car again madam. You may go. Perhaps in future you won't make light of what you may or may not be bringing into the country.'

And they are gone, ready to have a chat with the driver of the next car.

Her Ladyship starts to put all her luggage back on to my rear seat as The Lady, followed by Grumpy and then The Nice Mister Arthur, all happily pass through the green lane.

'Well, I don't think that was very funny, do you Old Girl? Come on, we have a long way to go after this; I don't think we can achieve it in one day. Perhaps we can stop off somewhere.' She starts me up and we leave the port.

I notice him first. Then Her Ladyship spots him.

'Can you see that man over there Old Girl? Why is he waving at us?' True enough, several hundred yards away someone is waving frantically at us and pointing to a turning. 'I think it's Chris,' Her Ladyship adds after a moment. The Nice Mister Chris, what's he doing here I wonder. He's supposed to be unwell.

'Hello you two,' he says as Madam applies my brakes beside him. 'Swing down there, I have a trailer waiting for you.'

'Oh you are a sight for sore eyes,' says Her Ladyship. 'A sight for sore eyes indeed. But you're not well, you shouldn't have come all the way down here.'

'Oh I'm not feeling too bad at the moment, and anyway I thought I would surprise you. Let's haul Miss Daisy up onto the trailer and let me take you both home.'

So here I am, back at home tucked up in my garage with some one thousand plus miles added to my odometer. It's hardly surprising that I am filthy, dribbling oil and exhausted.

'Good Morning Old Girl.' Her Ladyship bursts in to disturb yet another period of peace and quiet. 'My, you are a bit of a mess aren't you? Don't worry; we'll soon get you cleaned up again. Let's clear all my stuff off your back seat. Tell you what; I have a quiet morning this morning. Once I've done this, I'll get you outside for a good wash and polish, then we'll vacuum you out.' She starts to unload me, humming something tuneless to herself. There is something on her mind, but I don't know what. She glances at my Odometer.

'I bet you're relieved that we didn't have to complete that last two hundred and fifty miles, but looking at this you still did some twelve hundred and fifty. I'm so proud of you and what went wrong? Your dynamo failed, your plugs oiled up and you suffered a bit of oxygen starvation on the top of those mountains. That's all. Nothing too difficult.'

She wants to tell me something, but somehow can't get it out. Has she put me up for sale? Am I going to have to move on to a new owner, my eighth? She still says nothing and rolls me out for a wash and polish.

'This'll smarten you up. Tell you what; I'll change your oil before I take you out again. You'll be in need of some clean oil now. Let's have the radio on. You like Woman's Hour don't you?' She switches on the wireless set in my garage. The valves seem to take longer than usual to warm up and a presenter fades up talking to some man about single father families. It isn't long before Her Ladyship starts up the vacuum.

'There, that's the last trace of Spain out of your carpets. Let's get you back into your garage.'

She rolls me back in and starts to put the covers over me to keep the dust off. Winter must be approaching, so I expect she'll start using The Grey One now the weather is turning. Anyway, I need the rest after all that.

'Umm, Old Girl… look I've been thinking. I'm really not sure that our idea of driving round the world is such a good one.' What does she mean, 'our idea'? Your idea, Your Ladyship.

'The thing is Old Girl, we've proved we can do long and sometimes gruelling runs, but on all of those trips, we've been part of a group. I mean, when your dynamo packed up, it was Mister Arthur who fixed you up and when you broke down that time in France, it was Mister John. How would I manage in the Gobi Desert if you did have problems and there was no one to help me sort you out? No, I'm really sorry Old Girl, I think we should forget the whole idea of a round the world trip, don't you?' I know you'll be disappointed, but I hope you're not too upset.

Look, my ageing, confused old friend, this is the best news I have heard in the seven years I have lived with you. For heaven's sake, I will happily put up with the odd little journey – Ireland,

Normandy, even Birmingham where I was born, but thank you, thank you, thank you. I no longer have to contemplate the world.

She finishes straightening out my covers and turns for the door. She pauses and looks back at me.

'Tell you what Old Girl, I've got a much better idea. Why don't we just drive round the twenty seven capitals of the European Union instead? Yes, that's a good idea. Never too far from home. That's what we'll do now. The twenty seven capital cities. I like that idea, don't you?'

Oh for Heaven's sake!

Chris Williams
1945-2012